The Butterfield's

A fictional historical novel based upon two years genealogical research of my wife's family.

Charles Thomas and Joseph William Butterfield.
The Butterfield Boys

The Diary of Charles Jones, 1856

An Historical Novel

By Michael Stephen Harrison

The coffee was hot, very hot and Nicholas Mountsell was cold, very cold. He carefully climbed up the steps from the Mess Deck to the Sea Deck of the fishing smack Gnat. He had no shoes.

They had been sold together with all the other kit he had been given by the Mariners Society.

He was just 8 years old.

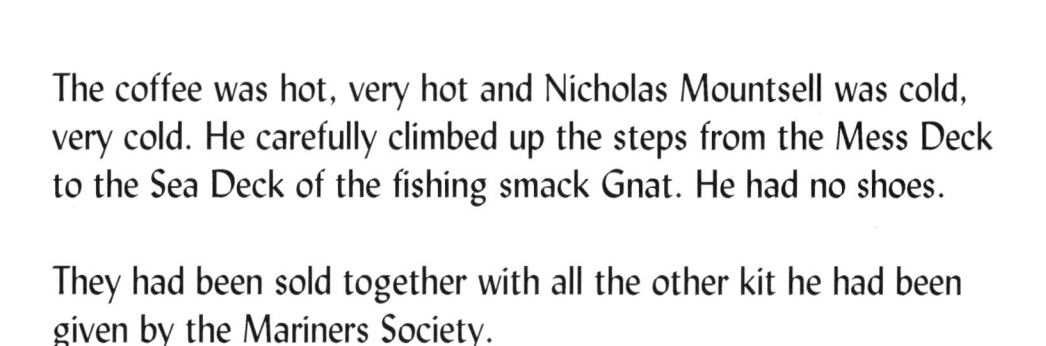

All was going well until he slipped on the wet deck!

The Butterfield's

The Butterfield's is an historic fictional novel written by Michael Stephen Harrison the husband of Marie Louise Howlett. She is the Great, Great, Great Granddaughter of Charles Thomas Butterfield and Ann Goodman Forge. The novel was conceived after the completion of my wife's Family genealogy.

Many of the people in this book existed since they are named in British Census Survey documents from 1841 through to 1911. The characters assigned to these names and the story itself is a work of fiction.

The novel is not intended to be a treatise on fishing techniques, the Town of Barking in Essex or Grimsby in Lincolnshire or on how to sail a fishing smack.

It is intended to be a "ripping good yarn" about the North Sea Fishing Industry and its cruel and inhumane treatment of orphans which were taken from Workhouses and sold into abominable slavery during the middle to late 19th Century.

It is the story of the Forge and Butterfield families' determination to end this situation. It was not ended whilst the families resided in Barking but ended in Grimsby when the Maritime Act of 1888 became Law.

That phase is dealt with in my second novel "Ann Kime" This is also available from Amazon and covers the period 1865 through to 1929.

This Historic Novel is set as being written by Ann Butterfield the only daughter of Charles Thomas Butterfield and Ann Goodman Forge. She married a certain Mr George Kime and bore him 12 children with only one being lost to the death sleep.

Happy sailing.

Michael Stephen Harrison

The Butterfield's Genealogy

William Butterfield born in 1750 married Martha Skinner and begot:-

William Butterfield born in 1779 who married Mary Ann Stevens and begot:-

Charles Thomas Butterfield born in 1815 who married Ann Goodman Forge and begot:-

Walter Butterfield born in 1852 who married Louisa Beckett and begot:-

Charles Beckett Butterfield born in 1876 who married Julia Elizabeth Ready and begot:-

Eva Valentine Butterfield born in 1909 who married John Howlett and begot:-

Marie Louise Howlett born in 1943 who married Michael Stephen Harrison = The Author

1851 Census
Fisher Street, Barking, Essex.

1861 Census
Heath Cottage, Barking, Essex.

[census search results](#)   [1861 address search](#)   [rede](#)

Name	Relation	Condition	Sex	Age	Birth Year	Occupation Disability	Where Born
BUTTERFIELD, Charles	Head	Widower	M	47	1814	...	Barking Essex
BUTTERFIELD, Charles	Son		M	13	1848	Scholar	
BUTTERFIELD, Ann	Daughter		F	10	1851		
BUTTERFIELD, Walter	Son		M	8	1853		
BUTTERFIELD, Henry	Son		M	5	1856	Scholar	
BUTTERFIELD, William	Father	Married	M	81	1780	...	
BUTTERFIELD, Mary A	Mother	Married	F	71	1790		Brentwood Essex
BUTTERFIELD, Joseph	Brother	Unmarried	M	46	1815		Barking Essex
BUTTERFIELD, Sarah	Aunt	Unmarried	F	73	1788	...	
BYN, Emily	Servant	Unmarried	F	19	1842	General Serv	
JONES, Charles	Apprentice	Unmarried	M	19	1842	Ap Fisherman	London Middlesex
ADSON, Charles	Apprentice	Unmarried	M	19	1842	Apprentice	
MORTON, William	Apprentice	Unmarried	M	18	1843	Apprentice	London Middlesex

The Events

1 The purpose of this Diary..9
2 Tuesday May 20th 1856 ~ Butterfield Day..10
3 Fisher Lad John Hennecky..13
4 Wednesday Mrs Charnock...16
5 The Argument...26
6 The Fisher Lad's Interview..28
7 The Strike...32
8 The Ann Goodman..34
9 Kitchen Time..44
10 Hammock Time...48
11 Thursday May 22nd...51
12 The Angels..53
13 Getting Knotted...55
14 Friday morning May the 23rd..66
15 Repentance..75
16 East Pond Marsh..78
17 Saturday May 24th...85
18 Sunday Morning May 25th..91
19 Sunday Afternoon Picnic on the Water Meadow............................98
20 Barking Town Dance...106
21 Monday May 26th ~ The Goodman set free..................................119
22 On the Dragon..129
23 On board the Ann Goodman..132
24 Back Home..135
25 The Great Yarmouth Fiasco...145
26 Back at Barking...148
27 Shares..157
28 The Coroners Court...161
29 The Steam Paddle Tug...166
30 The Proposal..168
31 The Temeraire ~ Joseph William Mallord Turner.........................176
32 Fish, Shares and Bank Accounts..178
33 I Meet Mr Byes..184
34 North to the Faroes..188
35 Riby Square...192
36 Incidents..199

37 Appendix

Images and imagination..216

1   The purpose of this Diary.

This is my diary written by me after I was taught to write by Ann Goodman Butterfield and her maid Emily Byers. My name is Charles Jones and I am apprenticed to the owners of the fishing smack Ann Goodman. This vessel is owned by Charles Thomas Butterfield (16 Shares), Ann Goodman Butterfield (16 Shares) and Joseph William Butterfield (32 shares).

My apprenticeship is for 7 years from 1856. I thank God every day for this. It could have been so different.

2. Tuesday May the 20 th 1856
Butterfield Day.

My name is Charles Jones. The year is 1856. I believe that I was born in 1843 in Romford Essex and if that is true then I am fourteen. I cannot be sure of this because my parents, brother and sisters are dead and so I am an orphan. Many say that I am old for my age. I think about things all of the time, all kinds of things, all of the time. I live in Romford Workhouse. Romford is a suburb of London. Many other orphans live with me. We are crowded into rooms which at best might be described as cattle stalls. There are six beds in the stall. My closest friend in this place was John Hennecky. He was placed last year by Mrs.Charnock as a Fishing Apprentice with Josey Craddock, owner of a fishing smack named the Swallow. This boat is part of the McAllan fishing fleet. The fleet's home port is Barking. John did live with the Craddock family in Fisher Street, Barking, if it can be called living.

Mrs.Charnock is the Manager of the Romford Workhouse. Her husband Alfred is the principle of the place. She is a hard lady bereft of human kindness. She believes in fate, the order of things and the class society as it now is. She has told me that God rules and that nothing happens without his knowledge and approval. She is of the Elect. She explained to me that she had been born again and so had been called and chosen to be with Jesus in heaven when she died. She then added that I, on the other hand, was not called and chosen. This was the cause of my current situation as an orphan. She has told me many times that we both have immortal souls and as such cannot really die. At death both of our souls are freed from our bodies and we become spirits. We are both changed. Her soul will go to heaven and mine will go to hell. We shall be there forever. My mother and father died of typhoid as did my brother and three sisters. Alice died in 1850 aged 5. Ann and Eliza were twins and they were born in 1846. Ann died in 1851 aged 4 and Eliza died in 1852 aged 5. None of them were baptised or at least there was no wetting of the head. My Dad did not believe that this was baptism. I guess that my Dad did not believe at all, though I cannot be sure. They also have been changed and are in hell. Mrs.Charnock often says that's what the Vicar of St Margaret's Church in Barking teaches. I hate him though I have never met him.

Everything that has happened to my family and I was God's will. I am an orphan because this was God's will. I hate this God he worships. I loathe and despise him whoever he is. I think that heaven will be a really bad place if that is where Mrs.Charnock is going. I hope she dies of typhoid just like my family. It is a long horrible death. When I get to Hell, the Devil is going to torment me forever because I am not of the Elect. She says there is no end to this torment. My mum died in 1850 at the age of 28. She is in hell. So maybe she committed sin for14 years if it began when she was 14. It would appear though, that this has no bearing because she was not called and chosen and so she will be in hell forever and ever and ever. This is mad thinking. This will be my fate unless the God Mrs.Charnock worships calls me to be part of the elect. Apparently I can be called and if I am, then the Holy Spirit will do something to me. I am supposed to have an experience which will lead me to repent and beg forgiveness from Jesus for my sins. I will then stop behaving as a sinner. I will get baptised. I will be good. All of this is in the Bible but since I cannot read or write how can I learn? How can I repent? How I can be called. Mrs.Charnock keeps on about it all being in this book. She says that the Holy Bible will help me and put me on the right path. But I cannot read it. I have to listen to Mrs.Channock's ravings. I have asked to be taught to read and write so that I can read not only the Bible but other books that interest me. Mrs.Charnock says this is not to be since I am a pauper and was born a pauper.

None of my kin could read or write so our place is as labourers and slaves or worse still mudlarks searching through human shit in the Thames at low tide to find something of value. Being a fishing apprentice is worse than this because you are indentured for seven years and during that time the skipper owns you. Mrs.Charnock gets twenty pounds per year from the Governments poor chest for each person in her care. This is provided so that we can be fed, clothed and educated.

The Workhouse is intended to be my home. If however, she can place me as an apprentice, then she is really better off since, in the case of the fishing smacks she pays the owner, Skipper or Company fourteen or better still ten pounds per year. She keeps the rest. There are over 400 orphans in this place. Last year she placed two hundred and seventy two boys with Barking smack owners. There are normally three to four apprentices needed for each smack. Work it out. The apprentices are just sold as slaves. Slaves, whose lives are dominated by cruelty, the apprenticeship period is, as I have said, seven years. During this time I am owned. Most of the smack owners are born again Christians. They have all been chosen. They all go to St Margaret's in Barking. Many are Magistrates. There is a great need for fisherman in heaven.

It seems God likes cod.

3 Fisher Lad John Hennecky

Here is what happened to my friend John Hennecky. He was always clumsy. He was a thinker and day dreamer, a bit like me. He was apprenticed to Josey Craddock. The "boys" as the apprentices were called did all of the mundane jobs that must be done for a smack to operate well. When the fishing lines were out deck activity was hectic. It got even more hectic once the crew started to haul the lines in. There could be twenty, thirty and sometimes forty hooks on a line and if it was a good run each hook might have a fish on it. These fish, if they were cod, were very valuable. A crewman called the hauler would free the fish from the long line hook as it came aboard and then throw the fish to John for placement in the well. This was a wooden four sided deep water well with auger holes though the hull so that the sea water could get in. The smack did not sink because the sides of the well were above the deck transom. This system kept the fish fresh. John kept dropping the fish on the deck. Fishing took place in all seasons and the weather in the North Sea especially over the Dogger and Holland Banks was wild. After his watch Josey Craddock strapped John to the capstan as punishment for his clumsiness and then lashed him with a knotted rope. Left exposed to March's winter weather off the Holland banks he nearly froze to death. One of the other apprentices sneaked on deck and cut him free. He took John down below and sat him near the mess deck fire wrapping his feet and hands in warm towels. Craddock found out and took him back on deck and again tied him to the capstan. That is where he died. John was fourteen years old just like me.

How do I know this? Mrs.Charnock called me into her office one day and read the account to me from the London Mail.

"Let this be a warning to ee lad" she said.

There had been an inquest and guess what? Six of the jury were smack owners. The report said that a member of the Medical profession had given evidence about John Hennecky's wounds. He had stated that the wounds in themselves were not death dealing. His conclusion was that John had died from exposure to the very bad weather. The report said that John had been lashed many times judging from the scars on his back. The report said that some of these had turned rotten and that gangrene had set in. I have seen and smelt that. I hate the smack owners and Scrimey McAllan is the worst. All of them including the Doctor who spoke at the inquest are born again. All of them are members of the elect. I cannot understand people believing this rubbish.

It was while she was reading the article in the Mail to me that Mrs.Charnock added that I would be leaving the Romford Workhouse. "I have placed you with smack owner called Charles Thomas Butterfield". I was to be delivered to his address on Fisher Street tomorrow. I shall be sorry to leave this place. I shall not be sorry to leave Mrs. Charnock. She often read passages from the Bible so that I would truly appreciate my place in life. Sometimes she would also read to me letters she received in the Post about her duties and how privileged she was. One of these letters contained details of a report sent out in 1834 a report was made to Parliament about us, me, the poor. She read this to me from the newspaper:-

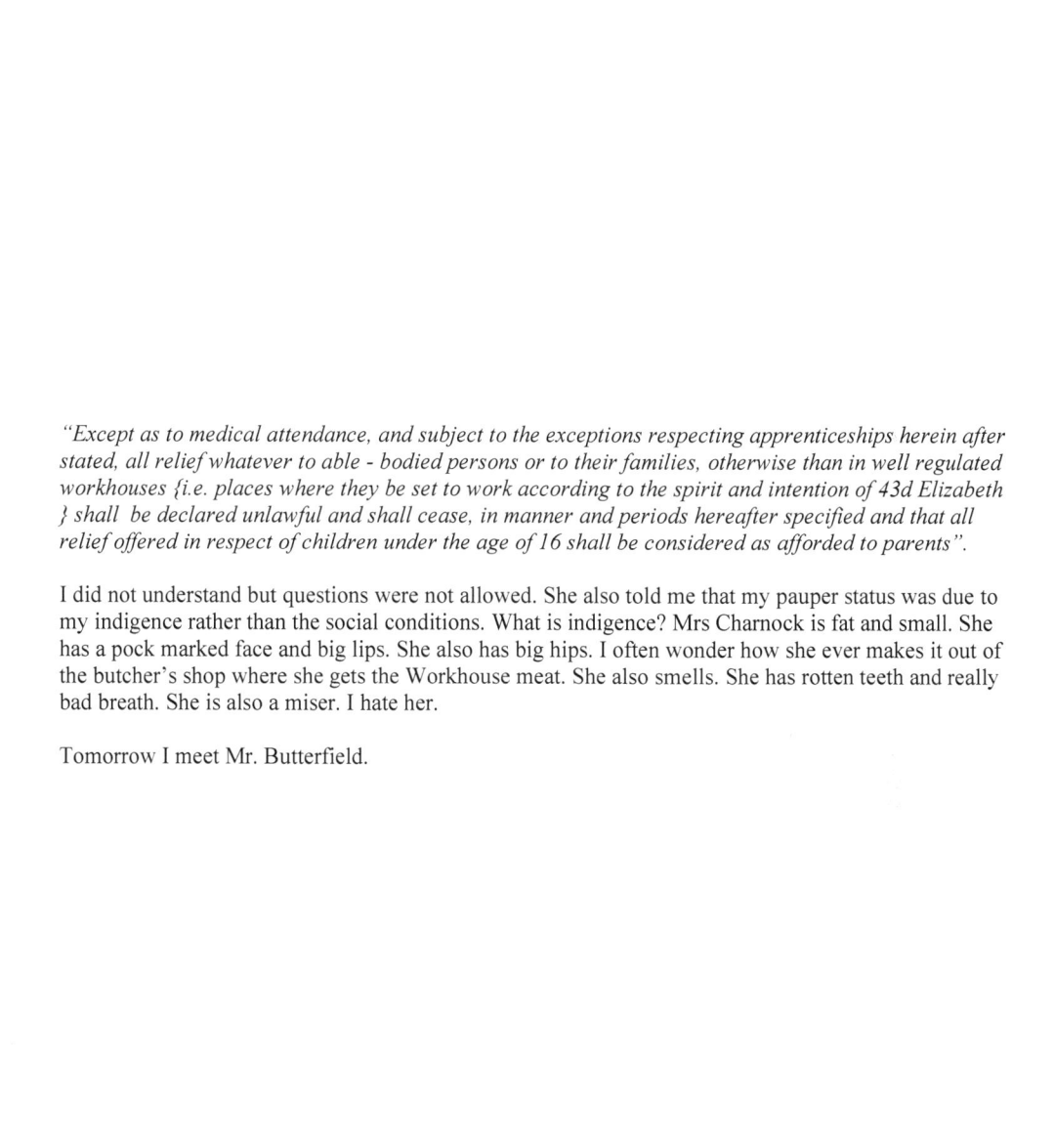

"Except as to medical attendance, and subject to the exceptions respecting apprenticeships herein after stated, all relief whatever to able - bodied persons or to their families, otherwise than in well regulated workhouses {i.e. places where they be set to work according to the spirit and intention of 43d Elizabeth } shall be declared unlawful and shall cease, in manner and periods hereafter specified and that all relief offered in respect of children under the age of 16 shall be considered as afforded to parents".

I did not understand but questions were not allowed. She also told me that my pauper status was due to my indigence rather than the social conditions. What is indigence? Mrs Charnock is fat and small. She has a pock marked face and big lips. She also has big hips. I often wonder how she ever makes it out of the butcher's shop where she gets the Workhouse meat. She also smells. She has rotten teeth and really bad breath. She is also a miser. I hate her.

Tomorrow I meet Mr. Butterfield.

4 Wednesday ~ Mrs Charnock

Mrs Charnock and I set off to cover the seven miles to Barking in her pony and trap. The Thames was on the ebb, the tide was going out and the wind was blowing from the west, from the City of London. The day was hot. The Thames, the Thames, the stinking river Thames. All the human excrement from five million people was dumped into the River. There was nothing living in it. The smell was every where. It was in the air, on the trees and flowers. It seemed to soak into the very ground. The stench took your breath away. Breathing was very bad for you. TB was rampant. I do not know what TB is but everyone fears it because there is no cure. Just like there is no cure for Typhoid. Mrs.Charnock of course had a scented handkerchief. We finally got to Fisher Street and Mrs.Charnock alighted from the trap, pulled me off it, and punched me in my back whilst at the same time telling me to stand straight.

She knocked on the door of number twelve. Fisher Street was a row of semi detached three storey houses. There was no front garden just a stone step in front of the front door. We stood on the gravel street in front of the step which was remarkably clean. The door opened and a girl about my age stood there. She looked at Mrs.Charnock and then glanced at me. Looking back at Mrs.Charnock she asked who we were.

"I am Mrs. Charnock of Romford Workhouse and I have an appointment to meet Mr.Charles Thomas Butterfield."

"Please come in" the maid said. I later learnt that her name was Emily, Emily Byes. "I will let Mrs. Butterfield know you are here. The Master is at the Pond with his Brother Joseph".

She seemed clean and cared for and spoke well. Maybe she could read. I liked Emily from the minute she glanced at me. She had a lovely smile. We entered the lobby which felt homely or at least what I imagined a home might be like. It was also warm. There were stairs on the right going up to the first floor. About six feet up attached to the side of the stairs there was a large brass bell with a striker easily within reach. Strange I thought, little realising the power of that bell and how it would control my habits. There was a passage with a door on the left and another next to it. There was then a door at the end of the passage. We were shown through the first door into what turned out to be the sitting room. There were six leather chairs in green and a very nice suite of dark wood furniture. On the walls, which were painted cream, were many pictures. Several of them were of fishing smacks.

"Please sit down" said Emily.

Mrs Charnock shook my wrist and said: - "Sit down boy and say nowt. I'll do the talking".

Emily left the room. She was wearing a black maids skirt with a white apron. Her blouse was white and she was wearing a black cap with a white ribbon and bow tilted to the left. She was the same height as me. I guessed she was about my age. Her breasts were lovely. She had a thin waist with a belt drawn tight with a bow at the rear. I like breasts and legs and waists and bottoms though I have been told "All that glitters is not gold". Someday someone will explain this to me but for now I liked the look of Emily Byes.

About two minutes after Emily had left a lady entered the room. I say lady because that is what she was. As soon as Mrs Butterfield entered the room things seemed better.

"Hello Mrs.Charnock, pleased to meet you".

Turning to me she said "You must be Charles Jones"

I looked at Mrs.Charnock.

Mrs Charnock spoke "Pleased to meet you Mrs Butterfield and yes this is Charles Jones, strong lad. Good teeth and a strait back. As you can see he has good strong legs and arms. He has worked on the wharf at Creekmouth"

I slaved on that wharf working for the Lawes Company as they built their fertiliser works and the Thames boat quay.

Mrs Butterfield spoke "Yes I can see". Looking directly at Mrs Charnock she asked? "You said he had worked in boats before?"

"Well it would be better to say he has worked on boats. I sent him to McAllan's dock at Creekmouth where he unloaded fish from their smacks and construction stuff for the fertiliser works"

"So he has never been to sea fishing?"

"No" said Mrs Charnock. "Do you want the lad or not, I have the fourteen pounds on me but you need to commit now. I do have others interested".

"Now, now, Mrs Charnock I did not say that I was not interested".

Mrs Butterfield looked at me for I was just staring straight ahead not daring to look at her.

"Excuse me Mr. Jones but it is not polite to stare into space when someone wants to talk to you. Please look at me."

I turned my head and looked. It was a pleasant face. She looked directly into my eyes; she never blinked but just looked at me. Funny though, I was not upset for they were kind eyes. She did not look at my legs, my arms, my teeth or my stance but then she said

"Hold out your hands"

She took my hands in hers and then turned them over to look at my palms.

"I see that you have been unloading coal, the coal dust always gets into the creases" she just looked at me. "We will take you Master Charles Jones."

Mrs Charnock was pleased and spoke "You will need to sign this Apprenticeship Agreement here and here and then I sign there. It is for seven years. Once you have done that the lad is your responsibility. He has no family and has been with us for three years ever since his family died."

Mrs Butterfield seemed annoyed. She gave Charnock a look that would have turned others to stone. She signed the Apprenticeship Agreement and received the fourteen pounds. Mrs Butterfield picked up a small bell and rang it. Emily reappeared.

"Please show Mrs.Charnock out Emily she has no time for tea".

Mrs Charnock stood up. "Well I never, I can see that you are not one of God's elect. Good day to you". She left.

"Now then Charles would you like a cup of tea. I have made some fruit cake which is really good, if I say so myself".

"Yes please ma'am I would love some thank you, thank you"

"Good, this is Emily Byes, my housemaid, though she is really like a daughter to my husband and I"

"Pleased to meet you Miss Byes" I said.

Turning to Miss Byes Mrs Butterfield said. "Emily please get the tray you laid earlier from the kitchen. It has three cups so please join us."

I was in paradise. I was human. I was a person with feelings I was. I was just so happy. I hope she is the Captain of the smack. I bet her husband is as hard as nails. At that moment I heard the front door open and the loud voices of two men. They seemed very happy. I heard something about the Ann Goodman, sails and Red Ochre.

In walked two huge men. Both had beards and long hair. One wore a captain's cap. Both men were in sailors gear. They both had huge arms and very muscular hands. They were about six feet tall with great wide shoulders. Charles Thomas and Joseph William Butterfield would, in my opinion, make an impression entering any room, anywhere, and to think that these two men were my new owners. Both suddenly grinned as they saw the fruit cake. "Now then, Ann Goodman Butterfield, what about some of that fruit cake?" This was said by the wilder looking of the two.

They both laughed and then stopped. They both turned to look at me.

"You will be Charles Jones, said the slightly taller of the two. I am Charles Thomas Butterfield Skipper and co owner of the smack Ann Goodman. This is my brother Joseph. He is first mate, co owner and cook and he is a very, very good cook indeed. He is also a pigeon fancier. Now how would you like to be called shall it be Chat, Chas or Charlie because Charles is taken. What name would you prefer?"

In all of my life no one had ever asked me this question for I thought I would just be called "Boy" since that was what John Hennecky and the other apprentice had been called.

"I prefer Chas sir" I said

"Oh dear, that is not the right answer and I should not have included it since we are interviewing two other apprentices today and one is called Charles Adson. How would Jonesy sound".

"That is fine sir, Jonesy it shall be"

"Move up Emily and let us sit down". Emily smiled at Mr. Butterfield.

"Sorry sir she said, I seem to be getting bigger every day"

"That's all right lass, time to worry is when your not. Now when you have finished your tea I want you to take Jonesy, for that shall be his new name to his berth upstairs and then down to the Pond to show him the Ann Goodman. Did you clean our cabin like I instructed?"

"Yes Sir" she said "but I cannot get the crew or mess deck really clean until the fitting out is finished"

It was then that I realised the Ann Goodman was a new smack. After we had finished the tea and cake Emily turned to me and said under her breath.

"Now Jonesy, you had better follow me. You will be on the third floor and there are to be two other apprentices. We are waiting for them to arrive".

I followed her out of the door. She turned right and then at the foot of the stairs she looked straight into my eyes and with a grin said "please follow me".

She began to climb the stairs. She was wearing one of those fashionable maids' outfits with a bustle and bow at the back. She had a really small waist. The bow swayed as she began to rise step, by step. It was a truly wonderful site to behold. There must be a God, I thought, there just must be. When we arrived on the landing on the third floor she opened the door and we entered an attic space. There were two dormer windows, one on each side. One faced Fisher Street and so you could see all the comings and goings as traffic passed by from the right making their way into Barking. Traffic going left right down Fisher Street was heading to the wharf and on to Creekmouth about two miles away.

The Fishing Smack Public House was almost opposite. The other dormer window faced the garden looking out onto Barking Pool. You could see the Water Mill and wheel race connecting the River Roding to Barking Pool. There was a road which I later learned was called Wharf Road which made its way in front of many buildings. It then went over the Mill Race by means of a bridge. I later learned it was called Six Bridges. The road then led to the West Bank of Barking Pond and you could see the foundry where the Water Mill was.

The River Roding entered Barking Mill Pool via the wheel race. From the pool to the Thames it was called Barking Creek. The tide was out and a really beautiful fishing smack was resting in a cradle which sat on the Pool mud. The Ann Goodman was kept upright by this cradle but leaning toward the wharf. When I worked at Creekmouth I learnt that Barking Creek has an eighteen foot tidal surge. The wharf edge to which the smack was leaning was about fourteen foot above her deck. The mooring ropes were loose. She seemed long compared with the other smacks sat on the mud. They had just one centre mast and bowsprit whereas the Lady Ann had two masts. The main mast was central and the second towards the rear. She also seemed to have a deep keel where the others where more flat bottomed. The Lady Ann seemed to have a much longer bowsprit than the others and there were two sails attached to it rolled up. .

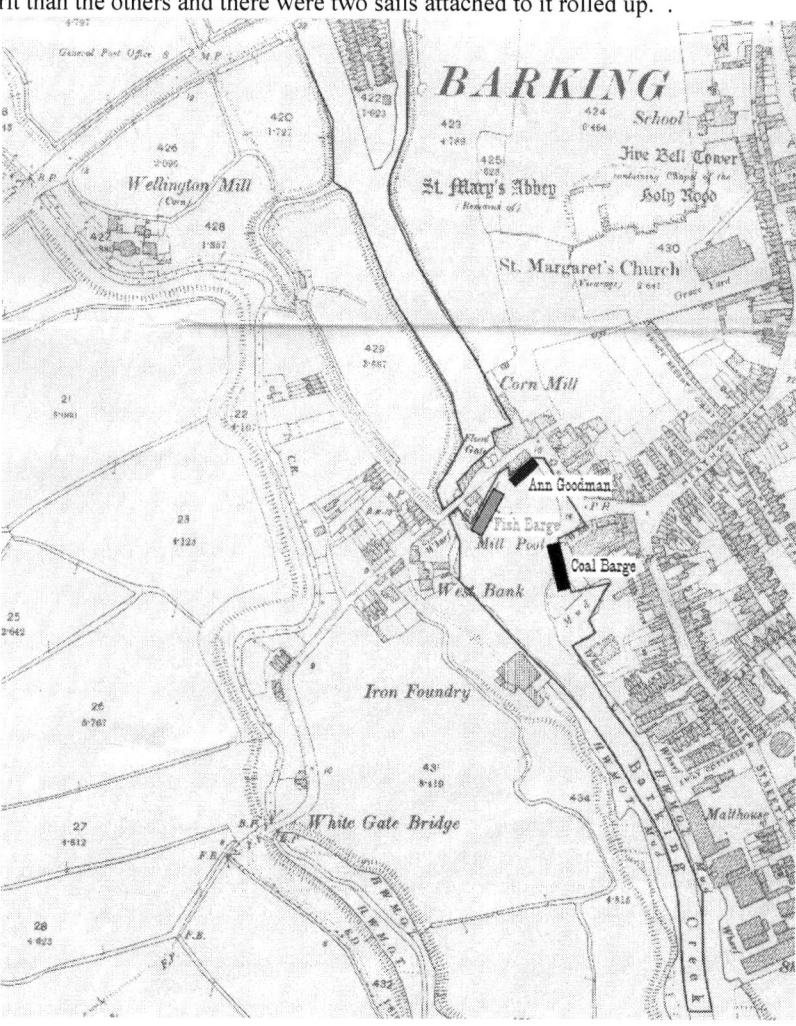

Barking 1894 British Ordnance Survey Map

All the other smacks that I had seen had a vertical bow whereas this smack had a sloping or as I later learned a schooner bow. There were two long deck boards hanging down and fastened to the hull sides. They seemed quite long. The hull bottom below the "Lloyds line" was painted red. The line was painted white and the hull blue. The deck was wood of a light colour but I could not see the detail. There was much activity.

Emily spoke
"This is where you will sleep. See the two posts. They are for your hammock. You need to get it from the cupboard there under the window and swing it between the posts on those hooks. You then need to make your bed. The bedding is in that sea chest with your name scrawled on it. There will be a proper nameplate but that has to be made. I will go and get the waterproofs. Now then Jonesy here is my advice. Make sure that your hammock and the area around it is ship shape and tidy. The Butterfield's like things to be in their place particularly when they are at sea. They both say that's how you sleep on a stormy night. There is a place for everything and everything must be in its place. The Skipper is NOT tolerant in this area because I have heard him say many, many times that when things are not in their place it can cost lives. You are entering upon a dangerous career Jonesy. Over forty seamen died last year. Charles and Joseph have lost two brothers at sea. Alfred died in 1846 and then John in 1850. John was married to Elizabeth Spashett for just five years. He drowned at sea and she had just had a baby. She was waiting for John to come back from his cruise for the baptism and the naming"

The cupboard had a large bowl on it and a very large water jug. There was also a chamber pot for the jobby and piss.

"Thanks, Miss Byes, may I call you Emily?"

"N0 you cannot call me by my first name, we have only just met and so I am Miss Byes to you."

"Sorry" I said. "Miss Byes is that the Butterfield's boat? "

"It's a smack Jonesy a smack and yes that is the Ann Goodman"

"Thanks, I have shall to do a pencil drawing of her, though not in the Pond but at sea".

"You can draw?" said Emily raising her eyebrows

"Yes I can draw; some say I am good at it though I need to get new paper pads and drawing pencils. I had a really good set given to me by one of the patrons of Romford Workhouse after he had seen a sketch I did of his dog. He didn't know I had done it until I gave it to him for a kindness he had shown me. They were all in a nice wooden carrying case. It was mine but Mrs. Charnock would not let me bring it here saying it was her property and she was going to sell it."

"Can you read and write?" she asked.

"No" I said and then "Can you?"

"Yes, Mrs Butterfield is teaching me. This is a very good place to be Mr.Charles Jones, Jonesy as you are now to be called. Masters Charles and Joseph are very good men. They have been very kind to me. I come from Creekmouth. My Father Frederick Byes is the Supervisor at Lawes Chemical Works there"

"Oh I know him, Mrs. Charnock placed me at Lawes for two months but your father would not take me on as an apprentice"

"I see, he will not take anybody on, anybody, not even his own children. I will be about five minutes and then after you have made up your hammock I will take you to the Pool."

She left through the door and then on the landing she turned and curtsied and then laughed and ran down the stairs. I took the hammock out of the chest and strung it between the posts. They were about 8 feet apart and the hammock sank between them ending up four feet at it's lowest from the floor boards. I then got what appeared to be a heavy quilt made up of squares stitched together. I noticed a grey mattress. It looked like the saddle cover you would place on a horse before placing the saddle on the horses back. It was about six foot long. I placed this into the hammock.

There was also a grey cotton sheet that appeared to have been made to fit the mattress. I put it in place with the edges under the mattress. I then pulled on the edge strings and watched as this action fastened the sheet tightly to the mattress. I then placed the flock headrest into position facing the wall. When I was in bed I would be able to look right and left out of both dormer windows, one looking onto Fisher Street and the other, though not close, looking out on the Creek.

If there were other apprentices as Emily had said there would be then they would block this view. I placed the quilt across the hammock at the bottom so that I could pull this up when I was in the hammock. All I had to do now was climb aboard. At that moment I heard a knock at the front door downstairs. I heard the door open and Emily Byes say

"Hello, who shall I say is calling?"

"My name is Iris Plant, I am the Manager of Dagenham Workhouse I have an appointment with Master Charles Thomas Butterfield ".

"Please come into the parlour" said Emily "I will get Mrs Butterfield"

"But my appointment is with Mr .Butterfield" said Mrs.Plant.

"You have to see Mrs Butterfield first" said Emily "Please come in"

I moved to the window so I could get a better view. Mrs Plant was tall and slim and dressed well. There were two boys with her. One seemed to be my age and the second was much younger and looked to be about eleven. I moved away from the window and approached the hammock at speed raising my right leg as I did so. I was in and then it twisted and dumped me on the floor with a whack. I heard laughter both male and female from downstairs.

About five minutes after this Emily came into the room carrying sea boots in black. There was also a full waterproof coat with a built in hood. Then there were waterproof legging over trousers and a pair of waterproof gloves. They were all in bright yellow.

"Are these NEW" I asked?

"Yes" she said. "They were bought from Charles and Mary Howlett's on the Isle of Sheppey. The Butterfield's bought all of their deck gear from the Howlett's until they moved to Grimsby."

WOW!! I said to myself, they were NEW and not hand me downs.

"I think these should fit you Jonesy, sorry about the laughter but the hammock throw is a family tradition"

So I now knew that Emily Byes had taken more notice of me than she might be prepared to let on. I was very happy.

"Are their other apprentices?" I asked.

"There might be if they get past Mrs Butterfield. She is from a seafaring family and knows what she is looking for in apprentices. Seven years is a long time. Her father John Forge makes sails for all the fishing smacks in Barking. It was Mr. Forge who introduced the Red Ochre dye to the cotton sails making them waterproof. Mrs Butterfield's full maiden name was Ann Goodman Forge. She met Master Charles when he was boarding at her mothers house on Heath Street. Master Charles had been the skipper of the Eastern Star, one of McAllan's smacks. Now are you ready to go to the Pool?"

"Yes" I said "please lead on".

As I left the house I peeked in through the front window and saw Mrs Plant sat where Mrs. Charnock had sat about two hours before with me. She seemed to be talking to the two lads. I later learnt what took place from Charles Adson now to be called Chas. Mrs Plant was re-assuring the boys that Mr. Butterfield was a very good skipper. He had learnt his trade under the McAllan's but did not like the way they ran their business. At one time when McAllan's were running welled smacks the skippers had to sail up the Thames to Gravesend where they placed the live fish into cast-iron fish pens awaiting small rowing boats or cutters to take them up the Thames to Billingsgate. The smack would then return to sea. The well or wet hold in the smack was connected to the sea via auger holes in the hull. The crew would puncture the fish bladder. The fish were thus kept alive and fresh. This meant that the crew might be away for two months. Scrimey as Scrimegour McAllan was called came up with the idea of fleeting. Now cutters would sail out of the Thames estuary and other North Sea ports and meet the smacks off the fishing grounds. Each smack had a rowing boat and the fish were now gutted and placed in wooden cases. These cases were marked with the smacks port of registration number. These would be ferried to the cutter. This was very dangerous work. Many of the seamen were drowned or injured. The Butterfield's did not join the fleeting operation. They caught the fish and then sailed straight to ports like Grimsby.

All the Skippers would deploy rowing tubs when the cutter arrived on station. It was a madhouse with two men to a tub working between the smacks and the cutter. As I have said the fish would be gutted on the smacks and placed in ice boxes.

These boxes were off loaded onto the rowing tubs and then uplifted into the cutters and the fish placed in the ice hold for transport to Great Yarmouth or Grimsby. From there they were then taken by steam train to Billingsgate. Fleeting was very, very, dangerous work because the rowing tubs became unstable with the number of boxes ferried across. There were sometimes sixty boxes of fish per boat stacked really high.

Though Scrimey did not know it at the time he had written the death certificate of the Barking fishing fleet but that story comes later. With "Fleeting" smacks would be at sea for four months.

This was a long period of time. It was much too long for Master Charles. Charles Thomas Butterfield married Anne Goodman Forge in December 1842. She was the love of his life. Neither he nor Joseph Butterfield would get involved with Fleeting and their stubborn refusal was to cause a great deal of trouble.

When I was undergoing sail training with John Forge he told me the following story.

5 The Argument

"You will be out for four months" Scrimey McAllan said to Charles.

"I will take a two month ticket and *that* is too long".

"Listen to me Butterfield, I own the Barking Fishing fleet all one hundred and forty smacks and you will do what I say. If you do not do what I say then you will never get another ticket and you will never sail another smack. I know what you are thinking ,well, I will make sure that the other smack owners, what few there are , can't get sails or anything else they need if they give you a two month ticket"

" I regret Mr McAllen that I am NOT taking a four month ticket and I warn you that I am not the only skipper who feels this way. If you will not see reason you will have no fleet for we shall all strike".

"What, how dare you threaten me? I am a Magistrate and member of Barking Council and a regular attendee of St Margaret's Church. What are you? The son of a Butcher, so do not dare to threaten me."

"I am not taking a four month ticket" said Mr Butterfield, "I have three children and they need their Father. I love my wife and am determined to be her husband. I have made vows before God which, if you truly are a Christian, you will want me to honour. I am determined to be a good husband and father to my children. I cannot do this if I am away for all of this time, which is an end to it! Just give me a two month ticket so I can sail on tomorrows tide".

"NO! If you disobey me on this you will never sail again, so take notice"

Mr Butterfield is reported to have said in reply

"Thank you for the warning Mr. McAllan but do not be surprised at the consequences of your actions. Remember that phrase in the Bible *Whatever a man sows, this he will also reap*. Cast your mind back to 1797. That was the year the British Navy experienced its first mutiny? The whole fleet mutinied. It took place not far from here in the Thames estuary at the Nore where Hangesor Creek enters the river. It's just sixty years ago. Even the Navy had to give in"

"I know where the Nore is Mr Butterfield. Don't you dare lecture me about the Bible what are you thinking? Do you fancy becoming a Minister of the Church? I will need to let the Vicar of St Margaret's know."

This conversation became common knowledge after the strike.

6 The Fisher Lads interview

Emily opened the door and entered the parlour and Ann Butterfield followed her.

"Please to meet you Mrs Plant, now who do we have here?" she asked looking at the two orphans.

"This is Charles Adson who is fourteen and this William Moreton who is eleven."

"Pleased to meet you both" said Mrs Butterfield. "Have either of you boys had any experience with fishing smacks?"

The boys looked at Mrs Plant.

"Go ahead boys"

Charles Adson spoke up

"Well we have been working at McAllan's dock at Creekmouth off loading and loading cargo. We have also been loading coal onto smacks and barges. Sometimes we have been employed punting the smacks up Barking Creek on the tidal flow but neither of us has been to sea."

Mrs Butterfield noticed that William Moreton did not speak.

Addressing William Moreton and looking him straight in the eye she said

"Now then William the sea is a taskmaster to be sure but if you are well trained, work hard and respect it then it can be a very enjoyable career. Lord Nelson joined the Navy when he was just twelve William and look where he got to".

Looking at both of them she asked "Is this what you want?"

William looked at Mrs Plant who said. "Speak up now William for this is not the moment to be silent."

"Excuse me Mrs Butterfield but where will I live"

"You will live here when you are not at sea. There is a hammock for you on the third floor. I have just taken on Charles Jones as an apprentice. Will you take tea Mrs Plant?"

"I will most certainly and thank you. They are good boys Mrs Butterfield and have never given me any trouble"

Emily brought the tea in and then there was a very loud thud followed by a cry. Ann and Emily burst into laughter and Mrs Plant could ear two male voices laughing in the next room. Emily left and after a short while they saw her carrying sea faring gear upstairs. They then heard footsteps descending the stairs, the front door opened and then closed. Mrs Plant partook of the tea and the fruit cake Ann had baked. Ann signed the apprenticeship documents and then received the twenty eight pounds from Mrs Plant.

At this point Ann rose and excused herself and went out of the parlour into the kitchen. She returned and was followed into the parlour by Charles and Joseph Butterfield,

"Pleased to meet you all" said the Brothers almost together .They then both laughed. I was told by Chas and Billy later that it was the most wonderful sound. It did of course come from two massive full grown fisher men. It had affected me and I know it affected them. We talked about it when we were getting ready for bed.

"WE have a problem Master Charles Adson. I am Charles Thomas Butterfield; I have a son called Charlie and a new apprentice called Charles Jones who has accepted the name Jonesy. Would you mind if we called you Chas"

"Eh no sir, Chas would be just fine"

"You need to write a shanty about this Joseph, what shall it be called? The Ann Goodman and three Charles at sea" Both men laughed again as did Ann and Mrs Plant.

"Now don't you worry Mrs Plant I shall take good care of the boys on land and the same will be true when they are at sea. Charles and Joseph will train and look after them. Charles is the Skipper and Joseph is the chief mate and cook. I cook all the food, buy all of the stores and make all of the trousers, shirts and socks. The twenty eight pounds will be put to good use."

"Thank you Mrs Butterfield and now I must be going there are still many boys to place. I am glad that the strike is over. Your husband and his brother were the only skippers to have ever stood up to Scrimey "

"I know but times were very hard during the two months that Charles and Joseph could not get a smack. He was not intent on organising a strike Mrs. Plant. He simply wanted to catch fish, make good money from his time at sea and be a good Father and Husband. He could not do that and neither could the other skippers if they took four month tickets"

"Tell your husband to be careful. Two skippers on their way home from the Fishing Smack Pub over the road were beaten up on Monday because of this four month ticket business".

Chas then told me that Mrs. Butterfield had told Mrs.Plant about their good fortune and why they were seeking three apprentices. The good fortune for the brothers was their Great Grandfather's will. Charles and Joseph's father was William Butterfield who operated as a Butcher out of shop on Hart Lane in Barking.

It appears that he furnished the salted pork and bacon to the skippers and owners of many smacks. William had married Martha Skinner the daughter of Ambrose Skinner the Second and his wife Ann Pitman. They lived at Longbridge Farm. William bought his pork from Ambrose. He was a skilled slaughter man and had agreed a special price with Mr.Skinner for this pork. Ambrose had said that if William would slaughter all of his cattle and pigs at Longbridge and then prepare the cuts for the victualler's throughout Essex and Kent then William could have his meat at a very special price. It was Ambrose plan to provide the entire industry in both Counties with the meat they would sell to the skippers.

The deal was that William Butterfield could have a long term price for the pork. During the time he spent at Longbridge Farm William met Ambrose's daughter Martha. She was a plain but loving girl and the marriage was a success. They had three children. Their first child was named Sarah and she was born in 1782. Their next child was William who was born in 1780. Sarah died in 1787 when she was five and so when the third child arrived and proved to be a girl she was also named Sarah in memory of her deceased sister. She was born in 1787. Their second child, William, met and married Mary Ann Stevens and they too had a good marriage.

They had six children. Charles Thomas; born in 1815, Joseph; born in 1817. George: born in 1818. John and Henry, twins, born in 1825, and then, came Alfred who was born in 1827. Alfred died at sea in 1850 aged nineteen. John died at sea aged twenty five in 1850. The Skinners were a wealthy farming family. Back in the 17th century Ambrose's father Ambrose senior had been robbed by Dick Turpin and his gang. Ambrose junior had walked in on the raid with his new wife. Turpin stole money and goods to the sum of three hundred pounds but did not hurt anyone. Ambrose Skinner the second, Charles and Joseph's Great Grandfather had just died at the age of ninety six and he had left £500.00 pounds in his will to Charles and Joseph with the specific instructions that it was to be used "to build that fishing smack you always wanted". This was the source of the money for the Ann Goodman.

7 The Strike

Charles and Joseph had a good relationship with their Grandfather and they often talked about the inhumane treatment of the fishing apprentices and the four month ticket issue. Charles had refused Scrimey's ticket and this seemed to be the flint needed for the strike.

Longbridge Farm was on a hill and could be seen for miles. The Skinners were respected by farmers all over Kent and Essex. Charles, Joseph and their Grandfather decided to build a huge bonfire at Longbridge and Ambrose arranged for similar bonfires to be located at strategic points on the Isle of Sheppey, Gravesend, Southend, Gorleston and all up the East Coast to Grimsby. They were roughly 20 miles apart. It was decided that if the Fishermen's Committee could not get Scrimey to yield over fleeting and the four month ticket issue they would strike on November fifth 1854. The lighting of the bonfire at Longbridge would signal all smacks at sea or in port to strike.

The Committee failed to get agreement and so on November fifth 1854 the bonfire at Longbridge was lit. The following morning the whole fleet struck.

It did not take long for the affect of the strike to be noticed by the owners. The smacks stayed at sea and the fish went off. Fish was silver currency and soon swayed the owners into negotiating. The wages paid went up and a bonus of sorts was agreed of the value of the catch.

The issue of fleeting was not resolved however. Any skipper could choose NOT to join in but then how would the catch get to market. It was back to the Thames and the fish cages but the Thames was much polluted and so many skippers stayed with fleeting.

8 The Ann Goodman

Whilst the tea party was going on downstairs I was upstairs rehearsing getting into my hammock. The door burst open and Emily strode in, yanked my arm and said "Come on Jonesy I have to take you to see the Ann Goodman".

She went rapidly down the stairs, out the front door and then left along Fisher Street. At the end of Fisher Street Emily turned left. I followed. Looking over her shoulder I could see, about two hundred yards ahead, the Ann Goodman leaning against the wharf. I had seen her from the bedroom window but from that view I had not appreciated how long she was. She was sat in a cradle which, because it was low tide, sat on the Barking pond mud. Men were stood on the mud working on the smacks hull. As we approached a small, strong, stout man came towards us.

"Hello Emily who's this with you? "

"Hello Master John please meet Mr. Butterfield's new apprentice Mr. Charles Jones, now to be called Jonesy by all."

" Charles Butterfield senior, Charles Butterfield Junior and now Charles Jones or Jonesy you say"

"Yes Mr. Forge and there is another Charles being interviewed right now from the Dagenham workhouse His name is Charles Adson" she laughed that sweet enchanting laugh.

"There is a shanty in that Emily. Hello, Jonesy, my name is John Forge and I am your mistresses' father. My family lives on Heath Street. Right Emily, ask Master Charles if I can have the apprentices tomorrow because I am ready to set the sales to the mainmast gaff, stay and foresails".

Turning to me he said "Tomorrow I will teach you three important rope knots. There will be a test at the end of it with a written certificate. This certificate has been requested by Mr Charles. Excuse me both of you but I must get on, the Ann Goodman's maiden voyage approaches"

He then turned and went across the wharf into a large open building with sails laid out on the floor. I watched him go. I then became aware of the activity on the wharf. The place smelled of tar, rope dip, paint, salted pork and of course fish. On the wharf side there were boxes and boxes of cod waiting to be loaded into the barges. There were large blocks of ice from the ice house farther along the quay which were being broken up and barrowed into the barges. I learnt that this ice was harvested every winter when the brooks and small rivers were damned causing them to overflow onto the flood plains. It would freeze and there was then an Ice Harvest and winter party for all who took part. The barges were shallow draught Thames barges with huge sales and stabiliser paddles. The paddles were hauled up so that they were or out of the water. Once the hold was spread with ice the fish would be taken aboard. The barges were being loaded for the incoming tidal flow and then the rapid journey on the ebb tide down to Creekmouth. At the estuary the skipper would turn West or starboard and sail up the river to Billingsgate. It was a tricky manoeuvre and required great seamanship. I was told later that this business was gradually being affected by the Railways. The line into Barking was opened in 1856 and had just started taking cargo. After Mr. Forge left us Emily headed to the boarding plank connecting the smack to the wharf. She descended to the Ann Goodman's.

It was steep but easy. The plank had slip ribs fastened to it about every three feet. These ribs worked well and I did not slip. Emily walked down the plank with confidence, her hips swaying and the breeze blowing her skirt. Wonderful! Arriving on deck she headed toward the stern and I followed.

"The Ann Goodman is the largest smack ever built. She is eighty five foot long and her beam is thirty feet"

"Beam what is beam Miss Byers?"

"It is the width, Master Jones and I have heard Master Charles say that when she is fully loaded with her catch she will draw eight feet six inches. She has a schooner bow and a rising counter stern. The main beam is fifty five feet and the bowsprit is twenty five feet"

"What is the main beam?"

"The main sail anchor pole nearest the deck see, it is attached to the mast with that saddle thing"

"Oh yes; I guess the bowsprit is the long pole going forward"

"Yes, well done"

She walked toward what appeared to be a large wooden bath with its sides about eighteen inches above the deck. The sides were about six inches thick and beautifully varnished. As we got nearer I saw that there was a wooden seat facing the bow. The tiller arm was about one foot above this. I noticed that the seat could be placed in different positions. About six feet in front of the seat was a raised wooden semi circular structure with doors and a sliding cover which was pushed back. This gave access to the decks below.

The doors were open and Emily daintily climbed over the step of the cockpit and then began descending, down some steps to the crew deck. There was a banister on both sides. The one on the port side fastened to a wooden divider running from stern to bow and the one on the starboard was a free banister fixed top and bottom with newel posts fastened into the steps. Both banisters were very strong. There was no movement. I followed Emily down into the bowels of the smack. As I went down the wooden divider wall was on my left or port side and an open space beyond the free banister was on my right or starboard side.

Emily stopped at the bottom of the steps turned and looking at me descending she lifted her skirt and curtseyed saying

"This Master Charles Jones is the Crew Deck."

Immediately ahead and behind her there was a space of about five feet and then a bulkhead running port to starboard with a door in it on the starboard side. To my immediate left or on the port side looking to the bow there was an arch through the wooden wall. This arch led to an alcove with an open clothes cupboard. There were many hooks on the right hand side.

"Excuse me Miss Byes but what is that stuff on the steps and the deck, it also seems to go into these alcoves?"

"Its caulk, thick caulk, I helped fit it, Stops you slipping when you are wet, and you will be wet Jonesy. The mess deck, where you eat, is through that door" said Emily pointing to the bulkhead in front of us. She pointed toward the bow.

She turned round and headed to the stern with the steps on our right or port. A bulkhead faced us spanning the smack port to starboard. Beyond was the skipper's cabin. As we approached there was, on my left or starboard side, an alcove with a thick curtain tied back with rope. There were two hammocks already in place all set with pillows and bedding. Emily saw me looking.

"This is the crew deck sleeping quarters. Those two hammocks are for the crew. Your sleeping quarters are beyond that wall. You get to them by going through the arch and then walking to the stern. Just a minute, follow me"

We went through the arch at the foot of the stairs and she gestured to three large hooks fastened into the bulkhead and to another three immediately on my right which were fastened into the dividing wall separating the clothes hanging area from the sleeping area.

"This then, is where you and the other two apprentices sleep. See the hooks fastened into the bulkhead; they are for the hammocks. You will hang yours when you board. You close that thick curtain when in bed by hauling on those pulleys. So the three hammocks on the port side are for the apprentices and the two on the starboard are for the crew. As you can see both have thick curtains. These were made by me, that is, by me with Mrs.Butterfield's oversight"

I pointed to the crew hammocks which appeared to be ready for the crew to sleep in "What are those bed coverings, I have never seen anything like them before."

Miss Byers groaned

"Oomph, I finished them last night and closed the curtains because the shipwrights and carpenters were supposed to be finished in there. It has not even been painted".

All of the walls, the sea deck roof and other fittings were painted light green. The deck beams and the bulkheads were painted black. Looking directly at me Emily said

" What is it about men? I told them to leave the curtains closed but they just do not listen".

"Excuse me Miss Byers but what are those bed coverings, they look really strange."

"They are eider downs from Torshavn in the Faroe Islands. They keep you lovely and warm. Mr. Butterfield bought them on his last trip. They are really large sacks filled with down from the Eider Duck"

We entered the door in the bulkhead facing us. It turned out to be the Butterfield's cabin. Immediately to the right of the door and backing onto the bulkhead was a large table. There were three chairs on either side plus one at the head. On the port and starboards sides were alcoves and in each alcove hung a hammock doubled up on one hook.

At the foot of the hammock towards the stern was an enclosed shelf and in this shelf was a brass jobby with a handle. At the bow end there was a raised cupboard with a copper sink in it. There was a huge water jug. In both alcoves there was a curtain going from the sea deck to the captain's deck. Beyond the alcove there was then a large desk going right across the smack port to starboard and embedded in this were a compass, barometer, Harrison chronometer, a sextant and an octant. There were numerous charts rolled up and placed in square wooden tubes joined together forming a shelf about three feet deep. On this shelf were two eider down quilts wrapped in brown paper .Emily examined everything very carefully. There were wood shavings and wood cuttings everywhere. She turned round and looking me in the eye said

"Still not ready"

She went back through the bulkhead door and began walking to the bow. As she walked she seemed to be muttering under her breath

"The port side is on the left when looking toward the bow and the starboard side is on the right".

Ahead of us was another bulkhead again going from the sea deck to the crew deck. The stairs to the sea deck were on the port, my left. At the foot of the steps on the port side, as I have already said, was an alcove. You could get to it as you left the Butterfield's cabin by walking past the steps and then turning to port or left under the arch toward the clothing bay and then left again so that the wall was now on my left or starboard. The three apprentice hammocks would be on my right or port side. She walked through this and turned left toward the stern. There were three hammocks fixings between the bulkheads. There was just enough room to walk between the dividing wall running bow to stern and the hammocks. There was sea deck to crew deck curtains. They were thick. As I have said there were two curtains with a pulley arrangement which enable the curtains to be closed or opened at each hammocks position. The pulley system was fixed to the Butterfield's cabin bulkhead and to a stern to bow deck beam. This arrangement was repeated on the starboard side but of course there were no stairs. Sorry for the repetition but a lot of events took place within the bowels of the Ann Goodman.

To get in to the top hammock on the port side was not that easy. There was a thick wooden handle fastened to the sea deck. You gripped this, placed your left foot into the hammock and climbed aboard. When in the hammock the stairs would be on the starboard beyond the partition wall with the hull on the port. When in the hammock there was a wooden wall on the port side running from the sea deck to the crew deck and in this wall, at hammock height were three lift up doors and behind them there were cupboards for storing your personnel things

My observations were interrupted by Emily saying

"Make sure you are on the top hammock".

" Why" I asked

"The sea deck is your roof and so you can fix things to it" she said moving down the alcove towards the Mess Deck bulkhead.

As I have already stated behind these lift up doors were cupboards. Beyond this was the wooden hull proper. At the bow end of the alcoves at both port and starboard deck level was a closed in shelf. The shelf butted up to the wooden partition forming the clothing cupboard. In each case on the other side of the wooden partition were drawers with brass handles. There were two for the crew and three for us. In these drawers were the jobby pales. Each was made of brass and had a carrying handle. There were three brass fish heads with their mouths open and then metal tubing shaped like rope going through the wall into the shelf. This was repeated on the other side. Miss Byers pointing to the shelf said

"You obviously sleep with your pillow at the stern end of your hammock. See, I have already made the starboard side ready" she said pointing to the other alcove. Here were the two hammocks I have already mentioned.

She blushed when pointing to the jobby's

"I am sure you know what they are for. The contents go over the side and you must be careful to cast downwind. In bad weather you have to fix the lids with the clips you see fastened to the sides there"

Both alcoves were finished. Ours had a cosy feel. I could see myself laid in my hammock with the curtains closed. I tried the pulley system and it was easy and smooth. The crew deck floor had been sanded and was ready for painting. Beyond the second bulkhead was the mess deck. We entered into the mess deck through a door on the starboard side. To the right was a large kitchen area with a metal cooking stove running from another bulkhead to the third. This continued back along the second bulkhead wall ending in a deck to deck cupboard with ten compartments in it. Each had a hinged door fastened by a locking wooden peg. The front however was open with wire mesh. Emily saw my puzzled expression

"Oh those, they are for the angels" she said.

"What angels, I don't believe in angels"

"Oh, but you will Jones'y you will."

The large stove had a metal flu outlet pipe fed through the top of the sea deck. When topside you would see this metal flu pipe connected to a metal chimney about twelve inches tall. Facing me was the mess table with stores compartments on the port and starboard sides. The door on the port side was smaller than that on the starboard. There was a three sided seating area with a table fixed to the floor and the bulkhead. It also had a bench seat on either side. The store rooms formed the port and starboard walls.

There was a chair with arms fixed to the middle deck but on slides. I could see that there were seven eating positions each with a copper ring fixed to the mess deck table. There were also seven smaller rings which appeared to be for the tankards hung on hooks on the starboard store room wall. On the port side, immediately as you entered the Mess Deck, was a very large room with double doors. They were locked.

"Doesn't it smell lovely, if lovely is the word" said Emily.

"Yes it does, just like you"

"So I smell of wood do I?"

"Eh yes, and no but, but the wood smell is really nice don't you think and since you have been working on the Ann Goodman it's not a bad thing, at least I don't think it is." I then added "I think that you are also wearing or have been using lavender"

"Oh, Mr. Charles Jones; Nicely done. I may let you call me Emily if this carries on."

Looking around she said to herself "They will have finished tomorrow so then I can get this place cleared while you are getting knotted" She laughed again.

"What is so funny Miss Byers? "

"That is my right to know and yours to wonder about. John Forge is a prankster so, be warned".

I pointed to the store room door on the starboard adjacent the start of the metal cooking range doors and asked.

"Excuse me Miss Byers but why is that one locked?"

"Well Jonesy, that is where the Rum is kept"

"But I have never drunk rum"

"That may be true today but when you are at sea and your watch of four hours finishes you will come in here. It will be warm, really warm. Master Joseph will have hot coffee on the brew and in that coffee will be molasses and rum, and you, Jones'y, will get to love it. You will not get drunk because the Butterfield's never get drunk but when its shanty time they might get merry".

"You will be expected to sing a shanty and if you do not know one you will have to make one up. I tell you what; after you return from your first fishing trip, which, I believe starts at high tide in one week, I will let you sing me your shanty. Oh! By the way, when do you intend to start drawing the Ann?"

"I need to get back into sketching first. Would you sit for me Miss Byes? Once I have made my first trip and have been paid I shall buy new pencils and several large sketching pads. Will you sit for me?"

Emily looked at me with those lovely eyes and said

"Me, sit for a sketch, um, I have never done that before, is it hard."

"No, but you have to let me pose you and set your head and arms and body so that your best features can be drawn"

She frowned "My best features and what are they?"

"Your eyes, your straight nose, your hair, your waist and your bosom"

Blushing Emily stepped forward and looking straight into my face.

"My bosom, my bosom what are you doing looking at my bosom"

"I am not looking at your bosom, though it is really nice because your waist is narrow and the white waist ribbon tied in a bow sets your figure off. Now please don't get upset, please, for I meant it from an artists point of view."

With her face blushing she said "This conversation is over, the cheek, you are here six hours and talking about my bosom"

She stamped her feet and stormed into the crew deck. She then climbed the steps to the sea deck swiftly hauling herself up by the banisters. I followed. She then walked up the gang plank at great speed and stormed off to Fisher Street. I was calling out at the top of my voice "Please don't be angry" She was about 100 yards ahead when she turned to look at me. Stuck out her bosom and laughed.

When I arrived back at number twelve I knocked and entered, to my surprise Emily was waiting. She was smiling and seemed happy.

"Tomorrow I have to take the three of you aboard the Lady Ann. What did you think of the Pool, did it give you any ideas about drawing?"

"Well, I did know something about it before. The entire fishing smack fleet collect at Creekmouth to take the flow tide up to the Pool; I have seen the tidal surge. The boys just pole the smacks away from the river banks as they are taken up stream on the flow"

Emily looked at me, her eyes seemed softer and the rage had gone.

" I have decided that you can call me Emily"

I smiled .She went on

"Did you know your Mother and Father and your Sisters?"

"Not really." I replied adding "I was five when they died. I know something about their death through Mrs. Charnock. Her view was that my family was destined from the beginning to be poor. We were destined to be of the lower class. She said that Cholera came to London in 1831 from Asia. The wogs brought it she said. They were heathens with no knowledge of Jesus. She had a water closet installed in their apartment in the Romford Workhouse. Everyone else used the piss pots or chambers as we called them. She told me that every workhouse had a huge cesspit as did nearly every house or group of houses in London.

These cesspits, though not perfect took the human shit, she called it excreta. The urine as she called it or piss was poured into the free drains. The adoption of these water closets in place of privies ended in huge amounts of water pouring into the cess pits which overflowed and so the sewers originally intended for rain water now carried raw sewerage into the Thames. The river water in turn was extracted by the water Companies to be drunk by their Customers. Before this, a long time ago a Dutchman had built a waterwheel in the fifth arch of the London Bridge and this was used to pump water to rich people's houses. Any way she told me that emptying a cess pit in the early years of this century cost a shilling. She told me there were over 200,000 cesspits in London alone. The government now allowed human waste to be dumped into the Thames. My parents and my sisters were "Toshers" or "Grubbers". They would enter the sewers looking for anything of value accidentally thrown away. One family found an engagement ring once which fed them for months. My Sisters also acted as "Mudlarks" searching the excreta of the Thames riverbed when the tide was out. They all died of typhoid. Night soil men removed human and animal waste from the cesspits and sold it as manure to the farmers. But this all ended when the guano works was built at Creekmouth. Bird shit imported from the empire to feed our soil. What a life BUT as Mrs Charnock explained to me it was God's will and I would have to put up with it. Not to do so would lead to revolution. "Just look what happened in France" she would say "They became a Republic with that blasphemer Napoleon as Emperor. Look what happened to him. I am sorry if I upset you about posing. You seem softer, why did you ask about my family?" "I heard Mr and Mrs Butterfield talking about the orphans, the workhouses and the really bad skippers. I was shocked and angry at the way they treated you and your class. I am glad you are here for you will find a home of that I am sure. Tell me Jonesy how do you know so much?"

"Well when you can't read or write you have to listen, pay attention and get people who can read and write to answer your questions. You listen. It upsets a lot of people you know, but it is, at least for me, the only way to learn. Emily, will you teach me to read, write?"

" Yes but since you are going to be at sea for weeks I will have to show you the method Mrs Butterfield used to teach me"

"Miss Byes, Emily, the Ann Goodman seems to be very comfortable almost like a yacht, not that I have been on a yacht. All the other smacks seem really basic when compared to the Ann, why is that?

"Yes it is comfortable. The Butterfield's have taken a lot of stick about that. The townspeople call her Mistress Ann, Queen of the Banks BUT they do not understand that the Butterfields are going after king cod off the Faroe Islands. Six feet long they are and weigh four and a half stone each. It's a fifteen hundred mile sail to the Faroes with no stopping on the outward sail. That is why the she has a long keel and two masts; she is very fast she can make fifteen knots with a tail wind. The Butterfields are also not fleeting, so everyone needs to be healthy and fit. This is the purpose of the Ann Goodman's design so that all will benefit in the bounty"

"What's fifteen knots and what bounty"

"Oh I don't know. The knot is a measurement of speed through the water and the bounty is an extension of the bonus negotiated at the end of the strike. You will get a percentage share of the value of whatever the catch sells for. That's why they are heading for Grimsby after each haul."

"What's a percentage share and how do you know so much?"

"I, like you, listen to everything the Butterfield's say. This is what I heard the three of them say. I wasn't snooping but they were in the front room and I was serving tea. I was in and out. You will have a share in the value of the catch. If the catch sold for twenty pounds, then, since there are twenty shillings to the pound the sum in shillings would be four hundred. I do not know what your share would be".

"Really, it seems hard to believe."

She looked at me with her jaw set.

"Yes, I know but that is what I heard. It will be in addition to what you get paid each week as an apprentice. Can you do numbers?"

"No"

"Well I can and that is what is being planned. It is on top of your weekly apprentice money.

Smiling I took her hand and shook it. "You will now have to add numbers training to the list"

9 Kitchen Time

The previous conversation took place just inside the front door after I had closed it. Emily's questions made me think about what had happened to my family. It had made me realise what a really sad end they had suffered. I followed Emily inside the house. I noticed the second door on the left was open. Emily strode towards it.

We heard a voice from inside "Is that you Jonesy"

"Yes Mrs. Butterfield it is I"

"Please come into the kitchen"

I entered through a door into the most wonderful room you could imagine. As you entered there was on the right a huge table that would easily seat twelve people. At each end of the table there were two armchairs and then five chairs down each side. Beyond this was a huge cooking stove. There was then another smaller table with a very large washing sink beside the stove with a hand pump. I noticed a dresser and several book cases with many books on them. One of these shelves contained many Bibles and Biblical reference works. I did not know what they were until Emily told me after we had finished the meal we were about to enjoy. There was a large open coal fire brightly lighting up the room.

"Ah there you are Jonesy," said Mrs Butterfield "we have been waiting. I believe you have met my Father John Forge" Mr Forge nodded.

"Yes Ma'am"

"Well this is my mother Mary and this is, as you can see, is my twin Sister Elizabeth Forge and here is Elizabeth Spashett our sister in law who we call Beth to avoid confusions. There are ten in the Forge family. Our older brother John is at sea and my nieces and nephews are with nannies. You will meet them later".

Her sister stepped forward with outstretched hand.

"Pleased to meet you, Jonesy."

"Pleased to meet you ma'am" I said.

Mrs Butterfield carried on with her introductions "Now Jonesy, this is William and Mary Butterfield my husband's father and mother and this is his Aunt Sarah."

We all shook hands and I must say that I never expected to be treated like this. I was just an apprentice after all.

Turning to Emily she said: "Go and get Chas and Billy I think they have fallen enough for one day"

Everyone laughed. My fellow apprentices came down and joined us. Charles and Joseph were in deep discussion at the small table when Mrs Butterfield summoned them both. Charles sat at the top of the table near the door and Ann sat at the bottom. Looking at Charles I heard Ann say

"Now husband please ask grace".

"Yes Dear, Our heavenly Father we approach you in the name of your Son Jesus Christ to thank you for the food we are about to receive and for the loving hands that have prepared it. We welcome into our family Jonesy, Chas and William and pray that we can take good care of them. Please give us the strength to continue our fight against the apprentice slavery. We ask this in Jesus name .Amen".

Everyone said Amen. I said Amen. Even though I had not done it before it seemed right. Another lady appeared one I had not seen before. Her name was Mrs.Shellicot. She loaded the plates with vegetables and Emily served the meat. It was roast pork. The pork had been donated by Mr. Charles father who though being a retired butcher still had contacts in the trade. There were peas and potatoes and golf balls {Brussel sprouts}.These were in a very large bowl with butter and Mrs Butterfield had fried some bacon and when it was crisp she had broken the bacon up and spread the small pieces into the sprouts. The taste was fantastic. There were roast turnips and she had tried roasting potatoes though not with a huge success. There was a plate of crackling and a bowl of apple sauce. No one seemed to mind that the roast potatoes were not cooked right. Joseph picked up a large metal jug and poured everyone, but us three apprentices, some ale he had got from the cellar It was called Goodman's Goblin. It had been brewed by Mrs Butterfield whose maiden name was Goodman Forge. I was so happy.

Master Joseph turned to John Forge and spoke "So John Emily tells me that you will be fitting the sails tomorrow"

"Yes, I will, with the help of your new boys"

"Good but call them fisher lads John for that is what they will become. Emily has also told me that you will be teaching them how to tie the navy knots? "

"Indeed I will though not all of them just the ones that we use in the fishing trade"

Both men winked, I do not know why.

We finished off the fruit cake we had tasted at my interview. Custard was available and so I poured some over my cake. Once everyone had finished eating the whole family moved toward the fire whilst Mrs Shillicot cleared the table. Logs were added and they soon burst into flames bathing the whole room in a lovely glow. Everyone had taken their seats with them. Many conversations were taking place. I spoke with Billy and the other Charles. Master Joseph reached behind him and picked up an accordion and began singing a sea shanty. The family new the chorus and joined in. I tried but did not know the words. It felt so good to be a part of this. Let me tell you that over the many years of my apprenticeship everything happened in that room good and bad. At around ten thirty we were sent to bed. Mrs Butterfield stood at the bottom of the stairs.

"Goodnight you fisher lads it's an early start tomorrow. Breakfast is at six thirty" she then coughed and went back into the kitchen.

I heard Master Charles say "You all right Ann?"

"Yes my love, what a wonderful night lets go up, time for sailing".

Much, much later when I had really got to know Master Charles he talked to me about marriage and how to treat a woman. He explained what had happened that night, my first night at Fisher Street. Ann had settled into bed. She was not wearing her usual nightgown; in fact she was not wearing anything. Charles however was still dressed. He sat down on the chair and removed his trousers and shirt. He had noticed that Ann had combed her long hair and had draped it by her neck onto her bosom. He pulled back the sheets and smiled. It was, he said, lovely to feel desired.

"Sailing it is then. You know we might get another child".

"yes dear, Charles is now nine Alfred is now seven and Ann is now five 5 and I would like another daughter"

He told me that he had not been paying attention and that he was distracted by something else. He said to my mistress

"Ann, why, when I say grace why do I always say in the name of the Lord Jesus Christ and yet when I address Almighty God I just say Heavenly Father. Surely the Creator must also have a name".

"Yes dear, I know and I know that you will someday find that name since you are a great fisherman but right now Charles I want to go sailing so please plot your course and let us get under way".

That night Walter Butterfield was conceived. As it turned out Ann was the only daughter they were to have. She was beautiful and like her mother in appearance and ways. There was a real closeness between Ann and her Father which, as time passed, was plain to see.

10 Hammock Time

The three of us entered our room on the third floor. Someone had lit all the oil lamps, even those on our tables. We were soon settled into our hammocks. I was the last to be ready and so put out the three bedroom wall lamps until only my table lamp was left on. I reached, turned off my lamp and as I fixed my pillow I felt something. I pulled the things out and there was a new sketchbook and three pencils. I smiled. I pulled the bedding up to my chin. Emily was absolutely right about the eider down quilts they were really warm. The three of us were really comfortable and hopefully at last we all had a home.

The silence was broken by William. "Jonesy are you an orphan?"

"Yes, go to sleep"

"I am an orphan; I never knew my mother or father. I have never had a home. Its funny but I think I might have found one"

"I think you may be right for Billy for I feel the same way" said Chas.

I added "Well, well, were all in agreement, were all orphans now it's time for sleep. Goodnight all."

Early in the morning I was woken by Billy.

"What is the matter William and what time is it?"

He looked at the clock on the wall. William could tell the time. I couldn't

"It's quarter past three. Sorry Jonesy but I can't sleep. This is all very new to me ~ all of this".

As he said this he pointed around the room. He then continued.

"The hammock's good, better than the poorhouse and these quilts are so warm. I have never felt or seen anything like them. I feel that, at last, someone cares for me. Stupid really since I have only been here a few hours. Do you feel the same?"

"Yes I do and I admit it is a strange but nice feeling. Now try and get back to sleep"

"Yes I will, but I don't want anything to spoil this. I woke you up to show you something, come and look at this"

He pulled the dormer curtains aside on the window looking out on the Pool. The oil lamps were out and as William had said it was three fifteen in the morning. We could just make out the Ann Goodman. It was a cloudy but moonlit night and the smack was occasionally lit up by the moonlight. Most of the she was in deep shadow from the Dock buildings and then suddenly the moon would break free and the Pool would be bathed in white light. It was a lovely sight. The tide was in and we could see her bobbing on the incoming flow. Suddenly she was bathed in moonlight. Near the gangplank were two men.

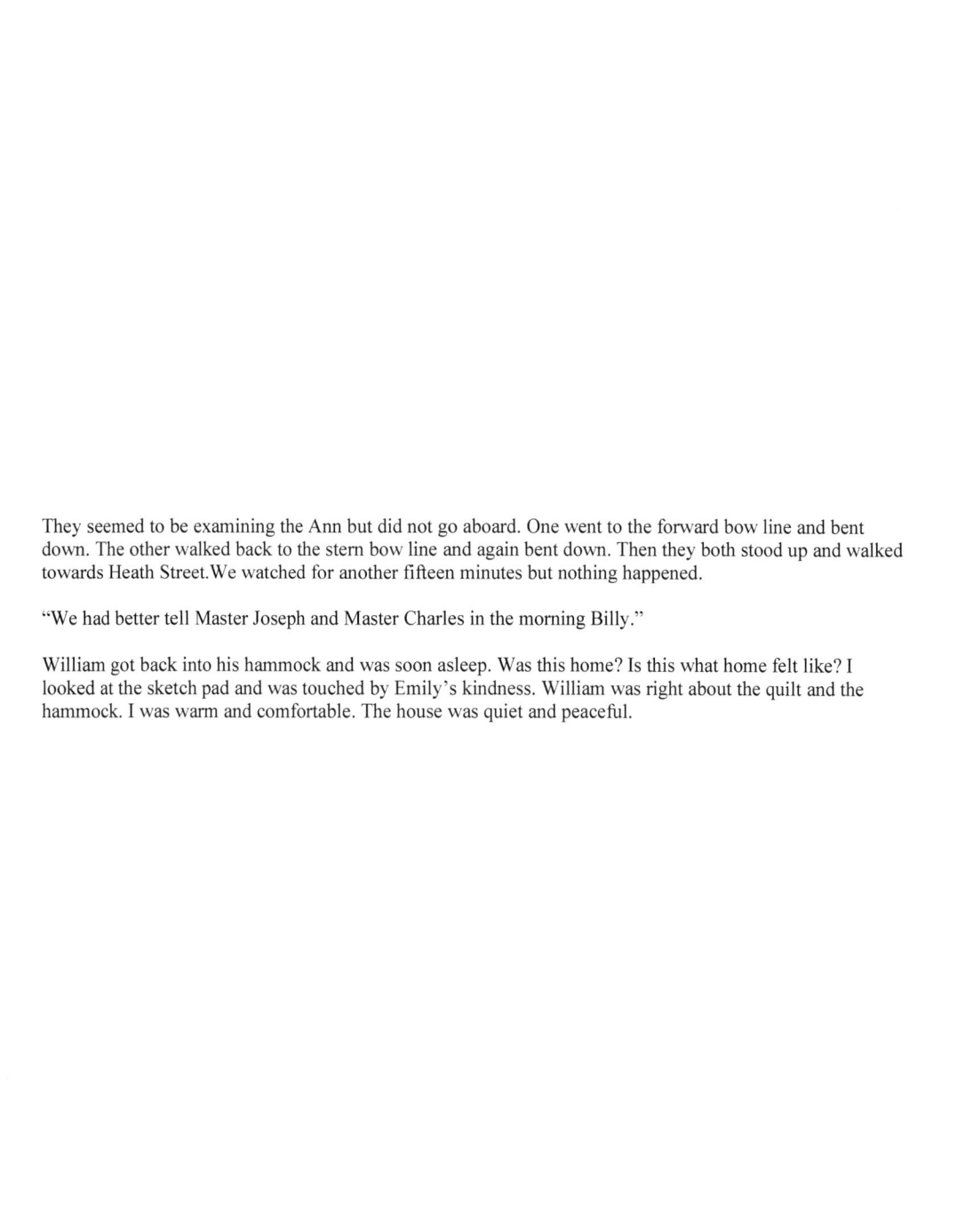

They seemed to be examining the Ann but did not go aboard. One went to the forward bow line and bent down. The other walked back to the stern bow line and again bent down. Then they both stood up and walked towards Heath Street. We watched for another fifteen minutes but nothing happened.

"We had better tell Master Joseph and Master Charles in the morning Billy."

William got back into his hammock and was soon asleep. Was this home? Is this what home felt like? I looked at the sketch pad and was touched by Emily's kindness. William was right about the quilt and the hammock. I was warm and comfortable. The house was quiet and peaceful.

11 Thursday May the 22nd

I suddenly heard a bell ringing. It was coming from the bottom of the stairs. A male voice was calling out

"Breakfast, breakfast "

All three of us staggered out of our hammocks. There was hot water in the wash basins and each had soap and towel. We washed our faces, dried, dressed and then went downstairs.

 "Chas and I have got to have a bath later today" said William "I have not had a bath for four months, Mrs .Butterfield says we smell"

 I had been made to have a bath the morning of the meeting with Mrs Butterfield. Mrs Charnock had forced me to. A cold water bath is no pleasure.

The three of us entered the kitchen to be hit by the smell of breakfast. Porridge, honey, eggs, bacon, fried onions, fried bread, tomatoes, toast, coffee, huge amounts of coffee as it turned out. Mrs. Butterfield was cooking and Emily Byes was serving. The porridge came first. Emily ladled the stuff into the bowls of Charles and Joseph Butterfield, next came Charles Junior, Alfred, Ann and then Chas, Billy and I.

I caught Charles Butterfield's attention "Excuse me Mr Butterfield"

He put up his hand "call me skipper Jonesy"

"Excuse me skipper but Billy could not sleep last night. He woke me up around three o clock. He had been looking out of the window towards the Pool. He saw two men near the bow and stern of the Ann Goodman and they seemed to be up to no good. I saw them to"

"Really" He replied "well I will check things out when we get to the smack. Let's get breakfast finished and then we must go. No more than ten minutes now for John Forge will be waiting."

Turning to Joseph he said: "Are you seeing to see to the angels Joe or are you coming now?"

"I will see to the pigeons first and then I will be over.

"About 30 minutes then"

"Yes that should do it"

"Good; see you aboard"

12 The Angels

Joseph Butterfield was a pigeon racer. He had a large pigeon loft with thirty homing pigeons. Ten of these pigeons had been trained to fly home to Barking from the Ann Goodman wherever it was. The Butterfield's were the only fishermen to use this messaging method. Though there were male and female homing pigeons they were all given female names taken from the Bible. The strongest pigeon, the one used for the greatest flight distance was called Abigail. Abigail, Billy was told, would be set free once we arrived off the Faroe islands. She was the strongest though not the fastest. The distance from the Faroes to Barking was one thousand miles. Abigail made this journey in about three days. The other pigeons had the following names and were released as we past the following places:-

Sarah	released as we passed Aberdeen on the way back
Rebecca	released off Edinburgh.
Rachel	released off Tynemouth.
Leah	as we entered Grimsby docks to offload the catch.
Ruth	released off the Holland Banks
Naomi	released off Great Yarmouth.
Bathsheba	released off the Dogger Banks.
Rahab	Hangisor Creek The Nore Thames Estuary.
Mary	Creekmouth at still water.
Martha	Creekmouth on the start of the flow.

It was Joseph's idea. It meant that the family could be kept aware of the Lady Ann's position and the well being of the crew. Charles and Joseph would write notes and messages and place these into the small containers on the angel's legs. Both men had huge hands but could write really small.

13 Getting Knotted

After breakfast at around seven o clock we arrived at the Ann Goodman's berth. The tide was nearly out so there was about two feet of water left in the Pool. The Lady Ann was resting on her cradle. Master Charles headed for the bow line and seemed to be carefully going over the cable. John Forge was waiting. "Right my fisher lads today I am going to teach you to tie six Navy knots that you will use everyday you are fishing. These knots and splices are really important so please follow me".

As the three of us entered the sail shop I noticed out of the corner of my eye Master Charles talking to a lad who looked to be about eighteen. He was leaning against the wall opposite the bow. Master Charles seemed upset.

"Come on Jonesy there is a lot to do". It was Mr. Forge.

Mr. Forge took us to the back of his premises where there was a wooden wall with kegs attached to it. These kegs rose steadily upwards until they reached a platform about 40 feet above the floor. At floor level there was straw about ten feet deep and on the top of that several mattresses.

Mr Forge spoke "Attention you fisher lads. When you have completed each knot or splice on the rope given you to work on you will climb that ladder and loop it over the baton pins you see at the top of the wall and then you will use the rope to descend the wall"

He then laughed. I could see what Emily meant when she said we were to get knotted. He took the three of us over to a bench where there were three ropes each coiled with a loop on one end. The other end had been cut. There was then a second coiled rope which had again been cut. The other end was neatly bound and butted off. Taking the line with the loop on the end and the line which had been cut he said

"The Ann Goodman is a long line smack with the longest and deepest keel in the Thames fleet. These are the line ropes. Since you are going after king cod off the Faros these lines will need looking after because they will split. This is a split long line and I am going to teach you to splice it. This work is money my young fisher lads because there could be twenty to forty king cod on this line if you are lucky. They can weigh four stone each. Your job is to inspect the lines after they have been wound on board and the cod detached and placed in the fish hold with the ice. The seamen will detach the cod and throw them to you and you will then cast them down into the ice hold. You then coil the rope inspecting it as you go. This is cold, wet and very hard work especially in a strong sea. The line will be about one mile long though some of the skippers use lines ten mile long. The hooks are tied to the line with tallow as bait"

We worked on the ropes splicing and tying all morning. After each knot or splice was ready we had to use the rope to climb the wall. It was very hard work on the arms. William fell once but it was nothing to do with rope splicing just muscle fatigue in his arms. We were working on bow line knots with Mr Forge when Emily Byes turned up with a spring in her step. Emily looked lovely and we all smiled. Mr Forge looked up and said "Pay attention lads. Complete the task by looping up in the dock cast iron mooring blocks"

We did as we were told. He then smiled at Emily and said "Right on time Miss Byes we are all ready for coffee and toast. Joseph then appeared on the wharf after climbing up the plank from the Ann. I had not seen him go aboard and then I saw Charles walking briskly along the wharf from the direction of Heath Street. Mr Forge put a large piece of decking on two trestles. Emily poured the coffee, out came the rum, just a drop in each cup and then the lid was placed back on the coffee pot and we scoffed the toast.

Looking at his brother Joseph asked "So who was it then?"

"The boy doesn't know because he was asleep, he woke up when one of them tripped, He thinks it was Craddock but cannot be sure"

Turning to us Joseph said "Right you fisher lads you are going to be on watch sooner than we thought. Jonesy you are going to take the night watch from midnight until four. You are excused Billy but Chas you will take from four until eight. I will take from eight until midnight"

Turning to his brother Joseph said "How did he take being sacked?"

"Not good, we have made an enemy there"

Joseph paused as if trying to recollect something. "Didn't Mrs. Plant say something to Ann about two seamen being beaten up over the strike?"

"She did, that was John Harrison and Fred Scattergood" said the Skipperr.

"Do they know who did it?" asked Joseph

"Don't know" replied Charles. "They are both at sea right now but are due back on the flow. Thought we might offer them crew tickets. What do you say?"

"Fred Scattergood is a drunk so I don't think we should use him." said Joseph.

"Well, he has four sons and four daughters and the Town gossip says he was forced to marry Florence by the Barber clan because he made her pregnant out of wedlock"

"You seem to know a lot." Joseph replied.

"I spoke with Florence one Sunday after the Service at St Margaret's. She had been crying. She is a sweet gentle soul forced into a loveless marriage by the Barbers. Fred does not love her and never did and so they are both miserable. The only thing in Fred's favour is that he does work hard to provide for his family. Life is tolerable for Florence as long as he is not on the Drink. Toby won't serve him at the Fishing Smack so he runs a tab at the Stanhope Arms.

Joseph frowned and said "that's Richard Scattergood's place isn't it?

"Yes, Richard is Fred's grandfather and it is to his shame that he allows Fred to get drunk there. If he is at sea with us then Florence will have peace ~ that's how I'm thinking"

"Hm ~ OK BUT there will be NO drink for him of any kind whilst he is at sea. I need you to understand this Charles. We carry Rum on the Lady Ann in the drinks cupboard. I will get a padlock. Agh! A padlock on me own smack."

"Thanks Joseph ~ I agree. My plan is to use them both on all the trips so long as they fit in and work hard"

"We will have no trouble with John Harrison. I know him; he is Reuben Rodgers's son in law. You know Reuben; he is the hostler on New Road. John married Alice and they have three children with another on the way."

"Do you think Harry might know who beat them up?"

Harry was the owner of the Fishing Smack pub.
"He might, I will ask him tonight after dinner, you coming with me? Asked the Skipper.

"Of course, you fool, perhaps the saboteurs will be there and a ruckus might well occur, I have not been in a good fight for months."

"Yes I know what you mean but what did Cut Bunton teach us?"

I noticed that Emily was rapt in attention taking in everything that was being said. My ears pricked up when I heard the name Cut Bunton. That was short for Uppercut Bunton. He was the best bare knuckle street fighter ever to contest in Barking. Barking was the centre of the London street fighting sport. People came from all over to watch the fights. It was outlawed in 1851. Cut was retired but could often be seen around Barking. He had never been beaten and always went for the knockout usually with an uppercut punch.

Joseph replied "As far as it depends on you be peaceable with all men".

"Where does it come from?" asked Charles.

"From the Bible you self righteous prick" said Joseph "You and your Bible Mr.Charles Butterfield wear me out, anyway what is a bloke like Cut doing quoting from the Bible considering what he did for a living"

Charles replied.

"He was teaching us how to fight and also reminding us that WE catch fish for a living and do not fight for a living. We are NOT street fighters. "

Joseph looked straight into his Brother's eyes, close up and said

"What else did Mr .Nathaniel Cut Bunton teach us Mr. Charles, Bible bashing, Butterfield"

Charles winked at his brother who immediately broke into laughter.

"He said that if we could not avoid a fight then there was no point in losing and we should go for the knockout because an unconscious man was not dangerous"

"So, me dear brother have you ever knocked any body out?"

"Er, yes, must we always do this"

"How many punches?"

"At the most three, I know, not like you; punch em out Butterfield. You down them with one punch"

Turning to his audience the Skipper said

"Joseph Butterfield, my beloved Brother and friend is not to be messed with, he has no patience and enjoys knocking people out: but in his defence I would have to say that they have all deserved it"

Joseph smiled at his Brother "and you Bible Bashing Butterfield have you never enjoyed a fight? "

There was a long pause "err yes, now let's get back to work."

Everybody laughed including Emily; she set off back to Fisher Street as we entered the sail shop.

"Seeing them fight is a sight to behold" said Mr Forge "especially when they do the capstan, Charles grabs them by the arm and spins them round to meet the incoming bone crushing fist of Joseph, proper seamen's hands he has shaped by hauling in long line cod and you know what? I could do with seeing a good fight. I tell you now boys that if anyone is trying to damage the Ann there will be a great fight and we must all be there though the Butterfield boys will try to do it in secret. Let's hope they fail. I do so like my Son in Law and he loves my Ann with all his heart. Did you know she has a twin Sister Elizabeth, oh of course you do you met her last night"

We spent the rest of the afternoon tying knots, knots and more knots and then splicing, splicing and more splicing. Chas Adson was a natural. He picked it up much faster than Billy or me. He also had very strong arms and seemed to enjoy the rope climb. I saw Mr. Forge looking at Chas. I wonder what is going on there.

At four o clock our Masters came up the plank from the Ann Goodman

"Come on my fisher lad's time to wash and change for dinner. Mustn't keep Mrs Butterfield waiting"

This came from Joseph.

We entered Fisher Street and Charles said:

"Go up, wash and change and then bring the clothes down with you. Mrs. Shellicot, our char lady, is washing tomorrow"

The three of us entered the house and went up to the third floor and sure enough there on the hammocks were a fresh set of clothes, shirt, vest, trousers, pants and crude thick sock slippers. There was hot water in all three bowls which Emily must have taken up. There were three jugs full of warm water as well. The bell rang and a voice sounded from below:-

"Thirty minutes to mess time"

I could not count the time but William could. He pointed to the clock over the door and said

"She means five o clock. We have about fifteen minutes"

William climbed into his new duds. Chas and I did the same. He pulled something bright and shiny out of his pocket. It was mouth organ.

"Who gave you that "I asked.

"Master Joseph gave it to me. He is going to teach me to play alongside him and his accordion so we can get a good tune up for his sea shanties."

At five o clock we walked into the kitchen but tonight there were fewer members of the Family. Elizabeth Forge was there helping her sister, Mrs Shellicot, Emily, Aunt Sarah, Charles, Joseph and us three. The children were at their Grandmothers for tea.

"Excuse us Mrs Butterfield but where shall we place our dirty clothes"

Turning towards the back door Mrs Butterfield shouted "Mrs Shellicot, where do you want these?"

A char lady appeared "In the back boys, follow me"

We followed her outside to the washhouse.

"Put them there with the others"

She looked at my new shirt and trousers and seemed to be very impressed. "Mrs Butterfield is such a good milliner"

"Excuse me Mrs Shellicot what is a milliner" I asked.

"I guess you cannot read or write Jonesy, she can make clothes that is what it means. I guess you are wondering if I can read and write, well the answer is yes. I used to be a teacher but have fallen on hard times still that has nothing to do with you does it?

"Err, No sorry for asking"

When the meal was finished and we had drunk tea by the fire Ann Butterfield said

"Right who's for writing, reading and poetry"

William, Chas, Emily and I raised our hands and then so did Joseph.

Looking at us Joseph said "I only go for the poetry"

Smiling at her brother in law Mrs.Butterfield said "Ideas for sea shanties is it, Master Joseph, pull the other one. Come on then into the drawing room."

She got out an easel and gave Emily a white chalk. She gave us small tablets and chalks. She proceeded to teach us the alphabet and then the sounds. She then asked Emily to go through the numbers. Standing in front of me Emily said

"This is the number two, Jonesy"

Mrs Butterfield guided my hand as a tried to copy the number.

"Please say it again Miss Byes" I said.

Pouting her rose red lips together she said "two"

"Thank you" I said, "can you say it once more", I added.

"Two "she said.

Under my breath I said "wonderful lips" thinking she would not hear. I looked up to face a blushing Emily Byers "That's enough of you Mr Charles Jones" and she then stormed out.

Mrs Butterfield nudged me and said:-

"Oh dear, dear Jonesy and you were doing so well".

Turning to Joseph she said with a laugh "and what have you got for us Joe"

Joseph stood up

"This is not finished but
A   is for ash wood the deck is made from
B   is for Barking where we all come from
C   is for Charles my Brother and friend
D   is for the Dogger and a really bad end.

Alphabet, Alphabet, letters you see help me to write down my long sea shanty

E   is for Eliza my sister in law
F   is for fresh fish on Billingsgate floor.
G   is for God who Charles name needs to know
H   is for hauling fish in a big blow.

Alphabet ,Alphabet letters you see help me to write my long sea shanty

I   is for indigents Jonesy will say
J   is for any job coming his way
L   is for laughter when you fall out of bed.
M   is for mourning our fisherman dead

And on it went. Mrs Butterfield encouraged us to learn it well since it would help. She then said: "OK your time is now your own"

Joseph turned to us and said "would you fisher lads like to meet the angels?

"Err yes sir" we all said.

"Follow me then"

We went through the back door of the kitchen into the garden. At the bottom of the garden was a small tree with a seat beneath if for two looking out to Barking Pool. Before this on the left was Master Joseph's pigeon coop. We went through a latched door and up some steps. The pigeons were all there in cages. There would have been about thirty. They all moved to the front of the cage and then Master Joseph dropped the single door and they took flight. Up they went all together sweeping over Barking Pond and circling the wharf and then they all alighted on Mr Forge's building. They then took off again circling Heath Street and Fisher Street.

"Thank you Mr Joseph" I said "I am going to get my pad and pencils while the light is good"

"Wait a minute Jonesy and watch what happens".

He took a whistle out of his pocket and blew on it .Immediately twelve of the pigeons broke away and headed straight for us. As they got closer one of the birds separated from the flock and landed on Joseph's hat. She then popped down onto his shoulder and when he raised his hand the bird leapt onto that. He gently placed the other hand over her wings and picked her up

"This is Abigail; she will be released by one of us when we reach Torshvaal in the Faroes. One of you will have to learn to feed and look after them on the Ann Goodman. They cannot be set free to fly until we get to the right place. So who shall it be?"

William pushed through "Could I do it Master Joseph?"

"You most certainly can, but there has to be a back up"
Chas Adson said "that will be me sir""

"Good that's settled then so here is what you do as regards the messages. You see this ring with the clip on it on her right leg. I or Master Charles will give you a small cylinder and you will simply grip the ring, NOT Abigail's or any of the other pigeons legs and then push the cylinder into the clip. We will have written a message and rolled it up inside the cylinder. If you can write or should I say when you can write you can also put a message inside it."

"Excuse me Master Joseph but how far is it from the Faroes to Barking?"

"Well for Abigail it's about 1000 miles in a straight line. She can do it in about 20 hours non stop. She can and does fly through the night. I do not know how she does it but she seems to be able to read the stars, but don't ask me how. Ask the Skipper. He will tell you it's because God made it so, agh. One of my friends in Barking sold a long distance racing pigeon to a man in Canada. She escaped from St John's in Newfoundland and was home in 55 days. She probably flew over Greenland; then to Iceland thus avoiding a long flight over the open sea. She would make land at the Faroes, then fly on to the Orkneys and then down the centre of Scotland and England to home"

I pulled Mr Joseph's arm to get his attention "Can I go now and get my sketching stuff"

"Yes and I will teach these two how to feed the birds"

I left and went back into the house, through the kitchen and upstairs. As I passed Emily she looked at me and said

"What do you think of the Angels?"

"Great idea if you can read and write. If I could write I could send you a message"

She lowered her head and then looked up

"You would want to do that"

"Yes, if that would be good with you"

"Err, yes, that would be good so we need to teach you quickly. Master Charles will take over once you're at sea"

As I was going up the stairs I heard an agitated voice "Agh Emily" said Mrs Butterfield "Have you seen those shirts pants and trousers the boys brought down"

I left and went upstairs, got my sketch pad and went back out down to the bottom of the garden where the tree was. The light was good. I could see the Ann Goodman really well. The tide was now out and she was sat in her cradle on the wooden beams which were placed in the mud right along the wharf. Just to my left was one of the Thames barges full of coal. She had come up on the flow and was now sat on the mud moored to a wooden jetty which was part of Morgan's Wharf.

A small road ran between the buildings and houses connecting to Fisher Street. The coal was being unloaded into wagons even as I sat down. They carried about one hundred tons. I learnt this at the collier peer at Creekmouth. I had loaded coal onto barges just like it. It was very hard work.

 Emily Byers walked up and said "What are you going to draw" "

"I thought I might draw the Ann sat in her cradle. I thought you were helping Mrs Butterfield with the clothes washing"

"No, she didn't want me for that. It seems two shirts, a set of trousers and some fishermen's socks have gone missing. Anyway, I thought you wanted to sketch me."

 "Yes, Yes, Yes but I was afraid to ask. Thank you for the gift it was a real surprise. Can I do a head sketch?"

"Not my bosom then"

It was my turn to blush. "Now just take your hat off and loosen your hair. Loosen the button at the top of your dress. Sit here and turn your face so that you are looking at the pool. Look at the Ann"

"Is this Ok"

"Perfect now there is just one rule. You must not move until I have got your features right. I can get the details later. Now pull a thick strand of hair down and twist it so its hangs in front of your ear. Her hair was really long, deep brown but gold where the sun caught it". She sat perfectly still; she really was pretty perhaps even beautiful but even those words did not really do justice to Emily Byes. Yes she was beautiful but she did not know it. She said she was fifteen but she looked more like eighteen. I was lost and completely taken with the moment. Time passes so fast when you are having fun and loving life. The light was good and though I kept making errors I soon got Emily's face shape, profile, hair and neck just about right. No detail but, I was pleased.

"That's it I said"

"Let's have a look "said Emily "well it is definitely me but why is it all blank and not filled in?

"You have to do the outline first. I'll start filling it in later tonight ".

"But how will you do that"

"From memory"

"I am in your memory?

"Oh yes, Emily Byes, an artist always remembers when he has been affected by what he is drawing. I will remember every line but perhaps another sitting will help"

"Oh, are we doing this tomorrow then?"

"Well, yes, if that's OK with you. Will you have the time?"

"Yes Jonesy, I will".

At that moment we heard Mrs Butterfield call out "Hey Jonesy, it's time you were in bed. Your watch starts at midnight"

"Coming Mrs B" I said. As I climbed the stairs Emily looked up and said

"I enjoyed sitting for you Jonesy, see you for breakfast".

14 Friday Morning May the 23rd

Sabotage

It was about two in the morning. I was sat on a bench I had set up on the wharf at the stern position of the Ann Goodman. There was some moonlight but it was mostly dark with the occasional moonbeam. The Flow was coming in and the Louisa kept bumping into the wharf. I had gone aboard and adjusted the bow and stern ropes as I had been shown. I was practicing bow line knots in the light of a small oil lamp when I heard some footsteps on the cobbles. It was Emily Byes I smiled.

"Thought you would like some hot coffee and rum and most of all my company"

"Yes, yes, that would be so nice, thank you for thinking of me"

"Do not get carried away Jonesy, Mrs Butterfield told me to do this last night after you had gone up"

"Oh" I said quite disappointed.

She had a large coffee pot in a thick towel. It felt hot as she poured out the coffee into the mug she had given me. I took a drink. It was really strong but sweet with the smell of molasses.

"This is delicious, are you having some"

"Try and stop me, the molasses sets the coffee and rum off don't you think"

Our hands just touched as she gave me my drink. One was warm and the other was cold. I gently took the cold hand and rubbed it.

"Oh, oh, oh that's nice, look there is another moon beam."

It passed over number twelve and we both looked. We talked about how long she had been at the Butterfield's and her gaze again wandered towards Fisher Street. I followed her gaze

"Sure is lovely "

She tensed.

"What is the matter", I asked. "Jones'y do you think that coal barge is moving or am I seeing things."

I looked at the barge. You could only see a dark shape. It was about four hundred yards away. The Creek flow was really strong and there was some noise from the barge but that would be expected.

"It is probably just the strength of the current working her lines against the jetty".

We carried on talking suddenly there was the sound of a splash. We looked towards the barge and saw two shadows leave the barge and enter the road on Morgan's Wharf. Then they were gone.

Suddenly Emily grabbed my arm and shouted "Jonesy the barge, the barge it's free look"

"God it is free! Quick, run as fast as you can and get the Butterfield's"

I dropped down onto the Ann Goodman's deck and tried to loosen the stern line from the cleat but I could not undo the knot. I did not know what to do. I climbed back onto the dock to release the stern line from the mooring pin but could not get the loop over the lip of the pin. The barge was moving slowly but steadily towards the Lady Ann's stern. With all that coal on board she would be crushed. Just about then Charles and Joseph arrived with Chas, William, and Charles Butterfield Junior.

"Cant get the stern free sir, I can't get the rope free from the cleat, the knot is really tight"

"I'll free it Jones'y from the mooring pin and come aboard".

"Damn, damn, look at this Joseph someone has fastened the slip knot with thread and needle I cannot get it free"

With that Joseph jumped on board and ran to the cleat to which the stern rope was tied.

"Someone's tied this with a devils knot"

He suddenly ran down the steps into the crew deck. In seconds he emerged with an axe. He ran up the plank this time and with one blow severed the cable at the mooring pin. Looking at me he said

"A place for everything and everything in its place Jonesy remember"

Charles and Joseph got back onto the Ann Goodman and grabbing the new punt poles fastened to the deck began pushing with me so that the Lady Ann pivoted on the bow line. Five minutes later with the Louisa moored against another smaller barge the coal barge hit the wharf with an almighty crash. The current swirled and fastened her against the right hand wall of the wharf. Charles and Joseph jumped onto the wharf and ran to the coal barge climbed on board and found that the bow and stern ropes were dragging in the water. They pulled them up and found that they had been cut. They quickly retrieved them, tied bow line loops and then dropped them round the mooring pins for and aft and then sighed with relief. They climbed back onto the wharf and walked quickly toward us.

"That's what caused the splash then" said Joseph "Now, Emily, what else did you see"

"Well sir it was dark and I couldn't really see anything but two dark shapes did leave the barge and head up the alley to Fisher Street"

"So someone deliberately cut the barge free to sink the Ann Goodman" said Master Joseph.

"Let me shake your hand Jonesy your quick thinking saved the smack"

"Mr. Joseph, just look at your hands! They are covered in coal dust"

The dust was very difficult to get rid of because it was so fine getting into all the skin creases in your hands. It took me days to get rid of it when I was loading coal at Creekmouth.

"So they are" looking at Charles Joseph said "You thinking what I'm thinking"

"Yes, they will be in the bothy at the bottom of the Fishing Smack's garden washing their hands ~ come on"

"Just a minute Joseph, we need to get the Ann back into position over the cradle"

"Right, come on then the faster the better".

"All three of us punted the Louisa back over the sunken cradle "

"Jonesy tie her off with a bow line now and then we have got to go"

Both ran off at some speed turning right into Fisher Street. The dawn was just starting. Suddenly we saw lots of oil lamps. People were coming from Fisher and Heath Street down to the wharf. Mr John Forge was there with his wife Mary and Mrs Butterfield's twin sister Elizabeth. Then up came William, Mary and Sarah Butterfield. Following them was Ann Butterfield with Alfred in her arms and her daughter Ann. Others were approaching including Chas Adson to take over my watch.

"Where on earth are they going and what happened, the house shook and woke us all up "said Mr Forge.

I spoke "Someone tried to sink the Lady Ann Mr. Forge. They cut the mooring ropes on the coal barge"

"Did they indeed, well I'll be damned". All the townsfolk present were shocked and angry. It was, after all a Town dependant on its fishing trade.

"There will be hell to pay over this, you mark my words. If Joseph ever gets hold of who did it they just won't survive"

I later learned at breakfast that when the brothers got to the Fishing Smack pub Joseph crept down the side of the pub and then down to the bothy in the garden. He had taken his boots off. There were five men in the bothy drinking in the light of an oil lamp. Joseph heard Craddock's voice saying that what they had done would finish the Butterfield's. He then heard another voice which he new was Stump Slater, a man Scrimey used for any bullying he needed doing. Both men were washing their hands with a scrubbing brush. Joseph returned and told Charles what he had heard.

"Time for capstan then" said Charles

"Aye but not in secret, this needs doing in front of the whole of the fishing community, tonight in the Pub after work"

"Absolutely Joseph it must be done before all"

A large smile crossed Joseph's face. What about "As far as it depends on you"

"Perhaps they will say sorry and tell us who paid them to do the deed"

"And if they don't what then"

"They must right the wrong, that's what repentance is ~ writing the wrong."

"Do not preach at me Brother"

"I am not preaching at you" and then with a wink Charles said "Craddock will not say sorry and neither will Stump ~ you will get your fight and so will I"

Stump Slater only had one leg. He lost it in a bad situation at sea. He was a bitter man because he could no longer go fishing for no skipper would employ him. He was a big bloke.

Turning to Charles Adson, the Skipper said;

"Do not, whatever you do, do not go to sleep Chas"

"I won't"

Everyone began to leave.

"Come on you two; time to go home" said Mrs Butterfield with Alfred in her arms, She coughed

"Come on, I will get my death out here hold onto my hand Charles" she said to her firstborn son.

Home, time to go home, I had a home now and much much more I had a family. Emily slipped her arm into mine and we walked back in silence. It seemed so natural. What a night it had been.

Friday Evening
By the end of the week the Lady Ann was finished. All the sails had been fitted and all of the ropes and pulleys adjusted and tried. She looked great. Emily had been down and cleaned the Butterfield's cabin, the crew and mess desks and so the smack was now ready for provisioning. It seemed like a never ending column of carts and horses and then suddenly all that was left was for the food, water and fishing tackle together with bad weather clothing to be loaded. This was to come from Fisher Street with us the Fisher Lads being the mules.

It was Friday night and after dinner Mr. Charles and Mr Joseph were going over to the Fishing Smack pub to see if Craddock and his crew were there. I was to accompany them. Joseph had disappeared and about fifteen minutes earlier and the Skipper was upset.

"Where is Joseph Jonesy?"

"I do not know Skipper but he left in a hurry, I saw him going up Heath Street towards St Margaret's"

"Um well he wasn't going to Church; Joseph is not a believer; so where was he going?"

"As I say Master Charles I don't know"

At that moment Master Joseph arrived with a horse and wagon.

"Where have you been?"

"I have been to Rueben Rogers to get transport for the bodies"

"Bodies, what bodies, are there going to be bodies? What are you talking about?"

"The bodies after the fight we are going to have in about fifteen minutes .Do not forget my brother that they are all going to be out for the count"

At that moment Mrs Butterfield came in from the kitchen to the front door. She put her hand on her husband's broad shoulder causing him to turn round.

"Now my dear I know that this has got to be done but please be careful. Please try to avoid a fight remember the Apostle Paul's words,

"Remind me"

"As far as it depends on you be peaceable with ALL men" she said.

"Oh yes, now I remember, but what if it is not possible?"

"Charles, I do not think that it will be possible due to Craddock's nature. He is a snake Charles and snakes do not fight fair as we have already seen with the coal barge. Don't drag it out, do what Cut Bunton taught you and knock him out cold. See you later"

Joseph had already moved on with the horse. He guided the cart to the front of the Pub. It was only fifty yards. He went inside. We followed. The Pub was crowded. Joseph walked straight up to a bloke sat on a stool at the bar. He was a bruiser of a man really tough looking and his face was scarred.

"Excuse me, Skipper but who is Master Joseph talking to"

"That Jonesy is Nathaniel Bunton known among the street fighting community as CUT. What he is doing here is anyone's guess"

"So he is the street fighter all of London talked about. I even heard Mrs. Charnock talking about him. Never lost a fight I was told?"

"No, never lost a fight but he gave it up five years ago"

The Skipper looked at me and said "Do you want a lemonade"

"Eh, no sir I will just stay by the door"

Master Charles went over and pushed his brother to the side.

"Steady now Brother don't be rough"

"Well, well, well. CUT Bunton if my eyes do not deceive me. It sure is good to see you, must be 3 months since we had a good chat. How are you?"

"Aye so it is, and I am well and living comfortably off my ill gotten gains and now I hear you have your own smack just like you wanted"

"You want a Morgan's" asked Master Charles.

"Aye that I will "

"What are you having Joseph"

"With what I am going to do I will just have lemonade"

"Why are you here Cut?" asked the Skipper.

"News travels fast. I was over in Ilford and heard about the barge. I also learnt that Craddock's coming but he won't be on his own. So we need to take them all out, he knows what you intend to do"

"Well how does he know that?"

"Mrs. Shellicott. She is the char woman for his wife just like she is for yours. Everyone knows my Butterfield boys, everyone that is why the Pub's full; remember though that most of the people here are your friends. Your stand on the strike is well remembered everyone's life got better cos of it.

"I see"

"I warned you about Mrs. Shellicot" said Joseph. "She is not to be trusted. Ann is missing some of the clothes she has made for us"

"Well how do you know that?"

"Because she's been loading up the Ann"

"I see"

"You don't see because you are always looking for the good in people"

"That's bad is it?"

"No, it's not bad Charles. I love you for it but sometimes it's daft, but do not change, for you see I love my brother just the way he is"

Master Charles raised his eyebrows "Why are you so sweet all of a sudden?"

"We have a scrap on tonight Charles and I do not wish for either of us to get hurt, you get that Cut, we need to take em down quick"

"We sure do so are you both ready because a gang just past the window"

At that moment the door swung open and Craddock marched in with five others. I dropped down in front of him just like master Joseph told me to and so he tripped and began to fall forward. Master Joseph move like lightning and as Craddock fell forward he met Master Joseph's giant fist moving toward him with speed and certainty. It landed on his jaw. Thwack, and down he went out for the count. Stump Slater stepped over him with a scaling knife in his hand. He lunged at Charles who nimbly stepped to one side grabbing Stumps outstretched arm and shouting at the top of his voice "Capstan". He spun stump round and as Stump rotated his face met with Joseph Butterfield's renowned uppercut. He went out for the count. Now there were two bodies on the floor and the crowd in the pub was going mad. At that moment Cut stepped into the ring that had formed and shaped up to the other four thugs and within minutes two were out for the count. The remaining two tried to run for it but the crowd had blocked the exit. Charles stepped forward.

"Who put you up to this, come on speak up"

"Piss off Butterfield you don't scare me, neither you nor your fishwife"

It was as if something was ignited inside the Skipper for he stepped forward and hit the man with a right hook. The man staggered to the left and then Charles punched him in the stomach with his left fist, the man bent over and then was caught by a right to the jaw. He went down. Charles then did something shocking, even though the man was dazed Charles jumped on top of pounding him with both fists until his face was a bloody pulpy mess.

"Leave him be Charles leave him be" cried Joseph but it took Cut and Joseph to drag Master Charles off.

He was not right for days.

"Right lets load up then"

Joseph said turning to me and Cut.

"He'll be no use now" he said nodding at Master Charles.

"Go home Charles, Cut and I will do the rest"

Master Charles said nothing but just got up and headed for the door. The crowd moved aside to let him pass. I heard one of the fishermen say to his mate

"He just shouldn't have mentioned Ann, when they were courting Charles Butterfield put a bloke in Hospital over a remark he made about Ann. He had a fearsome temper. Some say that it was after he met Ann that he got religion. Ann Goodman Forge certainly calmed him down."

I had never seen Master Charles anywhere near being angry. In the Pub everyone had enjoyed the scrap until Charles went berserk. I heard Toby the owner saying at the Bar

"Now you see what Charles Butterfield was like before he found God. You could always be sure of a good scrap for no reason at all. Why, even when he was provoked by Scrimey he kept his temper. You mark my words he is going to feel bad"

All six bodies were loaded into the cart. They were still out. Joseph and Cut tied their hands behind them and then their feet with fishing twine.

"Where we going Joe" said Cut.

"We are going to the fat pits at Creekmouth. Are you coming Jonesy?

"You bet sir I would not miss this for anything"

Creekmouth was two miles down the bank of the Barking Creek.

We went down Fisher Street and soon left the Town behind heading along the well worn wagon track

15 Repentance

It was some time later that I heard what took place when the Skipper got home. Emily told me this:-

Charles opened the door of number twelve and staggered into the parlour.

"Charles is that you" Ann said "That didn't take long". She entered the parlour to see her husband in tears silently sobbing.

"Oh my dear, dear love, what is wrong"

Gradually the sobbing stopped. Ann held her husband close and tight, she didn't speak.

Master Charles gasped

"The anger, my anger it came back, I, I would have killed him if they had not dragged me off. I wanted to kill him"

He sobbed again

"Of what use am I to Him if I cannot control this rage within me"

Ann looked at her husband with tender loving eyes

"I guess I was the cause ~ yes"

"Oh yes, yes he threatened to hurt you"

"And you are never ever going to let that happen are you my love ~ even if it the cause of you being sent to prison. Now how did he threaten to hurt me?"

"He called you a fishwife just like that other skipper that I put in Hospital. I just want to really, really hurt them ~ vengeance, true and pure vengeance. How can I be a Christian if I act like that when provoked?"

"Charles please listen to me ~ I fell in love with you because you care about people, the fisher lads, the orphans and about the cruelty. I saw that you were going to fight this and I wanted to be a part of that fight. The fact that you found the your Heavenly Father and his loving Son through me is one of the blessings of my life. You are a good man Charles, you may not be totally righteous but you are totally good. Remember when I told you about the Pharisee and the sinner"

"Yes I think so"

"The Pharisee stood before God and listed out all his good deeds, the sinner just bent his head and simply begged for forgiveness and Jesus said that it was the sinner HIS Father listened to not the Pharisee. Why even Peter slipped back into his fishermen's ways when Jesus was on trial denying him three times and then cursing"

"I remember"

"Jesus heard all of this, his back was to the patio wall and the fire around which all were gathered was only nine feet below, When Jesus was led away he looked at Peter but the look saved him Charles, it saved him. It was not a look of condemnation was it for he became one of the most used apostles. Now my love go and do what you have to do and then come down for supper"

Charles went upstairs passing Emily on the way down. He glanced at her; she saw that he had been crying. He gave her a small smile and then entered his and Ann's bedroom. She heard him drop to his knees, the gentle sobs followed and then the prayer but she knew that must be private so she hurried down into the kitchen. She was greatly affected as was I when she told me later. How can anyone feel like that, as if God is real, a real person that you can make happy that you can make sad. I had thought that if he existed at all he must just be power just power, right and wrong punishment. Master Charles and his wife seemed to be connected to a person. Emily and I agreed to talk about this later.

16   East Marsh Pond

Creekmouth was a small village with a school and Pub built for the workers employed at the Lawes Chemical Plant. There was also a Guano works. Close by were the Navy and Army Magazines. It was a dangerous place but always seemed peaceful. From Creekmouth you could see all the ships heading for the Royal Docks in London. Many lay moored in Barking Reach just where Barking Creek entered the Thames. They would wait there until they had a berth at the docks. On the northern side of the Thames just up from Barking Creek they were building a huge Gas works to feed London with Coal Gas. Becton Pier had already been built ready to take the sailing colliers from the North. The railway was under construction and the track went onto the pier enabling coal to be loaded directly into wagons and then taken by steam engine into Becton Gas works. The coal was also taken into London for house fires and so on. The worst thing about Creekmouth was that six hundred feet from the mouth of the Creek was Balzagette's Main Drainage sewer outfall. I was told when I worked at Creekmouth that the plan was to deliver all of London's untreated sewage into the eastern Thames estuary so that the tidal surge would then take it out to sea. It did not work. The tide did not carry the shit and refuse out to sea as expected. It all came ashore. There were banks of solid shit nine feet deep along the creek with animal guts, fat slime and other horrors. There were huge fat pits and the Creek's banks had collapsed at certain points. There were trees stretching out over the pits. The trees eventually also fell into the Creek. There was however one tree called Boys Oak that hung on seemingly unaffected. From this tree fishing apprentices would be hung over the pit. If the rope broke they would be dumped into the fat and slime. They did not drown but floated in the stench. They smelled for weeks. I knew that this was where Joseph was taking them.

Joseph was determined and quite but in a very unnerving way. It took about an hour to get to Creekmouth. When we arrived our guests were just coming round. Cut Bunson and Joseph pulled Craddock from the wagon. Joseph shinned up Boys Oak and out onto the large branch stretching out over the fat pits. Cut tied a rope to Craddock's feet and then tossed it to Joseph who looped it over the branch and then jumped back onto the bank. The two of them then hauled him up over the fat pit. They did the same to Stump but took his wooden leg off and threw it into the fat pit. It floated on the scum. Craddock was using foul language and threats so Joseph hit him again, knocking him out. He then took two bricks and smashed them into Craddock's tiller hand. He did this several times until the hand was busted. He then turned to Stump and broke his other leg.

Turning to Cut he said "We will keel haul the other three at the East March pond."

"Good job done then" said Cut

"Yep, they won't be bothering us anymore now. Craddock and Stump have hauled many an apprentice out over the Creek. They are both known for their cruelty to the fisher lads. They had this coming! What we have to do is find out who put them up to this "

"Let's go to East Marsh then and get this done" said Cut. As we left he turned round and said

 "I hope the ropes break soon"

"They will I nicked them with that knife Stump had."

"Good thinking. The longer they are in the shit the better".

I said: "They <u>will</u> stink if they drop into that fat pit Master Joseph. When I was working on the dock Craddock hauled two apprentices up Boys Oak and they fell in. One was only eight but we managed to get them both out. All the water in the world could not get them clean just carbolic soap."

I learnt later that when the Police finally arrived at Creekmouth they had been in the shit for nearly four hours. It took over an hour to get them out by which time the police stank .They later called at the Fishing Smack pub and spoke with people outside on Fisher Street but there were no witnesses and no one would talk. Their stench and appearance caused much laughter. As for Craddock and Stump though the Police asked them to name the people who had done this to them they remained silent. They left Barking and the last we heard were in Great Yarmouth. Stump was murdered there but Craddock, though badly wounded managed to escape with the help of Scrimey McAllan. He had offices there for his fleet. This happened after Stewart Neil's death. Stump had finally gotten a cruise and threw this eleven year "boy" overboard in rough seas and of course he drowned. Stuart's relatives are thought to have done the deed but no one really knows.

We arrived at East Marsh pond. The three gang members were tied hand and foot. A rope coil was attached to both ends. Cut went to the other side of the pond towing the rope behind him. The pond was about twelve feet deep and about forty feet across. It had been a small quarry. The sides were steep. Joseph cast the first man into the Pond and Cut dragged him across. As soon as he arrived at the other side Joseph pulled him back. They did this three times to each member of the gang. Needless to say at the end of this experience they were wrecked. Joseph made them lie on the grass with heir heads together and with their bodies in a star shape. Joseph knelt down and leaning over shouted into their ears.

"You're the guys who sailed with Craddock and mistreated or should I say murdered Robert Jones and Edward Mount, eight and ten years old those boys were. Apprenticed to Craddock from the Marine Society and kitted out by them which kit you sold. Now take note that you are alive, if only just , but I swear by all that is Holy that if I ever see you around these parts again and by this I mean Romford, Ilford, Dagenham, Barking and anywhere in between you will come to a very slimy end" He nodded toward Creekmouth. We left on the cart. They were never seen again.

Our arrival back at Heath Street was quiet and when Joseph handed the cart and horse over to Reuben Rogers, there was a brief whispered conversation and then we headed home.

As we walked Joseph pulled on Cut's shoulder. He turned round and I heard Joseph say to him

"Thank you Cut, thank you, you made a big difference"

"That's fine Joseph and now I suggest you get out of Barking on the next tide. The Ann Goodman looks ready. Is she?"

"Well, we wanted a few more days but, yes she is ready. My Brother and I will leave on Monday mornings ebb. See you when we get back. It's just a snagging trip out to the Holland Banks and back. "

Joseph turned to me and said

"Step lively now Jonesy we need to get home and console my Brother"

It took just twenty minutes for us to get to Fisher Street, everyone was there. William and Mary Butterfield the Skippers parents. Elizabeth Spashett ne Butterfield , John's widow. I then saw Emily, Charles Adson and William Moreton looking sombre and sad. The fire in the kitchen was bright and all the oil lamps were lit. Emily came and stood by me. She pulled on my sleeve and said

"Are you, are you all right Jonesy? "

"Yes Emily but much more important to me is are you alright, you look upset "

" I am upset I passed Master Charles on the stairs and he had been crying, though that is not the right word for how upset he was. He went into their bedroom and he must have just dropped onto his knees, I heard the thump and then he started sobbing. It was then that I realised he was praying~ thank you so much for caring about me."

At that moment the street door opened and in walked Ann Goodman Butterfield's twin sister Elizabeth Forge accompanied by her Father and Mother John and Mary.

"Why was Master Charles so angry it is just a fishing smack after all" I said to Joseph

"It wasn't about the Ann Goodman Jonesy. The man threatened my Brothers wife and that is why he went berserk"

"Ann" said Joseph "where is my Brother?"

"He is upstairs. He is quiet now, please go up"

Mrs Butterfield turned to the family and with a gentle controlled voice said: "He will be alright now. They are very close and yet so very, very different. I'll make some tea"

Turning to Emily she said "Come on dear lets do some cooking"

They moved away toward the cooking range.

"Hello you fisher lads, we have not been really though we have met. My name is Elizabeth Ann Butterfield. Call me Lizzie. You may know my brother Henry Spashett. He is in the fishing business. John, my late husband was the brother of Charles and Joseph. He died at sea five years ago. You may hear your Skipper talk about him because he was very close to John. These smacks are dangerous boats boys so please sail safe. When is the maiden voyage of the Ann?"

"Master Joseph said to me on the way here it would be Monday morning on the ebb."

Ann turned in my direction me and cried

"What was that Jonesy, did you say you sail on Monday mornings ebb?"

"Yes Ma'am at least that is what Master Joseph told me"

"Thank the Lord for that, once Charles is at sea he will forget what took place over the road. SO everyone Saturday is going to be a very, very busy day for all of us".

A general warm agreement was heard. We were moored in Torshavn some weeks later when Master Joseph told me something about his conversation with his Brother, not all of it I am sure, but the bit that mattered.

Joseph had knocked on the bedroom door and asked

"Charles can I come in?"

"Aye come on in and tell me what you have done."

"I have not killed anybody my Brother but all I wish to say is that we shall not be bothered again. Now we just need to find out who put them up to this"

"You and I both know who put them up to this, don't we"

"Yes, but he is very difficult to catch because he has so many connections even at St.Margarets"

"Look Charles you slipped up, you lost your temper, not over the Ann Goodman but over the threat to Ann. If I had a wife like Ann Goodman Forge I would have acted just the same."

"Yes but I am supposed to be trying to follow Jesus Christ! Now don't start Joseph, Ann has shown me the way, though we both still have so many questions. Jesus was threatened and did not go berserk~ He who lives by the sword shall die by It~ He who hits you on your right cheek turn unto him your left also ~ Love your enemies as yourself "

"Look you silly man this isn't about you is it? He was not threatening you was he ~ he was threatening Ann. That's right isn't it?

"He called her a fish wife, a harlot and I took that as threat after what the other Skipper did"

"She is <u>your</u> weakness. You told me that another fisherman had a weakness. You said he was afraid of men. You told me that when they said he was a Galilean and that he knew Jesus he swore and cursed that he didn't know him just like fishermen do"

"Yes, yes he did, what is your point"

"You told me that Jesus was up on a balcony and no more than eight feet away from Peter with his back to him leaning against the balcony wall"

"Yes, yes, please get to the point"

"So Jesus would have heard what was going on below"

"Yes, yes but what are you getting at"

"You said Peter had a weakness"

"Ann said he was afraid of men and not well educated"

"So, fisherman Peter had a weakness"

"Yes"

"I have a weakness, I do not have your fiery temper but I actually enjoy dealing out justice to these vile men. Your weakness is Ann. Just remind me what happened to Peter? Was he thrown back like a bad fish?"

"No he wasn't, but"

"No buts'. We sail on Monday morning's ebb"

"What!! There is still a lot to do"

"The Ann is ready for sea. The rest is comfort stuff like food, drink, clothing and getting the angels on board"

"Have the Kisby rings arrived"

"They are in John Forges shed. He loaded the long line hemp and the hooks and cork protectors very early this morning.

"You think we can make it"

"Yes"

The two men entered the kitchen and were welcomed by all the family. Lizzie Butterfield went up to him and put her arms round her brother in law and I heard her whisper

"You are a good man Charles. My family and I could not survive financially or spiritually without the kindness of you and Ann. Please forgive yourself and come sit with me by the fire"

She took his hand and they sat together. She told him about John Butterfield Junior who was five years old. He was born the year her husband was lost at sea on the fishing smack Upton which Lizzie and John had a mortgage on. So her money needs were taken care of but I do not how you care for someone spiritually. I will ask Emily what the word means.

17   Saturday May the 24th

Early Saturday morning after Breakfast all of the family that were there late on Friday night arrived including all of the children and grandchildren. The only person missing was Lizzie Butterfield but she was baking bread to be stored in the Mess Deck cupboards on the Ann Goodman.

John Forge was also missing because he had taken Daisy, his carthorse, and his wagon to the colliers in Barking to get coal.

It was a great morning and very busy, Chas, Billy and I were very happy because though orphans we were treated like family. It was truly wonderful. The three of us had mastered getting into our hammocks and true to Emily's word our names had been burnt into our sea chests which were now on board the Ann and located beneath our hammocks on the crew deck. The orange Kisby rings had been loaded and stored on deck with the Ann Goodman's name painted in black. Each had 100 yards of half inch hemp but even this was to prove not enough.

We had started early and so around eleven o clock the smack was declared ready for sea after an audit by Mrs Butterfield. I no not know what an audit is but it had been completed by my mistress. It was during this "audit" that Mrs Butterfield asked me about a pair of trousers, a shirt and two pairs of sea socks. She had made all of these things herself. I told her that I had placed them where she had asked me to in the wash house beyond the kitchen ready for washing day. I had done this on the Thursday night after my time with John Forge getting knotted. She seemed very puzzled.

"Well I cannot find them anywhere Jones'y, I suppose they will come to light eventually OK everyone lets head back"

"Chas don't forget you have the midnight till four watch tonight so when we get in go to bed"

We arrived at Fisher Street and everyone was in high spirits even Master Charles seemed his normal self. The children and grandchildren were in extra high spirits.

"Uncle Joseph can we let the angels out please" said Charles Butterfield junior

"It's too early, wait till later"

They all sighed. "We will be in bed later"

Joseph looked at them and a big smile stretched across his face.

" Come on then whilst it is still day"

Emily approached me, "I am in the mood to be sketched BUT are you in the mood to do it and is the light right?"

"Just go and change, put that white blouse on and open it at the neck. The light is not right but I will do a shadows sketch which is different to what I have been doing. See you by the tree"

"Just a minute" I heard Mrs Butterfield say, "Charles, what is the weather going to be like tomorrow?"

"The barometer shows high pressure so it will be fine and quite warm with a light breeze in the afternoon and the wind will be from the east so there will be little smell."

"When and where are you going to teach the apprentices to float?"

"Tomorrow afternoon in the Watermill race at the Roding River"

"Right, so St Margaret's in the morning for the service and then in the afternoon we will have a family picnic on the Water Meadow by the Wheel Race. Get the word out for Barking is ready for a picnic and then she paused."

"What"

"Nothing lets finish off"

There was a rousing cheer from the children and grandchildren together with the rest of the family including Emily and us. I looked at Chas and Billy. Neither of us could swim. Would it be cold?

Looking at Joseph Ann smiled and said "The vicar is going to ask a blessing on the Ann Goodman's maiden voyage, as is the custom, so we all have to go"

"I will not be going" said Joseph.

"You will be going Joseph Butterfield or no more meat pies from your Sister in Law".

"Ok, Ok, but I shall only be going if Nathaniel Bunton can come and attend the picnic afterwards."

"Well of course he can come but I thought you said he was going north"

"He is, but will not have gone yet"

"Off you go then and tell him to dress decent and be at St.Margarets by nine thirty. He can sit with us"

"Ok, but after the angels have flown"

Emily was sat by the tree. The sun was strong and so I positioned her so that her face was in shadow with her forehead, nose and chin lit on one side and in shade on the other. She had her hair pinned up.

"That is just about right can you unpin your hair and place it by your neck in the Sun" She did as I asked but it was not quite right.

"May I set your hair as I want it?"

"Yes"

I moved closer and adjusted the curls into the nape of her neck. I was very close.

"There that's it, so now please sit still, can you turn your chest, ah um bosom, a little so that the light and shadow are central."

"How is that "she said

"Great"

"I shall be seventeen tomorrow"

"I thought you were fifteen"

"No, I am seventeen but please do not tell them"

"Emily, what does it mean to take care of someone spiritually?" I asked as I began sketching.

"I don't really know. It is more than friendship. I think it is some way of guiding a person to do and live right. You will have to ask the Skipper or Mistress Ann."

"I can't, they will think that I am a fool. You ask them on my behalf"

"I don't think that will be possible Charles. I will have a lot to do tomorrow, as will you and anyway I won't be in the mood. We can talk about it more when you get back. You will only be gone for a few days. It is a shakedown cruise after all"

"Oh, Charles is it, that's really nice. Much better than Jonesy."

"Yes. When we are on our own it shall be Charles"

"What a lovely thing to say. We must make sure that we have a lot of time together, on our own. That's what we will do. Emily you truly are beautiful"

She blushed and sat still. I worked away on the sketch and got the framework down of the shadows. Then the light went and Emily rose and went inside.

"Now master Billy the last to go on board will be the angels. Since we are sailing out to the Holland Banks when we get there which angel shall we need?" asked Joseph.

Billy's face broke into a big smile

"I release Ruth when we leave the Holland Banks, then Naomi when we leave the Dogger. I the release is Rahab when we pass Haversford Creek at the Nore. Mary is released if we get to Barking Creek at still water. I release Martha once the flow sets in."

Joseph grinned "I am very, very impressed mate, now off you go"

The three of us entered the kitchen to find our Mistress waiting for us.

"Follow me" she said. We went up the stairs onto the first landing and then passing Master Joseph's bedroom on the right we entered the children's bedroom. Facing us was another door. We went through this into what appeared to be a workroom. There were dress makers dummies and cloth rolls everywhere.

"Right you three let us see if these fit. I cannot have my family going to St Margaret's looking like orphans can I"

She placed in front of us the following items of clothing. A white linen shirt, vest, pants, trousers and a three quarter jacket and black socks

"Please try them on, use the screens over there"

We went behind the screens, got dressed and came out. The clothes basically fitted but the trousers were too long. The trousers were cream. The three quarter coats were green, dark green. She pinned the trouser bottoms to the right length and then stood back.

"Now my fisher lads I know they look like uniforms but they are not. I bought the material in bulk so that is why they look the same. Um, you do look smart. I am pleased."

SHE was pleased; I looked at Billy and Chas and knew that the clothes and reference to family had really affected all of us. We were really pleased to be listed in one breath as part of the Butterfield family.

"It's just a shame about the shoes, they just do not look right. They are old and I just cannot get them clean."

At that moment I heard Lizzie's voice call out.

"Ann, Ann are you there"

"Up here in my workshop"

She climbed the stairs and came in. "After dinner, if you send the three boys to William Byford he will provide the boys with dress shoes. He has just made three pairs for his boys and has enough leather left for the lads.

"Oh, isn't that kind. So after dinner you lads do what Lizzie has asked but Billy, I want you in bed by nine o clock."

"Yes Ma'am I will make sure I am back for then"

After dinner we all disappeared up Fisher Street then onto Heath Street and then right into Mr. Balfour's shoe shop. It was on the corner of Hart Street and Heath Street. Mr Balfour was waiting for us.

"Come in lads and introduce yourselves. This is my wife Eliza and here are Edward, William and Thomas. Here are John and my baby daughter Eliza"

I spoke. Mrs.Butterfield had said that I should introduce the others first and me last.

"Pleased to meet you Mr Byford this is William Moreton or Billy, Charles Adson, now to be called Chas and me. My name is Charles Jones now called Jonesy".

"Good it was my hatch boat that you tied the Ann Goodman to the night Craddock and his men tried to sink her. I have a contract with Mr. Day to move his fish to Billingsgate but we are still loading. We are out on the Ebb Wednesday evening. The boys are going up to London to see my sister. I have had trouble getting a good helmsman that knows the Thames tidal currents. James Leach was recommended but he is a deep sea man, do you know him."

"I have seen him in Mr. Forge's chandlery sir but not spoken".

Looking at our shoes he said

"Ah, I see what Lizzie means. You will never get them clean enough for best. They look like Howlett's of Sheppey. Good shoes and they still have lots of wear. He's gone to Grimsby. Please sit down while I measure up."

Within two hours the shoes were done. He called them brogues. Billy' and mine were in brown leather and Chas was in black. They were new. They were made for us by a master shoe smith. They fitted and were very comfortable.

"That's it then sees you tomorrow at Church"

"Oh, are you going"

"The whole of Barking is going Jonesy, well all that are involved in the fishing business. It is a Town tradition that a smacks maiden voyage be blessed. Then we are all going to the picnic to watch you get soaking wet."

Everybody laughed.

"Don't worry; Charles and Joseph are really powerful swimmers"

"Come on Jonesy its nearly nine o clock I shall be in for it if we are late." said Billy

"Goodnight Mr Balfour we will see you tomorrow"

18 Sunday Morning
May the 25th

After breakfast Chas, Billy and I went upstairs and changed into our new clothes. We then went downstairs and walked into the parlour. All of the family were there. Everyone looked happy.

"My oh my" said Joseph. "Don't we look smart and handsome and new shoes as well!"

I glanced at Emily; she was wearing a white silk blouse with a red bow. She wore a red belt and a dark blue long skirt. She was also wearing a jaunty hat tilted to one side which really suited her.

"Come on everyone" said Mrs Butterfield "let's get going St. Margaret's will be full today"

Joseph walked out first holding Charles junior and Alfred's hands. Then followed Master Charles and Ann.

The Skipper was holding his daughter Ann's hand. They looked regal. Ann had her hand in Charles arm. He had combed his beard and tied his long hair into a pigtail as had Joseph.

As I crossed the door Emily followed and she just placed her hand in my arm and then slowly slid it down so that we were holding hands. It was electric.

"You look really handsome Charles; this is going to be a lovely day"

The Sun was out and strong just like Master Charles had said. There was just a slight breeze. When we got to the top of Fisher Street there was man in a Frock Coat and tall hat .He wore white breeches and had a very fancy cane. As Joseph approached the man took off his hat and bowed low to the children. It was Nathaniel Bunton. Ann stepped forward.

"Good morning Mr Bunton or shall I call you Nathaniel, would you please escort me to the Church? "

"What me escort you Ann, why I should be proud, real proud"

She placed her hand in Nathaniel's arm and walked up Heath Street towards St Margaret's. Master Charles let them get a few steps ahead and then he joined Emily and I.

I could just hear what Ann Butterfield was saying

"Thank you Nathaniel for helping my husband. It was very good of you. Did Charles really lose it?"

"He certainly did Ma'am. He was coping until the bloke called you a fish wife and then he went mad. THE trouble is Mrs Butterfield"

"Call me Ann please Nathaniel"

"The trouble is Ann that he is very, very strong. Stronger than Joseph, though there is not much in it"

"I know, I know but listen I have asked the Vicar to preach about forgiveness so that should really help"

We joined others and entered the Church and I could see it was filling up. The sun was streaming through the windows. One of them was made of stained glass in the fashion of a fishing smack. Ann rejoined Charles but noticed Mr. Bunton separating and hanging back

"Nathaniel, what are you doing?"

"Well this is for the family Ann so I will go and sit at the back"

"You will do no such thing Mr. Bunton; you are with us so step lively now you are holding the family up"

"Are you sure Mistress Ann?"

She pushed him into the row ahead of her and then said to all of us to follow them since all the family were to sit in the first two rows Butterfield's, Forges and Spashett's. What a crowd.

The Skipper turned and said

"Tread gently you two were walking on Great, Great, Grandad Ambrose's grave stone. He was such a poser"

I looked down and turning to Emily asked

"What does it say?"

"Later on the way out" she answered.

The minister called the Congregation together and then opened with a Prayer. After we all said Amen he spoke from the Pulpit

"We are gathered here today to bless the Ann Goodman who begins her maiden snagging voyage tomorrow morning at 6:30 on the ebb. Please join with the choir in singing "I will make you Fishers of Men"

The organ blasted out and the choir began to sing. The whole Congregation including all of family and Nathaniel Bunton seemed to know the words

"I will make you fishers of men

Fishers of men,

Fishers of men,

I will make you fishers of men if you follow me.

If you follow me.

If you follow me.

I will make you fishers of men if you follow me.

Hear Christ calling come unto me,

Come unto me,

Come unto me,

Hear Christ calling come unto me, I will give you rest,

I will give you rest,

I will give you rest,

Hear Christ calling Come unto me I will give you rest.

The music was very nice and it was easy to sing. I joined in, as did Emily. After we finished singing we all sat down. The Minister said that the reading was from the Book of Acts chapter three verse nineteen. He then added that the lesson was about forgiveness.

I noticed Mr Charles sit up and lean forward. He opened his Bible as did Ann, Emily, Joseph and indeed all of the family did the same thing.

He read this as I remember

"Repent ye therefore and be converted that your sins may be blotted out, when the times of refreshing shall come from the presence of the Lord. And he shall send Jesus Christ, which before was preached unto you. Whom the heavens must receive until the times of restitution of all things which God hath spoken through the mouth of all his holy prophets since the World began."

The Minister then spoke

"This is not an easy text to explain. It seems to say that history is going somewhere and THAT SOMEWHERE is said here to be the Restitution of all things. It seems to echo the Lord's prayer where we are told to Pray for God's Kingdom to come and for God's will to be done on earth as it is in heaven. This is not the subject of today's lesson. Notice the word in the text rendered as *blotted out*. It is the Greek word "exaleiphein" and it literally means to wipe clean. In those days writing material was very expensive. Papyrus was made from plants that grew alongside the Nile. It was rolled out and then dried. Since the inks were all vegetable dies the writing could be simply washed away and the papyrus used again. Now there is a similar word to "exaleiphen" and that is "chiazein". It means to cross out. It is the same shape as "X" a letter in the Greek alphabet. Sometimes contracts or debts were written on velum or animal skin. They were etched with a stylus. When the debt or contract was paid the Creditor would place the velum in a public place and just simply cross through the writing. You could of course still see the debt although paid up. With papyrus the debt was placed in a public place and then the creditor would take a sponge and wash the papyrus. The text was washed away. The papyrus was free to be used again.

SO

When God forgives us there is no trace of the debt. It has been forgiven AND forgotten. The word sin comes from the Greek word "harmatia". It is used in the Javelin contest in the final phase when there are just three athletes. A circle is placed on the ground at some distance from the throwing line. Gradually the circles are reduced in size.

Whenever a javelin landed outside the circle the crowd would shout "Harmatia" you have missed. This sin is not murder, lying, adultery. They are bad acts. The text is saying that we have missed being like God. We were made in his image but have sinned in that we have missed being like him. It is to cancel out that sin that Jesus died for us. But that is another lesson. We will now stand and sing "Eternal Father Strong to Save".

The organ thundered out and we or should I say the Congregation all sang. The Church was full and the sound of human voices praising God was very impressive.

Eternal Father strong to save Whose arm doth bind both wind and wave.
Who biddest the mighty ocean deep. Its own appointed limits keep.
Oh hear us when we cry to Thee for those in peril on the sea.

O Saviour whose almighty word, the winds and waves submission heard.
Who walkest on the foaming deep. And calm amid its rage did sleep.
O hear us when we cry to thee, for those in peril on the sea.

O sacred spirit who dids't brood. Upon the chaos dark and rude.
Who biddest the angry tumult cease, and gavest light and life and peace.
O hear us when we cry to thee, for those in peril on the sea.

O God of love and strength and power our brethren shied in dangers hour.
From rock and tempest fire and foe. Protect them where so erst they go.
Thus ever let them rise to thee Glad hymns and praise for land and sea.

The Reverend closed with Prayer and then went to the Church exit where he stood to thank everyone for coming. The mood seemed to me to be very positive. We all moved down the aisle following the Butterfields, Joseph, walking beside Nathaniel Bunton looked very uncomfortable. Emily tugged my sleeve.

"Look" She was nodding with her head to a flag stone which lay in the isle between the rows of pews.

"That is the stone recording the passing of Ambrose Skinner, Charles and Joseph's Great Grandfather. To read what it says we shall have to let everyone pass and then turn round."

That is what we did. Emily read it to me

"Here lieth the body of Mr Ambrose Skinner, of Longbridge in the Parish of Barking in the County of Essex Farmer, Who departed this life on the 5th of October 1778 aged 85 years. Also the body of Mrs Ann Skinner, wife of the aforesaid Mr.Ambrose Skinner, who departed this life Oct 14th 1781. Also the body of Ambrose Skinner grandson of the aforesaid who departed this life October the 14th 1781 aged 4 months."

"Emily when it says they departed this life what does it mean?"

"Well I think it means they have gone to heaven to be with Jesus, but I do not believe that. Master Charles has explained to me that they are all in the death sleep waiting for the Resurrection"

"What is the Resurrection?"

"Master Charles is sure that they will live again in the flesh here on earth. They will be raised up from the dead that is what resurrection means. Please ask him"

We got to the Church exit and saw Master Charles in conversation with the Minister. I heard this

"Thank you for the sermon Reverend, it was of great comfort to me"

I saw him smile and then wink at the Reverend.

"You're still wrong on the immortal soul but thanks for today"

"Well that is what the Church teaches Charles but let's not get into a deep debate. It's a lovely day and everyone is looking forward to the picnic at the Water meadow. Barking is united by tragedy. So many families have lost loved ones many of whom died through this awful practice of fleeting. It cannot be right to keep the smacks at sea for months and transfer the catch by rowing tub to the schooners. Any way you know more about this than me. See you later this afternoon and later at the dance"

"What dance?"

"Oh dear, the dance that all the ladies of your family have arranged with Toby Mullins of the Fishing Smack they are erecting the marquee during the picnic"

Charles turned and looked at his wife with surprise and delight.

"Look, you are going to be away for weeks aren't you? So we all decided that today should be a day to be remembered by all. Anyway I needed an occasion to wear my new dress as does Emily, Elizabeth and Lizzie".

I looked at Emily. She looked at me.

"Can you dance Charles?"

"At Christmas in the Workhouse we used to have a party and yes there was dancing but the only dance I can do is the Barn Dance,"

"Can you do the St Bernard's Waltz?"

"No, is it difficult?"

"Well it is different but I can teach you, what about the Gay Gordon's"

"Yes I can do that. It's where you hold hands and walk three paces forward and then kick your leg"

"No, No, No she interrupted I will show you later"

19 Sunday Afternoon Picnic on the Water Meadow

At that point Mistress Ann summoned everyone together and led the walk back to Fisher Street via Heath Street and was again escorted by Nathaniel Bunton. Nathaniel spoke to Mistress Ann

"Well done Ann, the Vicar's sermon has done the trick"

"Yes Nathaniel I think it has and the rest of the day should be just what everyone needs"

When we arrived at the house all the picnic preparation had been done. There were hampers of food and Joseph's lemonade and beer. The day had turned really warm so everyone got changed out of their Sunday clothes ready for the water meadow.

"Nathaniel"

"Yes Ann"

"Please can you get the changing tent from the back garden and go ahead of us. There is a barrow in my Fathers' workshop which he has left open. Take the tent to the Water Meadow and set it up by the small jetty. Can you also get the three Kisby rings from the Ann Goodman?"

"Aye Ann, I'll see you there"

"Excuse me, Mrs Butterfield but why do we need a changing tent Chas, Billy and I can change behind the tree I saw in the meadow"

"So you can BUT several of us ladies fancy a swim don't we "

Emily, Elizabeth and Lizzie all shouted "We certainly do and so might Aunt Sarah and Charles mother so we need somewhere to change."

I looked at Emily. "You can swim"

"Yes, when you work in Barking on smacks cleaning them and so on it is a good idea to be able to swim don't you think. Mrs Butterfield taught me at East Marsh Pond"

"That's really deep"

"How do you know that Charles? have you been there?"

"Er, well I have heard about it but I am glad the three of us are learning to swim in the Wheel Race".

Soon the family started off, about twenty of us. We walked up Fisher Street and turned left joining many other families walking along the quay in front of all the chandlery warehouses. We then we turned left again over the six gates bridge where the River Roding, having done its work with the Mill Wheel, entered Barking Pool. We soon arrived at the water meadow. Many Barking folk were already there. There looked to be about one hundred and fifty people. Up went the ladies parasols and very soon out came big summer hats. Before long the children had kites in the sky. Blankets were placed on the soft grass and the picnic began. I loved it. Just one great big family. Every one knew one another and there were many skippers present with their families. I truly loved the whole thing. It was after all just four days since Mrs. Charnock had delivered me to my new owners and yet I did not think like that any more.

I and the other apprentices had a home and family. It was great. I got out my sketch pad and started the framework of a picture I was later to call "Happy Days". Little did I know of the storms heading to the Butterfield family in the years that lay ahead?

Charles stood up. He shouted to two other families close by.

"John Forge, yes it's you I am talking to .It is time for Cricket".

Turning towards two other families he said:-"Come on George and Harry get your crew together and let's teach these Sail Makers and Provisions merchants how to play cricket"

At that John Forge stood up and turning to William Butterfield said

"You up for it William?"

"Certainly, time this lad of mine respected his elders"

Charles turned to Joseph."Are you coming?"

"No, I promised the children a game of rounder's so that's what I will be doing but first before that we have an important job to do ~ Chas, Billy and Jonesy. Get changed and come down to that small jetty. You will need to change to Charles so come on while it's hot."

The Skipper shouted to his Father."Give me ten minutes Pa. Joseph and I have got to teach the apprentices to swim"

"Aye any excuse will do to avoid a thrashing. Try not to make it longer than twenty minutes. We'll get set up"

With that we all headed into the tent Cut had put up and in a few minutes emerged in our bathing suits.

"Right lads" said Charles. "Joseph is going to go in first and then I will fasten the Kisby rings to the jetty. You will then get into the water and take hold of a Kisby ring. You then need to kick your legs and head out to Joseph"

We did as we were told. I got hold of my ring and held onto Billy's. When we were all in the water, which was not cold Master Charles dived in and then swam toward us.

"The skill I need you to learn is how to float, not how to swim but how to float. If you get swept overboard I or Joseph will spill the wind out of the sales and the Ann will quickly move into stays. We will then throw a Kisby ring out to you. All you need to do is stay afloat by paddling. We then need to make sure you know how to hold on. Joseph and I are good at this. We have practiced throwing the rings a long way and with some accuracy. If you stay afloat we can get to you"

It took about twenty minutes but after this we could all float and let go of the Kisby ring. The key was to keep our breath and avoiding water getting into our mouths.

Just then Ann, Lizzie and Elizabeth screamed and jumped off the jetty into the water. Their swimming costumes were black and looked like dresses. Emily slid in and soon all four were enjoying a swim. Many joined them and further up where the Mill Pond was shallower there was a sort of beach and so the children were playing in the water with their parents looking on.

We were floating in the Wheel Race when Master Charles swam away towards Ann and his in laws. Elizabeth Forge was Ann's twin sister and though they did look alike they were very different in temperament. Joseph turned to Billy and said.

"Billy, go and let the pigeons out and bring the angel's whistle back with you"

He shouted towards the bank where Cut Bunton was sat talking to Mary Ann Butterfield, Joseph's mother, "Hey Cut, pull Billy in will you"

Grabbing hold of the Kisby ring rope Cut soon had Billy at the bank.

Billy jumped up and without drying himself ran all the way along the wharf, passed the Ann and then turned right into Fisher Street. I watched him all the way. Just then I saw Emily climbing out of the river. She was further up where the children were paddling. The water made her dress cling to her body. I looked away; she really is a beautiful girl. What on earth have I got to offer her? I noticed Mistress Ann nudge Lizzie Butterfield and then they both waved at me. I waved back

At this point John Forge called out to Charles Butterfield who was still swimming

"Come on Charles are we having this cricket match or not, we really fancy our chances"

"Ok, on my way"

Joseph turned round and saw the dejected look on his nephews faces. Charles, Ann and Alfred were sad. Seeing there sadness he said, "Come on then get your cousins and we'll get the rounder's going but before that lets stroke a bumble bee"

The children shrieked in laughter.

"They will sting us"

"Not if they have been collecting pollen and are drunk. See there is one on the table."

The children approached.

"That's Bombus lapidarius, see how it pants and see how the pollen bags are full"

He took out a magnifying glass and let his niece Ann and his nephews Charles and Alfred look.

"Now listen Ann, place your little finger on the table in front of the Bee. Do it slowly so that it can see you. That's it. Now move your finger slowly towards it and then lift it up, slowly now, that's right now just touch the hairs"

Ann cooed with wonder. Then Charles did it but a really funny thing happened as his little finger moved toward the bee it put out one of its front legs and touched Charles finger as if too say "That's enough, no more, I just want to rest"

"Sorry Alfred it seems to have had enough, right let's set up for rounders"

I got to play stump. Chas and Edward Forge got their chance at bowling. It was so simple, so good and so easy to be happy.

Emily came over to bat. I was still on stump.

"You will not be able to stop any ball whilst I am batting Jonesy"

With that she took the rear of her dress and passed it through her legs and pushed it down her belt. She was not wearing any shoes. Wow.

She saw my face and laughed.

"Told you"

With that she whacked the ball about 40 feet through the air and began running. She made it to the third base. I was in the wrong spot. I shouted out

"Edward come and take over stump"

I walked across to the fourth base and gave Emily the nod and said

"Try your best Miss Byers but I do not think you will make it to home base"

"Oh, Oh, Oh Jonesy we will see about that"

The ball was pitched and the batter missed. It was pitched again and the batter missed again. The bowler pitched again and the ball glanced off the bat along the ground straight toward me, I bent down to pick it up only to feel Emily's hands on my back as she leaped frog over me and struck for home.

She was jumping up and down with joy for her team had won. We all went back to the tent for lemonade. The cricket match was in full swing but since I do not know anything about the game and have no appreciation for it all I can say is that it looked good. Twenty over's each and then the team with the most runs wins. It was still a lovely day. It was now around four o'clock. Ann was looking at Charles who was in to bat. Ann, Elizabeth and Lizzie had all got changed.

Mary Ann, Charles and Joseph's mother was serving up ham carved from the bone and Mary Forge was carving up huge slices of home made bread and layering on home made butter when the pigeons arrived. They were circling above the Water Meadow and then flying back over the Pond, over the wharf and then back again.

Joseph called all his nieces and nephews together with John Forges children.

"Now my lovelies would you like to see some angels"

"Oh yes please Uncle Joseph"

"Billy" Joseph shouted "Did you bring the whistle"

"Yes Master Joseph just like you said it's in my pocket"

"Good take it out and give it a good blow"

Billy did just as he was told. Immediately ten of the birds broke away from the circling flock and headed straight toward Joseph.

"Now stand still" He said to the children, "do not move your heads and you will see the angels"

With that the ten carrier pigeons landed on the children though Abigail as normal landed on Joseph's hand.

"Now hold out your left hand"

With that Joseph placed feed into each hand and the birds simply dropped down onto the children's hands to feed. The children were delighted, excited and laughing. Soon the birds had fed and again took to the air. Cut Bunton walked up and went inside the tent. He came out with a large flat wooden base made of the teak decking left over from the Lady Ann. He put this down on the ground and went back inside the tent this time bringing out ten whip and tops and a box of chalk crayons.

The children gathered round.

"Now you all know what to do. Draw patterns on the tops and then make them spin with the whips. For every nice pattern there will be a prize"

"Ooh "They all cried.

"What's the prize Uncle Nathaniel?"

"Joseph and I shall be the horses and you shall be the jockeys and we shall race to that tree"

The children again were delighted.

"Who's for a game of leap frog" This came from Lizzie Butterfield.

"I will join you "said Elizabeth Forge "but we need competition".

At this Emily stepped forward and said

"Jonesy and I will race you. What do you say Charles Jones, are you up for it"

"I certainly am"

"Can Billy and I play?" asked Charles Adson

Again Lizzie and Elizabeth pulled their long dresses from the rear through their legs and into their belts. Emily did the same. Emily bent down as did Elizabeth and Billy.

"Go" shouted Mary Ann Butterfield, Aunt Sarah and Mary Forge.

So off we went. The first leap was easy and I was just in front of Lizzie and Chas and then had to bend down. I heard Emily running and then felt her hands on my back and she was over. On we went.

We were ahead on the ninth leap and would have won when a strange but wonderful thing happened. Instead of leaping over me Emily landed on top of me and not expecting it, I fell to the ground with Emily falling off and then rolling over. I pushed up with my arms and was now over her face when she raised her head up and kissed me on the lips. She then jumped up and ran off back to the tent screaming with laughter. Lizzie and Elizabeth were laughing as were Chas and Billy. This was all I needed to get me laughing to.

Charles, Nathaniel, John Forge and William Butterfield walked up. The Cricket match was over. Ann stood up. "Right everyone let's get back to Fisher Street for we ladies have a dance to attend"

Those close by heard this and it was soon relayed across the Water Meadow. United in sorrow and united in joy for a day. It was wonderful and the evening was yet to come.

Nathaniel had brought the tent on a barrow and it was soon dismantled and loaded up. Joseph pushed it as we walked back home. Nathaniel held the children's hands.

Ann Butterfield walked up beside me and said how much she had enjoyed the picnic watching how her new lads enjoyed themselves. As we continued walking she poked Joseph with her parasol. He turned

"Which sea shanties are you and the other skippers performing tonight dear brother?"

"Well, we had thought of Heave Away, Where Away, Drunken Sailor, Bold Riley and some others. I was thinking of finishing with the new one I have written, about the alphabet .Would you and Emily help with the chorus"

"Yes certainly, Emily is that good for you?"

"Eh yes ma'am but what is the Chorus"

Master Joseph does no more than burst into song

"Alphabet Alphabet we all must larn

To read and to write protects us from harm.

Alphabet Alphabet learn it by wrote

Then you can send your love a nice note "

Ann immediately spoke up with some alarm in her voice

"You can't use larn it's learn.

"I can do whatever I want, sister of mine. It's my shanty and through your larning Jonesy and I, and soon the other fisher lads will be able to send notes via the angels to you all whilst we are at sea. That IS something to sing about. However I have anticipated your attention to detail so there is a simpler one

"Alphabet Alphabet letters you see, help me to write my long sea shanty"

"Now are you going to help me?"

"Yes, yes, Joe we shall help, should be good fun"

"That certainly is good" said Lizzie Butterfield with a strange look in her eye. Elizabeth Forge reached out and held her tight. When we arrived back at Fisher Street the family dispersed. Joseph and Billy went to feed the Pigeons and the children and cousins were settled down for a nap.

I went up to the third floor and looking out of the window I could just see the marquee at the back of the Fishing Smack Pub. I wandered over to the other window and watched Billy cleaning his mouth organ whilst Master Joseph fed his birds.

When he got back I asked him

"Are you joining in with Master Joseph tonight Billy?"

"Yes but the only one I can really do well is Drunken Sailor"

20 Barking Town Dance

On the bed were shirts and trousers for all three of us. We put these on. The shirt arms were long and baggy but were met by a tight band at the wrist. The shirts had blue buttons. It looked like the same colour used on the Ann Goodman's hull. It was dark blue. On the bed were three scarf's but they were in a very shiny material.

"What do we do with these?"

At that moment Joseph walked in. He looked great. His beard was combed, his hair was tied in a pony tail and he was wearing a brightly coloured waistcoat, a black leather belt and a fob watch and cream seaman's trousers finishing off with polished boots up to his knees.

"These are cravats. They have to be tied in a certain way. I'll send Ann in she knows how to do it"

"Can you dance Mr. Joe" we all piped at once.

"Of course I can dance as can any seaman worth his salt".

"At that moment Ann Butterfield walked past the door. She was wearing a lovely dress in blue with a deep v from her shoulders to her waist. She had a narrow waist. She was wearing a white silk blouse, tight button collar with folds of white going down to her waist. Then the dress flowed down over her hips and spread out in four valances right down to the ground.

Joseph called out "Ah Ann can you tie the cravats"

"Certainly can, though Emily will want to do Jonesy's"

She turned round "Emily"

"Yes ma'am"

"Come and tie Jonesy's cravat"

I heard footsteps and then Emily stood at the door.

"Ta Da" and then she spun round.

What stood in front of me was the most beautiful girl I had ever seen. She was wearing a gown in cream . It was split at the waist and then flowed away over her hips heading to the floor. There was a large dark green bow tied neatly at her waist and then the front bodice leading to a square neckline with flared sleeves. She was wearing green ear rings and a small green necklace.

"Stop staring Charles Jones and turn round"

I did as I was told. Emily picked up the cravat and deftly tied it round my neck. Stepping in front of me she shaped and pulled it out so that it hung down over my shirt.

"My, oh my, aren't we handsome, I shall never be able to compete with you" She laughed.

When we got to the foot of the stairs we were greeted by Lizzie and Elizabeth. They wore different style dresses to my Mistress and were in different coloured fabrics. Lizzie was wearing white and Elizabeth was wearing deep red.

I then remembered that these were the colours of the fabric rolls I had seen in Mrs Butterfield's work room. So she really was a great milliner after all. When I was in the workroom I noticed on the floor something shining brightly. It looked like gold or copper in colour. I bent down and pulled it from between the floorboards. It was a curtain ring. There was also some silver thread thick and stiff. I took both thinking that it would make Emily a nice ring.

Nathaniel Bunton walked in from the kitchen. He was wearing a bandana in red with white spots. He had a false beard below his moustache and was wearing a white shirt like the cavaliers wore. There was a gold chain round his neck. His breeches flared out and he was wearing black leather boots. He looked like a pirate.

Charles walked up. He was wearing a waistcoat and a shirt like mine with flowing sleeves. He had a fob watch exactly like Joseph's. He saw me looking at it.

"This and Joseph's was a gift from Great, Granddad Skinner." The skipper said.

"Right, is everyone ready," and looking directly at Cut added "including Blackbeard".

"Yes" came the united reply.

Nathaniel opened the door and held it back so the ladies could get themselves and their dresses through. When everyone was through including the children he let the door close and stepped quickly forward. Ann led the way with Charles. Next came Joseph and Elizabeth and then Nathaniel and Lizzie Butterfield. She looked at him and began laughing.

"What?"Asked Cut. Lizzie was still laughing

 "I take it; Blackbeard has something to do later, but for now take my arm and stop fooling about"

Lizzie's children together with their cousins followed. Emily and I then followed the children with Chas and Billy bringing up the rear. It was a short walk of about one hundred and fifty yards and then we all entered the Fishing Smack. Toby Warren guided the party through and out of the rear doors into the marquee. A cheer went up from the assembled crowd. The marquee was large. Down the left side was a huge table with mountains of food on it. There was crayfish, lobster, tuna Ann's roast potatoes and salad. There was large bread loaves sliced into doorsteps. William Butterfield had provided chicken, beef and ham on the bone and of course there was Cod and chips. Outside there was a roasting pig. To the right offset from the food table was the dancing floor with tables and chairs set for a large crowd. Every one was expecting to have a good time. The marquee was lit with oil lamps in many colours

John Forge stepped forward. He stepped on the dancing floor and stamped his foot.

"Welcome to all of you. I am now going to call on the Reverend Jeffries to ask a blessing on the food and the entertainment to follow".

The crowd fell silent.

"Dear Father in heaven we thank you for this day. Please bless this food and those who partake of it. I ask this in the name of Jesus Christ our Saviour"

There was a solid AMEN. John Forge stepped forward again.

"There will be three dances and then we shall eat. Please take your partners for the Old English Barn dance".

Nathaniel stepped forward and bowing before Lizzie Butterfield said. "Would m' lady care to dance with Captain Blackbeard?"

"She would be delighted IF Blackbeard will remove his silly bandana"

"It shall be removed to please you ma'am"

"You may not know this Nathaniel but you are quite a handsome man BUT, look we have competition"

About thirty couples had formed a circle and then the band struck up. They and we all bowed.

Emily and I joined the circle. I was very nervous. She got hold of my right hand with her left and then the Barn Dance began.

"Three steps forward kick and then three steps back, Turn and face me move to the left with me spinning and then dotsy do round three times and then start again."

As she span her dress spun out and she moved with such grace it was absolutely wonderful.

"Charles look"

Charles and Ann Butterfield were dancing and they were completely gone. They were not in Barking but somewhere truly wonderful. As they moved to do the dotsey~do they paused, kissed and then danced on.

"Oh my, I see "

Then as we went for the dotsey~do I moved in close, paused, and kissed Emily"

A great shout went up and the leader of this was Nathaniel Bunton and of course every one else followed. I felt great. I felt wonderful in fact I had never ever felt like this before. Emily was laughing but not blushing. It seemed everyone knew what was happening between us and they all approved. We finished the Barn Dance and went for lemonade. About ten minutes passed.

John Forge took stage again and said. Please take your partners for the St Bernard's Waltz.

We all took the floor again but this time Nathaniel was Ann's partner, Charles took Elizabeth and Joseph took Lizzie.

Emily touched my chin and said "Right this time we face one another. Put you right hand on my hip and hold my right hand in your left. Ok"

"Ok"

"Now when the music starts we step three paces to the left and then stamp our feet twice. Then we take two paces to the right and then you move your right leg back one step and then your left, great and now stamp twice. Now spin me round three times walking to the left as I spin and then we dotsy do together three times and then we start again. Not bad Charles not bad, but this next time hold me closer when we dotsey~ do, that's it. Now your getting it lets show this lot how it's done"

I did just as I was told and felt the swing of the music and so I danced much better. There were several more dances and then Emily asked me.

"Jonesy have you ever tasted Joseph's sailor's coffee?"

"Yes you brought me some the night the Lady Ann was almost sunk"

"Ah yes, but that coffee was not long standing. This is."

She got hold of my hand and led me to a table where there was a huge coffee jug on a stove with a low oil flame. We had to join a small queue and there were ladies in it. Jane Ready turned round and looking me straight in the eyes said "You sure you're ready for this"

"Well Emily Joseph says that this is what I will get after a cold watch off the Faroes"

"I see. The secret is not to drink it quick. It is made with Morgan's rum and you have to add molasses to your taste. Keep it on your tongue for about five seconds and then swallow. Joseph is only allowing two cups but since this is your first time just take one, what do think Emily, am I right?"

"Yes ma'am I shall only be having one" said Emily

"Then I shall do the same" I said

John Forges voice was heard again "Ladies and Gentlemen take your partners for the Gay Gordon."

Emily jumped up and yanked me onto the dance floor.

"Oh Emily I cannot do this dance, I will just look like a fool"

"Listen Jonesy just look around" I looked

"Is anyone looking at us?"

"No"

And then the music started and it was wild for some of the families were from Scotland and really knew how to do the dance. Emily and I stayed on the dance floor until the dancing stopped.

John Forge stepped forward and shouted:"FOOD~ please let the Butterfield's go first."

We all lined up in good order and soon had full plates with lemonade as the drink. Some adults had beer but it was being tightly controlled by Joseph. The roast pig was not yet ready. I discovered that there was to be fireworks, a tradition on a maiden voyage.

Whilst this was happening a large wooden platform was brought in and placed on the dance floor. It was about twelve feet square and about a foot deep, within fifty minutes, everyone having been well fed was sat down waiting. They all seemed to know what was going to happen. I turned to Emily and raised my eyebrows.

"Just watch, it is truly great as you will see. The crowd will go mad for remember Jonesy these are all Sailing and Fishing families and so they know how to have a good time".

John Forge stepped up and shouted "And now with Joseph Butterfield on his accordion I give you Charles Butterfield and The Sailors Hornpipe"

Charles stepped on to the sound box, for that is what it was and stamped his foot on the stage. It boomed. Joseph began the tune and Charles began to dance thumping his feet on every fourth bar.

The crowd went mad. I went mad, Emily went mad and then suddenly Nathaniel Bunton stepped onto the stage and danced with Charles. He was wearing a bandana and a large false moustache. Ann was in hysterics. The two of them then danced another jig to a faster tune.

William Butterfield then climbed on stage. He seemed to have a guitar in his hand though it was not a guitar. John Forge climbed up with a huge skin drum in his left hand and a bone drum stick in his right. Then John Harrison, who was to be my shipmate climbed up with a fiddle.

William spoke

"For many, many long years this Town has been the centre of the fishing industry for London. Before that we provided many sailors for the Royal Navy through the press. "

A great boohoo went up from the crowd.

"All of our men folk have a long history of working sailing ships and from this comes that which we all love, the sea shanty. From sailing before the wind in raging seas and in gentle swells came the songs we all know. Ladies and gentlemen I give you the Shanty Drunken Sailor"

There was a great cheer with Lizzie, Elizabeth and Ann cheering.

Then, for me, came the most amazing thing of all. Billy Moreton got onto the stage. He stood close to Joseph and pulled on his sleeve. Joseph bent down and Billy seemed to whisper in his ear.

Joseph put his arm round him and smiled. Joseph shifted his accordion into the playing position. John Forge began thumping his arm drum and then Joseph nudged Billy with his knee. Billy then placed his mouth organ to his lips and began playing a haunting chord. We all clapped. Nathaniel stepped forward and began the song.

"What shall we do with the drunken sailor, what shall we do with the drunken sailor, what shall we do with the drunken sailor early in the morning."

Then the crowd joined in.

"Way hay and up she rises, way hay and up she rises, way hay and up she rises earlie in the morning."

Nathaniel continued

"Shave his belly with a rusty razor, Shave his belly with a rusty razor, Shave his belly with a rusty razor, early in the morning

Way hay and up she rises, way hay and up she rises, way hay and up she rises earlie in the morning.

Put him in a long boat till he's sober, Put him is a long boat till he's sober, Put him is a long boat till he's sober early in the morning.,

Way hay and up she rises, way hay and up she rises, way hay and up she rises early in the morning.

At this point William stood up and using his mouth organ played the chorus on his own. He was really good. John Forge was thumping away with his drum and then came:-

Stick him in a barrel with the hose pipe on him, Stick him in a barrel with the hose pipe on him, Stick him in a barrel with the hose pipe on him, earlie in the morning

Way hay and up she rises, way hay and up she rises, way hay and up she rises early in the morning.

Put him in the bed with the captains daughter, Put him in the bed with the captains daughter, Put him in the bed with the captains daughter earlie in the morning,

Way hay and up she rises, way hay and up she rises, way hay and up she rises early in the morning.

That's what we do with the drunken sailor, That's what we do with the drunken sailor, That's what we do with the drunken sailor,

Way hay and up she rises, way hay and up she rises way hay and up she rises early in the morning.

Way hay and up she rises, way hay and up she rises way hay and up she rises early in the morning.

Hey hey hey

"Thank you thank you and now St Margaret's Choir is going to join us in Haul away Joe. Join in the chorus Thump your feet and clap your hands one. two, three and four. Remember this is much slower.

"When I was a little boy so my mother told me.

Well haul away we'll haul away Joe

And if I did not kiss the girls my lips would all grow mouldy

Well haul away haul we'll haul away Joe

Well haul away Joe the good ship now is rolling ready

Well haul away haul we'll haul away Joe

When Louise was the King of France before the Revol~ution

Well haul away we'll haul away Joe

And then he got his head cut off which spoiled his constit~ution.

Well haul away we'll haul away Joe

Now the first time I met a yankee girl and she was fat and lazy

Well haul away we'll haul away Joe

And then I met an Irish girl she damned near drove me crazy.

Well haul away we'll haul away Joe

Well haul away haul away were bound for better weather.

Jo ——————e

It was blood curdling stuff. The ponderous slow beat was deafening and everyone and I mean everyone was singing the chorus and clapping their hands. I could have gone to war. Emily Byes was yelling at the top of her lungs and so was I.

Then Ann, Lizzie and Elizabeth climbed on the stage, the whole crowd cheered and then looking at Joseph they counted and began singing to the same tune.

So you're going away to Norway's isle

Well haul away we'll haul away Joe

Your going now will break my smile

Well haul away we'll haul away Joe

Catch King cod and come back soon

Well haul away we'll haul away Joe

I will wait in my swooning room

Well haul away well haul away Joe

Sail safe come home to me

Well haul away we'll haul away Joe

Don't get taken by the sea

Well haul away we'll haul away Joe

Ann Goodman please just make good speed

Well haul away we'll haul away Joe

Up Barking Creek and fill my need

Well haul away we'll haul away Joe

Looking direct at Charles Ann pointed her hand

I'll love you to the day I die so make sure that you do homeward fly

Well haul away haul away Joe

Send me an angel every day with a sweet message that will say

Well haul away we'll haul away Joe.

Miss you miss you my sweet wife you are the love of my life

Well haul away we'll haul away Jo~~~~~~~~~~e.

John Forge stepped forward and said

"The last sea shanty a capstan shanty is one you all know and love. Those that know the dance to Heave Away please take your partners."

About thirty couples took to the floor. Charles came down off the stage and bowing before his wife said.

"May I have this dance with the beautiful Mrs Ann Goodman Butterfield or would you prefer another sailor?"

"You will be gone long enough my dear so please dance with me and any way, you know how good we are at this"

They formed a circle and John Forge began thumping his drum in a fast rhythm. Then the choir joined in with their tambourines

Joseph stepped forward and began thumping his foot on the stage. All those on the dance floor did the same. The beat was great. The dancers had not yet moved. Then as Joseph opened his mouth they all took three steps to the side and stomped. They then took three steps to the side back to their original position and then stomped. The they all took three steps back and stomped three times, A step backward stomp, a step forward stomp and then they all turned and began again with three steps to the side. It looked easy but it was fast.

What started the dance was this: "Come gets your duds in order cos were bound across the water

Heave away me jollies heave away

Come get your duds in order cos were bound to leave tomorrow

Heave away a me jolly boys were all bound away

Sometimes were bound for Liverpool sometimes were bound for Spain

Heave away me jollies heave away

But now were bound for old St Johns where all the girls are dancing.

Heave away a me jolly boys were all bound away .

John Harrison stepped forward with his fiddle and the crowd cheered. Emily grabbed my hand and said

"Come on Charles we can do this"

I smiled and said

"Yes I think I can"

"Quick get behind your Master and I will get behind Ann. Hold my hand tight"

I did as I was told and soon got into the dance.

Charles and Ann Butterfield were adding steps and twirls it was just great to see. The shanty carried on

I wrote my love a letter I was on the sweet Ann Goodman

Heave away me jollies heave away

I wrote my love a letter and I signed it with a ring

Heave away a me jolly boys were all bound away

Sometimes were bound for Liverpool sometimes were bound for Spain

Heave away me jollies heave away

But now were bound for old St Johns where all the girls are dancing.

Heave away a me jolly boys were all bound away .

John stepped forward again with his fiddle.

So Emily me darlin I am now leaving you

Heave away me jollies heave away

So will you wait and marry me when this trip is through

Heave away a me jolly boys were all bound away .

You promise now but please don t deceive me

Heave away me jollies heave away

Sometimes were bound for Liverpool sometimes were bound for Spain

Heave away me jollies heave away

But now were bound for old St Johns where all the girls are dancing.

Heave away a me jolly boys were all bound away."

John Harrison and John Forge stepped forward again and we all went mad.

"Sometimes were bound for Liverpool sometimes were bound for Spain

Heave away me jollies heave away

But now were bound for old St Johns where all the girls are dancing.

Heave away a me jolly boys were all bound away.

"Just once more cried Joseph

Sometimes were bound for Liverpool sometimes were bound for Spain

Heave away me jollies heave away

But now were bound for old St Johns where all the girls are dancing.

Heave away a me jolly boys were all bound away .

AWAAAAAAAAAAY Ha"

What a dance. It was great. Emily and I had not disgraced our selves and everyone was clearly hot. John Forge stepped forward again

"Right folks the pigs ready and the bonfires lit. Please line up there is plenty for all. The Ready's are doing the fireworks as they always do so please let the Butterfield's go first. Soon we were all outside with doorstep sandwiches and roast pork in apple sauce. We stood with the bonfire behind us and enjoyed the fireworks. I turned to look at Emily in the firelight. She turned and said.

"What are you thinking Master Charles Jones?"

"I am noting all of your beautiful and elegant features so that I can draw you just as you are tonight whilst I am away"

"Write to me Jonesy"

"Oh I will, I surely will".

Charles and Joseph Butterfield waved. The crowd turned in the firelight to see the rockets bursting overhead. Charles spoke with some emotion. "Well dear friends I am afraid the Butterfield's must go. We sail on tomorrows ebb on the maiden voyage of the Ann Goodman. We are not going far just to the Holland Banks. It is a shakeout cruise and then we shall be back. But two weeks later we shall be gone for eight weeks as we head for the Faroes to catch King cod. With a full hold I intend to sail straight to Grimsby. We shall do this four times and then sail home via the East Coast ports and the Dogger Bank. Ann will keep you all informed via the angels. Now Reverend may I call on you for a blessing"

Reverend Jefferies stood up and looking at Charles and Ann said

"I know what a student of the Bible you both are so on behalf of the community and all your friends and family I just want to read this"

Taking the King James Bible he read this

"The Lord bless thee and keep thee, the Lord makes his face shine upon thee and be gracious to thee. The Lord lifts up his countenance upon thee and gives thee peace".

Looking at the crowd he and they said AMEN.

The Skipper was genuinely affected. His voice was full of emotion when he said:-

"Goodnight all. Thank you for coming. Come on Billy and where is Chas?"

"He is over there with John Forge showing the children how to tie sea knots"

"Go and get him will you Jonesy"

All the family headed back home, though of course it was not far to go. Emily pulled on my arm and we went through the house and out into the Garden. She stopped at the tree. Turning to me she said

"I shall not come down to the wharf to say goodbye and neither will Mistress Ann. It's considered bad luck. I will wave to you from here as you go past as will Mrs Butterfield. So we must say goodbye now. Kiss me Charles for I think that I love you"

I was speechless. "You, you love me"

"Yes I think so but you know what they say"

"What do they say Emily"

"Absence is to love what wind is to fire ~ quickens the large flame and puts out the small. I will know for sure when you come back."

She looked so beautiful I carefully bent down and kissed her softly on those wonderful lips"

She kissed me back. We were both new to this but it felt just right.

"Emily Byes I have loved you from the moment I saw you, I am so happy"

"When you get back we shall have to go to Creekmouth so that I can introduce you to my parents. Hold me tight Jonesy for I am just so happy and it truly is a night to remember"

The next morning we set sail on the ebb.

21 Monday May the 26th
　The Ann Goodman set free.

Master Charles put the speaking trumpet to his lips and called out "Billy, let go forrard"

"Aye, aye, Master" Came Billy's swift reply.

With that command Billy looped the bow cable over the mooring pin and threw it to Chas. Billy then leapt onto the Ann's deck.

Master Charles spoke again "Ok boys punt her off"

Chas, John Harrison and Fred Scattergood laid hold of the punting poles and pushed the Ann Goodman's bow away from the wharf. She began to rotate with the stern cable still holding her to the wharf. The ebb was well on and I could tell it was pulling on the hull. It was well on even though it was just 5:30 in the morning. The breeze from Sunday had picked up but was now blowing from the West, from London, as the pungent smell in the air proved. Billy was coiling the bow cable when Master Charles turned in my direction and shouted through the trumpet.

"OK Jonesy let go the aft"

I undid the cable from the deck cleat and John Forge lifted the cable over the wharf bollard and dropped it into the pool. I hauled it on board, fastened it as I had been shown and waived to Master Forge, as did we all. The Ann Goodman was set free.

"Sharp now Jonesy she's under way" was Master Joseph command.

I ran forrard and jumped onto the stern deck landing just behind the tiller bath cockpit where the Skipper stood with the tiller firmly in his hand.

At last the Ann was free and in the element she was designed for. The narrow and calm water of the Creek was not of course her real element. Though I had lived in London all my life I had never been to sea. With her bow pointing downstream towards the Barking Creek estuary she began to steadily pick up speed. The rudder had no effect since we were just floating with the ebb. We passed the garden on number 12 and there stood the whole family waving us on. I had my sites set on Emily Byes and she waved and then blew me a kiss. Just a few more minutes and we left Barking Pool, passing out of site. We were truly on our way. We soon passed the Malt house and then the shipbuilding and engineering yard which were all on the port side. Smoke rose from the tall chimney stack so the boiler was well on. On the starboard side was the Iron Foundry which was quickly left behind.

Putting the trumpet to his lips the skipper called out "Billy set the foresail"

With that Billy bent down and picked up the foresail halyard and pulled hard so that the sail rose up the rope He really worked at his task pulling the halyard hard hand over hand tightening it via the deck pulley until it was taught. He then lashed it to the deck cleat prepared for it. The sail billowed with the wind and then Billy again hauled the sail in and as he did so the Ann picked up speed. The sail was now really taught and Billy again fastened it as he had been shown. When you looked at the Ann from the side there was a rope attached right at the tip of the bowsprit and this went to the top of the main stage mast. The main mast consisted of two parts. The main mast itself went through the deck and fish hold and was stepped on to the ships keel.

About fifty feet up the stage mast was attached with six u bolts taking the mast a further thirty feet. About the middle of the stage mast was the forestay rope. This was also attached to the tip of the bowsprit.

Then came the stay rope which was fastened to the bow. This rope gave the mast stability since it was attached to the ships keel via u bolts. The Jib topsail was attached with ropes to the jib on its top and via a single loop to the forestay rope.

Master Charles shouted "Well done lads raise the jib topsail as you have been shown and fix it." Billy, Chas and John Harrison pulled on the halyard raising the sail via its loops up the forestay until it was taught. They then hauled on the pulley at the bottom triangular part of the staysail until it was taught and then fastened it to the deck cleat. Both sails filled and when full and bye were drawing well. The Lady Ann picked up speed and the rudder bit. We could all tell because the Lady Ann heeled to port and Master Charles controlled this with the tiller.

"John, Fred keep her centre stream until the Creek widens. Be about eight minutes before we see the Thames.

Then the Thames came into view. Even though I remained at the stern I could see all of the ships moored in Barking Reach awaiting their turn at the Royal Docks. The number of sailing ships varied over time many waiting farther down river in the Thames Estuary waiting to be called into the Reach by Pilot Cutters. These ships came from all over the empire.

As we approached Creekmouth, Boys Oak came into view. The ropes were hanging free. Joseph turned and caught my eye and winked. The stench from human waste was strong. Raw sewerage nine feet deep was piled on both banks of the Creek. There was offal, fat, slime and other horrors. I had seen this before but not from the Creek. The main cause of all this was the Northern Outfall sewer from Balzagette's London sewerage network. I could now see the construction of the Becton Gas works. This was to produce coal gas to light the City of London and fuel all the Restaurants and Kitchens throughout London. Finally on the starboard side was Horse End mud bank and on the port the village of Creekmouth with Lawes Chemical and Manure factory clearly visible. As we swept out of the Creek the Master Charles shouted down the trumpet. "Staysail tighten off lads". Billy and Chas had already raised the staysail but had not fastened the bottom of the triangle so it was loose and simply flapping in the breeze. At this Billy and Chas tightened it off via the deck pulley until it was full and bye and then tied down to the deck cleat. Next came the command to Fred and John "ready the mainsl". They immediately raised the mainsl gaff which was like the boom but not so long and inclined upward instead of parallel with the deck. The mainmast end of the gaff and boom were like a Y and butted into a saddle which allowed both masts to rotate. The sail filled the space between the gaff and the boom as it rose up the main mast via its pulley system and the large loops on its front edge rose up the main mast. The boom moved out but was not yet taught and so had little power. The Red Ochre stained main sale flapped in the breeze. John and Fred had got everything ready on the way down. The gaff had been prepared on its saddle and the main spar roped and fed through the pulleys and at Charles command hauled into position. At the same time Joseph and I brought the mizzen mast stern sail into action and again hauled hard and then fastened the rope to the desk cleats. Charles turned the Ann Goodman toward the Thames Estuary and got her set into position prior to tightening all sails and thus increasing our speed.

With the wind blowing a westerly the Ann would be running before the wind. The Ann gradually began to increase speed. After about ten minutes more we were at Barking Reach "Full On " came the command and all sails were tightened full and bye. The main sail was hauled tight and filled with air. It had the most beautiful shape. The Skipper put the helm hard over and we swept into the River Thames heading due east. After about an hour of fast cruising down the Thames estuary following the twists and turns of the river the waters widened out. This was most noticeable from Lower Hope adjacent Stanford le Hope from which point I had a clear view of the Estuary with Southend on the Port side and the Medway Estuary on the starboard.

Once past Shoebury Ness we entered the North Sea proper where the sea conditions and wind altered. Small white caps were to be seen on the wave tops. The sun was out and there were many smacks lingering in the Thames off loading their catch into the float cages before heading back out to sea. These cages were emptied by other craft that filleted the catch on their way up stream to Billingsgate

"Haul away"

This shout came from Charles Butterfield at the tiller. Immediately we all hauled on the sail ropes to increase the pull on all the sails. The Ann Goodman heeled over and began to gain pace. Soon her schooner bow was slicing through the choppy sea with some, though not a lot, of the North Sea breaching over the deck. I could see what everyone meant about the danger presented by the low freeboard in smack design. Charles and Joseph had bitter experience of this. Some of their shipmates had been washed overboard in heavy weather due to the small freeboard. The Ann Goodman had been designed with safety ropes from bow to stern fixed to the centre of the deck. The ropes were separated by the main and mizzen mast. We were equipped with a safety harnesses with two loose ends about six feet long. The ends were fitted with a clip which we fastened to the safety rope. We fastened the free rope to the safety rope running between the main and mizzen masts. "Fasten on" was the command for the second rope and "loose off" was the command for the first rope. I could see that this was a very good idea for safety but it did restrict movement. We were all required to "Rope Up" on command though this was not popular with any sailor because of what I have just said. The Butterfield's insisted that all deck crew "Rope Up" on command. No one was excused. The deck now had a lean on it as the Lady Ann began to sail hard and fast.

"Rope Up" Charles shouted. We all obeyed. There was no real work to do since we were not long lining or fishing at all. The plan was to get to the Holland Banks as quickly as possible. The trip was to shake out all of the Ann's rigging and stuff and see how she behaved at sea. By twelve thirty the Holland Banks came into view. There were hundreds of smacks fishing for skate and other flat fish. The Long Mac fleet of Scrimey McAllans was out there in strength. Once on station Joseph stuck his head into the cockpit, through the sliding door and called out

"Breakfast, John, Chas and Billy"

He then disappeared below.

"Right Jonesy I'm heading North East and we will begin our run South long lining after they have finished breakfast. Prepare the line with bait and make sure the hooks are in their baskets with no kinks."

"Next"

This call came from Joseph who appeared from below deck as John Harrison, Chas and Billy resumed their stations. He then walked to the stern cockpit and laid hold on the tiller at which point Charles got up and together with Fred Scattergood and I went below deck for breakfast. Everything was ready. Joseph had cooked and served. The plates were in the wooden holding rings fastened to the table as were the coffee and cream jugs. The cups were hung up on hooks behind the bench ready for use. I was hungry as were Fred and Charles. We set to. The Skipper bent his head and muttered something and then he began eating.

Addressing Fred Scattergood the Skipper said

"She sails really well, better than I had thought she would. She will be really, really fast in a strong stern wind. What is your opinion Fred, on the sailing gear?"

"Well Captain as you know John Forge makes the best sails in Barking. He has done a great job of the rigging and it was really easy to haul and set. I think you have a great boat Master Charles."

"I think so to but heavy weather will prove it, what do you say?"

"Well Captain the schooner bow will cut through the water fine and the steep rising sides seem to deflect the sea swell really good though I think that in heavy weather we will still have breaching sea over the deck just like all smacks. She will probably be better than any other smack I have sailed on".

"I agree but the only time we will know is when we have gone through the experience. That is not going to happen on this trip if you look at the barometer it would seem we are due calm weather. However I am planning a fast sail to the Faroes in one go and we will probably hit the heavy stuff then. I reckon forty hours out of Barking will get us to Torshavn where we will port, take on ice and rest up before long lining the big cod. When the fish hold is full I will then head straight for Grimsby in one sail"

"We are not going into the Scottish Ports then Captain"

"No, Grimsby is where we will get the best price for the fish we are going to catch. We should get a very, very good price. From Grimsby the catch will go in ice wagons to Billingsgate. The railway track extends onto the Alexandra Dock. There are pontoons and we off load direct onto the pontoons. After mooring up the catchers will gut and box the fish and then they will be auctioned. After that we get our money and the fish will go south via the Manchester, Sheffield and Lincoln Railway to Billingsgate.

We had sailed round the Dogger Bank and headed straight for the Holland Banks. This was, I was told, shallow water leading to big waves even in calm weather and so it proved to be. None of us had been sea sick and this was seen as a good sign. Soon more masts came into view. Master Charles said that there were about 200 smacks all long lining for skate. We were not fishing and so headed into deeper water just of the shore seeking a good mooring spot. This was soon found and after anchoring and going through all of the checks Fred Scattergood remained on deck whilst we all went down for more grub. Joseph had done stew and it was great. After Billy had finished he went to the pigeon coop and took out Ruth. The Skipper had just finished a short note and this was inserted into the metal cylinder attached to Ruth's leg. He then went on deck and set Ruth free.

"Change the watch" I heard Billy say.

"Aye, aye lad," said Fred "she'll be home in about an hour. Good idea of Joseph's."

Fred came down the steps and entered the mess through the door separating the mess deck from the crew deck. We were all eating pudding with custard. Fred sat down and Joseph set the stew before him. Once we were all finished Joseph set before us his famous molasses coffee laced with Gordon's Gin. It was a single small shot for us lads but Charles, Joseph and John Harrison had the normal.

"No Gordon's for you Fred as we agreed and no hitting of Florence when we get back to Barking, you understand"

"Aye captain I understands. I got her pregnant you know, I know you know, everybody knows. I was drunk. The Barbers made me marry her. I do not and never did love her."

"Be that as it may you have made your bed and must lye in it and there must be no violence to her, understand"

"Aye I understand and I know it damages the kids but as I say I have never loved her and I have met someone I do love"

It seemed very strange to hear this conversation. I was embarrassed but apparently all in Barking knew about Fred Scattergood's drunken stints. His Grandfather owned the Stanhope Arms in Barking and let him run up a tab. Everyone thought that this was the trouble but it appears Richard Scattergood, Fred's Grandfather was against the marriage as was Fred's own Father Arthur. Arthur married Ada Post and got her pregnant at 16. She was a servant at Stanhope Hall. They married at the Church in Kibworth Harcourt. It was a double wedding since her sister Eliza was married on the same day to Willfred Collins. Arthur and Ada named their first child Eliza. Then came Arthur followed by William Frederick. This was the drunk now on board the Ann. It is true the he was a very hard worker when free of drink and he was sober all the time I sailed with him. Ten years in all.

"Thanks Joseph that was great" said the Skipper.

Turning to me he said

"Jonesy take Billy his coffee and make sure everything is ready for the night. We all need a good rest. I am going to our cabin Joseph."

"I will see you in a while" said Joseph.

Gradually the wind subsided just like Charles had said and within three hours the sea had calmed down and indeed by seven o clock we were becalmed. The water could be heard gently slapping against the hull. I went to my hammock and settled in for a rest. It gently swayed with the boat but I remained roughly in the same position. I could see why the Butterfield's preferred hammocks just like the Royal Navy. I had taken the top bunk just as Emily had said. I suddenly I heard the deck bell ring with four clangs. This meant a boat was approaching. Each smack had a deck boat which was used for fleeting. The Ann Goodman had such a boat but Master Charles said that he would never use it for fleeting because the practice was too dangerous.

With fleeting the fish were placed in iced boxes whilst on the smacks and then these boxes sometimes fifteen to twenty at a time were placed across the boats and rowed to the delivery schooner. These would then sail off to the Thames or east coast ports. Many, many seamen either drowned or had their limbs broken in such trips. John Scattergood, Charles brother and the husband of Elizabeth Ann Spashett had died doing just this.

"Boat ahoy, what ship" shouted Billy through the speaking trumpet, just as he had been taught.

"Esther out of Barking" came the reply. "Skipper Kitchin on board"

Charles immediately emerged from the Captain's cabin and went up the steep stairs. I heard the boat bump alongside and then the Skipper say "High Brian come on board ~ what's the crack, how's the fishing?"

"It's good even though there are so many boats out but I haven't come to talk about fishing but about murder"

"Murder "said Charles. "Come down to our cabin and let's talk"

"First things first Charles. The skipper of the Dragon is in the boat and I do not think he has got long to live. Can I get Harry and Michael to bring him on board while we talk?"

"Sure get the lads on board I'll get John Harrison to tend his wounds. Joseph will get the crew some grog."

The two men came down the stairs and went into the Captains cabin. I heard the boat banging against the Ann Goodman's side and then the sound of groaning as someone was lifted on board. A body was brought down the steps. Whoever it was he had been badly beaten. The Mess Deck door opened and Master Joseph stood there.

"What the hell is going on and who is that?

Brian Kitchin spoke up:-

"Its Zachariah Bass Joe, he's been beaten up by the crew of the Dragon"

Joseph noticed the other crew

"Oh hello Michael, didn't recognise you, Zechariah Bass you say, I bet the bastard has been up to no good. Bring him in here and lay him on the table. My, he is in a bad way. John can you see what you can do"

"Want some coffee mates there some still in the pot"

"Aye Joe that would be good, really good"

The Captains cabin door opened and Master Charles leaned through.

"Joe come aft. Brian Kichin's got news of a murder."

Master Joseph went through but left the door open.

"Sit down Brian, murder you say, who was murdered?"

"An eight year old apprentice called Nicholas Mountsell.

"What, oh no not another one, I thought that the London Times article about the death of John Hennecky had put an end to the really violent stuff."

I heard Skipper Kichin say "You sent for that Reporter didn't you Charles, the owners were trying to find out who did it. All the Skippers and crew knew but said nowt. The strike brought us all together"

"It might have been me or it might have been him"

Charles said nodding at Joseph

"but it seems it was all to no avail because it's not against the law. To stop this inhumane treatment of these children, for that is what it is, the Law has to change and neither Joseph nor I have any contacts in that area. All the Magistrates are smack owners and they control Barking. In fact they control all of the Courts up the East Coast ports including Yarmouth. All we can do is make what is done to these poor children public. So now please tell me what happened to Nicholas Mountsel"

I heard Skipper Kichin explain what had been done to this apprentice.

"He was a Navy orphan and so when he was signed up with Mister and Mrs Bass, Bass not only got the fourteen pounds but the Marine Society equipped him with ALL of the clothing and wet weather gear he would need. Bass sold all of it. The boy only had a cotton top and some draws. He had no shoes. Zechariah constantly beat him. He kicked him in the knee repeatedly until he could hardly get below decks. Even though it's May Charles you know what the waves are like over the Holland banks. Bass sent Nicholas down for coffee and when he came on deck with it his knee gave way and he slipped as he got near Bass. This resulted in the hot coffee shooting over his tiller arm. Bass does no more than grabs Mountsell by his shirt collar and just throws him over the side. Like most apprentices he could not swim and so he drowned. The crew were shocked and then mutinied. After we won the strike no crew worth its salt will put up with treatment to their mates like that. They saw Bass on many occasions mistreat the boy. He kicked him in the knee on the sail out as I have said. He could hardly walk never mind work. So the crew lashed Bass to the Capstan and whipped him. That's what you can see."

I heard Master Joseph say:

"Got what he deserved then, the bastard. I'll tell you what I am going to do and that is suffocate him for then it's done. No one will know, what say you Charles an Eye for an Eye? Yes? That is what the good book says isn't it. Hand for hand, for foot yes, come on that is what it says isn't it.?"

Charles looked troubled "Joe, what we need to do is use this as proof that the Law has got to be changed. The Ann is not being used for fishing so let's take Bass into Great Yarmouth and report what he has done to the Magistrates. I will also inform the Press.

"Is that what you will do then" asked Skipper Kichin

"Yes, we will head into Great Yarmouth in the morning and report the murder to the police" said Charles

Joseph groaned

"Nothing will be done Charles, nothing"

"Will the lads on the Dragon follow us in Brian?"

"I don't know, come back with me now and ask them"

Joseph spoke

"Aye my Brother let's do just that".

With that all three men came out of the cabin, they paused, Skipper Kichin called out for Harry and Michael members of the Dragon's crew to go on deck. With that I heard all five men climb the deck steps. They climbed into their smack boat and pushed off for the Dragon. I got off my bunk and went up on deck to see what was what and saw the men pulling strongly for a smack hove to in the distance.

I went back down the stairs and went into the mess deck. Chas, Fred and John were looking over Zechariah Bass. He was in a bad way. His right arm was broken and he had rope burns round his neck.

"Let's finish the swine "said Fred Scattergood.

"That is what he deserves but Master Charles wants him in Court. I heard them say that we are all going into Great Yarmouth tomorrow. That includes the crew of the Dragon if they will agree" I said.

"Get me that pillow John I'll suffocate him, there will be no marks and everyone will believe it was the beating that killed him"

"No Fred" I said "Master Charles wants this in Court"

"Who are you Jonesy to tell me what to do"

"I am no one Mr. Scattergood. All I am telling you is what I heard the Skipper just say"

"I bet Joseph was up for doing him in for that is what Bass deserves"

"Yes, Master Joseph wanted to suffocate Bass but the Skipper wants to get the Press up from London just as he did with the Hennecky case"

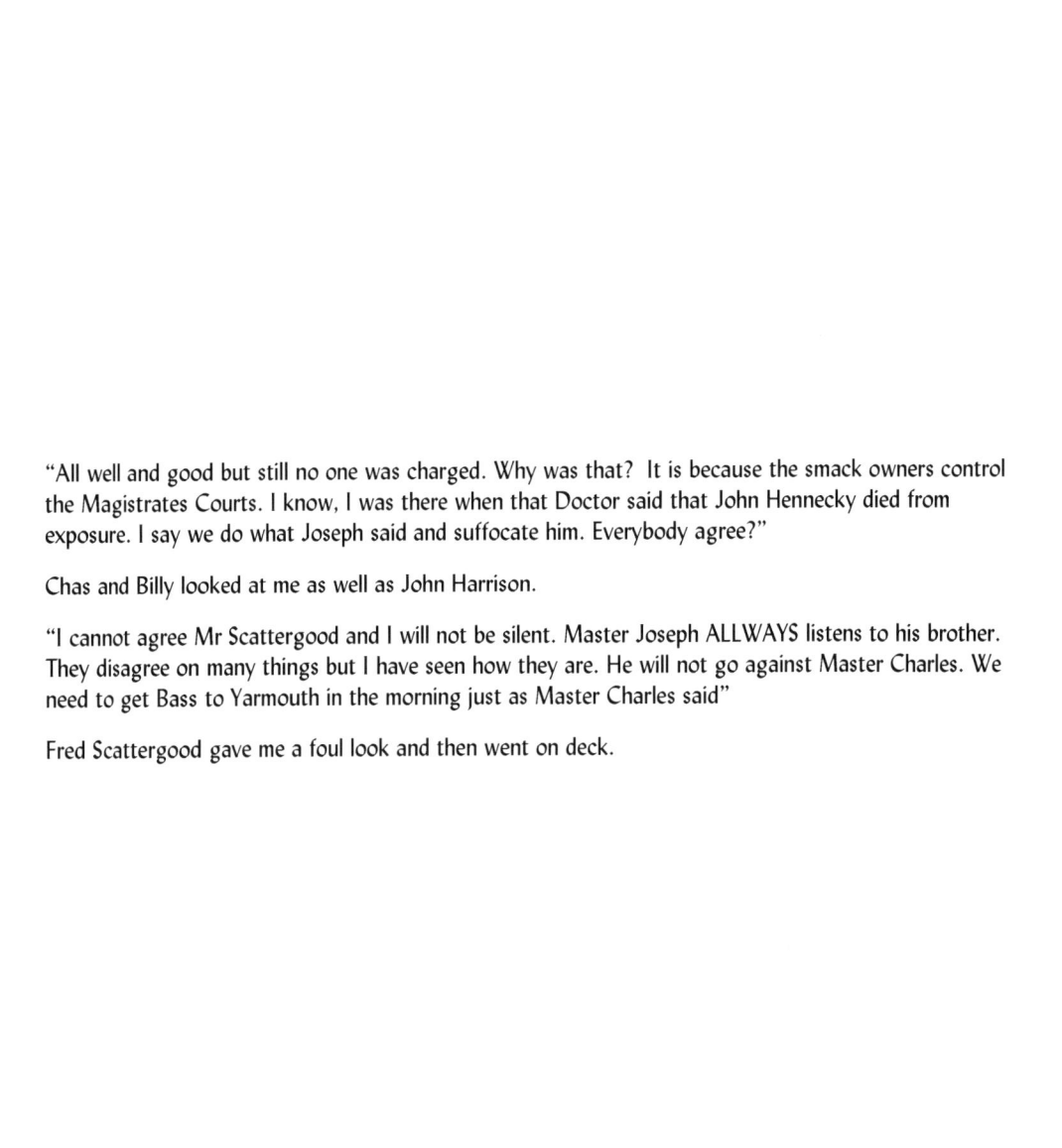

"All well and good but still no one was charged. Why was that? It is because the smack owners control the Magistrates Courts. I know, I was there when that Doctor said that John Hennecky died from exposure. I say we do what Joseph said and suffocate him. Everybody agree?"

Chas and Billy looked at me as well as John Harrison.

"I cannot agree Mr Scattergood and I will not be silent. Master Joseph ALLWAYS listens to his brother. They disagree on many things but I have seen how they are. He will not go against Master Charles. We need to get Bass to Yarmouth in the morning just as Master Charles said"

Fred Scattergood gave me a foul look and then went on deck.

22　On the Dragon

As we approached the Dragon Skipper Kichin called out

"Ahoy the Dragon, Ann Goodman approaching"

"Come on board Skipper we have been expecting you" came the reply.

The second mate was a man called John Stradling. He was a distant relative of the Butterfield's. Joseph reached out and shook John Stradling hand.

"Hello John, rum business this but Bass got what he deserved"

Master Charles spoke "Get the crew down to the mess deck John and let's get all the details. Who is taking the watch?"

"Simon Docket my nephew, he's one of my apprentices. I will get one of the crew to spell for him. He and the other apprentice will likely know the most about what happened".

They all went below decks but the Dragon was a fifty footer smack with just one mast and so the mess deck was cramped

"So you young fisher lads how was Nicholas Mountsel killed?

Josh Munn spoke first "Well sir we left the Thames alright and then hit a strong northerly breeze. Mr Bass had sold all of the gear Nick got from the Marine Society and unlike us he had no clothes from the poorhouse". He was always cold, we all were but Nick had no shoes sir. Just some cotton draws and a long sleeved shirt. There weren't any bedding and Mr Bass made us sleep on old deck mats between watches. We had no food for days. Nick and I got boils but Nicks were really bad. He treated him horrible sir, real bad. He kicked him in the knee once and it took Mr Stradling to put it back into line. He picked on Nick all the time. On the day he kicked him in the knee we all got him back below and wrapped him up real warm but Bass found out and made him go on deck. He whipped him with a rope end sir which caused some of his boils to burst and then they went septic, I think that is the word. The crew kept telling Bass that he would cause the death of Nick but he would not listen."

All the time both mates were nodding their heads.

"OK Josh now tell us about events leading to Nicholas Mountsel being thrown overboard." Asked Joseph.

"It was Nicks watch. The wind had dropped and everything was easier. Bass shouted "Boy" and when Nick got to his side near the tiller he told him to go and get him some coffee and to be "quick about it". He came below. I saw him; he was limping badly due to his knee not being right. He got the coffee and went on deck. Dragon was rolling with the waves but not bad. As he got near Bass his knee gave way and he fell pitching the cup full of hot coffee over his tiller arm. Bass grabbed Nicholas by the shirt and just threw him overboard. He couldn't swim sir. None of the crew can swim. We all saw and heard him crying for help and then he sank".

Josh began to sob. "We couldn't save him Master Butterfield was just had to watch him die"

"My God" shouted Joseph "the cruel bastard. He deserves death and nothing else"

All turned to look at the Skipper.

"Joseph's right but let's just be sure we have the whole story".

Turning to the Dragon's third mate, Bert Shore, the Skipper asked

"Then what happened with the crew?"

"We are all different since the strike Charles, we ain't putting up with this treatment any more. Nick was not the only one badly treated. The other apprentices suffered and so did the crew. Bass thought he was God. I ran for Bass and dragged him across the deck whilst Stradling took the tiller. Harry and I knocked seven bells out of Bass and then we tied him to the capstan and whipped him. It was during this that we broke his arm. We left him for about an hour and then set about him again. That's what you see"

"OK. We are taking Bass into Yarmouth tomorrow and Brian Kichin is coming with us. We will take him to the Police Station and state that he is a murderer. We have one big problem. There is no body so will you all come with us and tell the Police what you have told us?"

They all agreed to go into Great Yarmouth.

"Charles, Charles let's go back and suffocate the bugger and then let God sort it out" said Joseph.

"Look, all of you. The death of this poor soul may give us another chance to make public what is happening every day on board these smacks. Let's send an angel to Ann and get her to contact John Dill of the London Mail. If we can get him to the Yarmouth Court then all of London will learn what is continuing to happen"

Joseph went very quiet but was angry.

"We will never, never beat this lot Charles and you know it. They own the Courts, the magistrates the support yards, the shipwrights; everything. The poorhouses and the workhouses provide a never ending supply of orphan children. They themselves are terrible places and that's what the politicians want. They don't want to know about the orphans or the apprentices. You mark my words Bass will not be found guilty of murder. Look at the number of crews that die during fleeting. I ask you, rowing boats loaded down with fifty boxes of fish in ice across rough water and then trying to off load to a schooner in high seas. They do not care. Many fishermen still do fourteen weeks at sea even after the strike. Our brother John died doing that leaving Lizzie a widow with a baby no more than three weeks old. I say we finish him off tonight!"

"Joseph, what you say is true but somehow we have to get the Law changed. To do this we need someone in power with a love of humanity. In the meantime the best weapon is the Newspapers".

Turning to Brian Kichin the Skipper asked: "This will not be easy Brian. The crew may be charged with assault. Mrs Bass is wealthy and no sweet lady so will you come in with us and go to the Yarmouth papers "

"Sure but I can only be there for two days. After that I will have to take the Dragon back out to sea, will that do?"

"Certainly would. Let's get back to the Ann and get that message sent"

23 On Board the Ann Goodman

I heard Billy call out "ahoy there, who approaches" and then heard

"Dragon with Skipper Butterfield"

The boat banged alongside and we tied off. Joseph and Charles came on board and we then released the boat which sheered off back to the Dragon

"See you at nine bells Brian and don't forget Josh" said Master Charles.

The Butterfield's went into their cabin. I later learnt that the message for the Angel was as follows

"Dear Ann, Nicholas Mountsel aged eight murdered by Zechariah Bass. Contact John Dill at Time. Get him out to Yarmouth. Will send message tomorrow from Yarmouth"

Joseph gave the message tube to Billy and said

"Billy get Naomi, attach this message and set her free"

Billy did this and then went up on deck and set the pigeon free.

"Right everyone let's hit the sack, we have an early start in the morning." Said Master Joseph.

Chas went up on deck and all of us settled down in our hammocks. I was the next watch and went to sleep almost straight away. I woke at four o clock and made my way to the Crew Deck to get coffee which Joseph always kept on tap. I got my coffee and walked past Zechariah Bass who seemed very still. I looked closer and was sure he was not breathing. I woke John Harrison. He moaned at me and then came and looked.

"He's dead Jonesy. Dead and he's cold so I would guess he died around three hours ago. I'll tell the boys."

John walked through the door into and through the crew deck and knocked on the Butterfield's cabin. Master Joseph opened the door. I told him about Bass. He woke his brother and they both walked into the Mess Deck to look at Bass.

"He sure is dead Charles, seems that your God is just after all."

"Yes, I can see that he is dead and yes, that is probably just, but it makes my goal much harder"

"You said that we would not get a conviction because there was no body. So yet again Bass would be found to be innocent"

"That is true. If however, he had been alive, we could have got the Coroner to interview him after Josh had testified. This would have been recorded by the Press and that would make London aware of the cruelty"

"Oh, I see, umm does that mean there will be no investigation at all?"

"No there will have to be a Coroners Court and an investigation into the circumstances into Nicholas Mountsel's death."

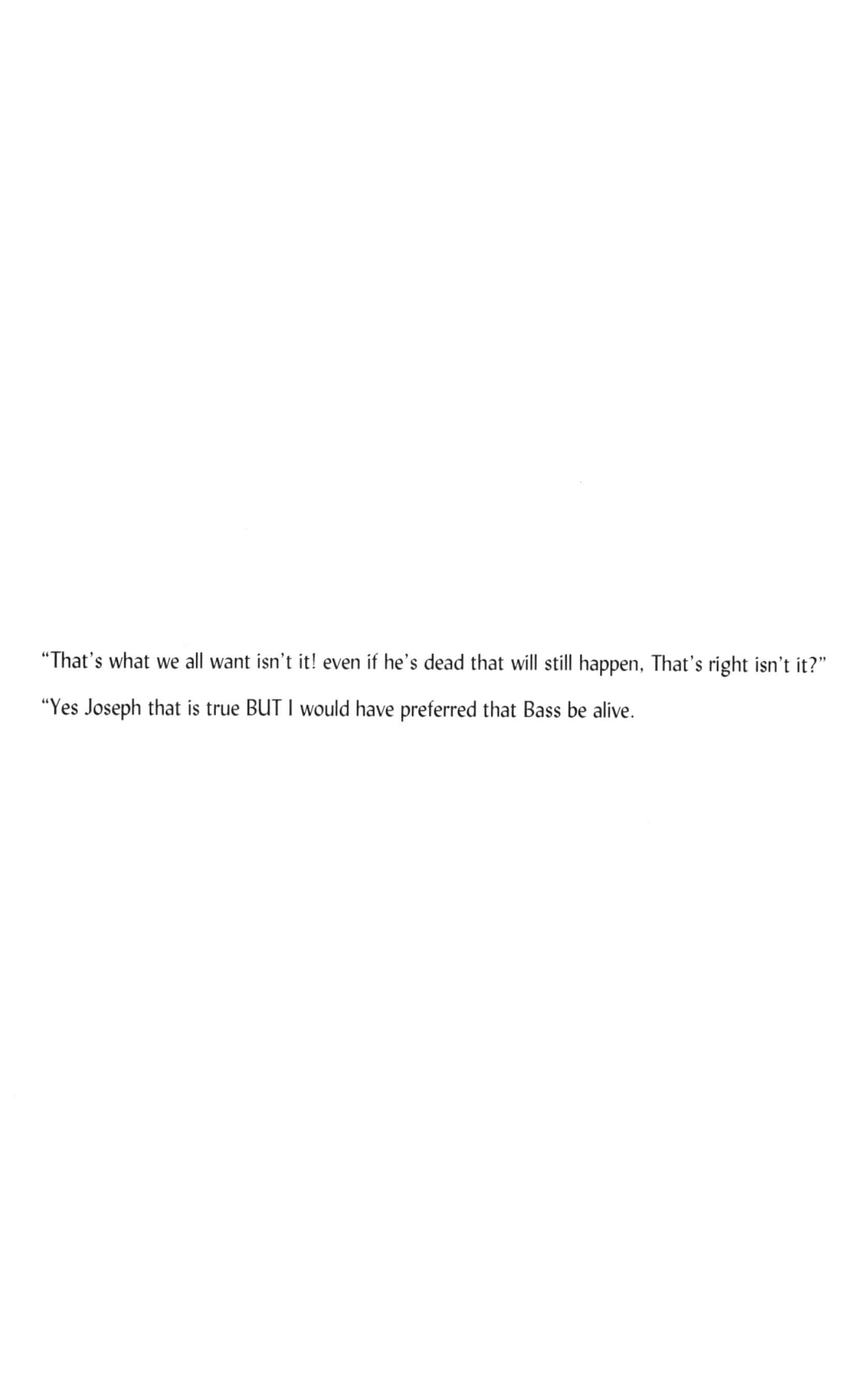

"That's what we all want isn't it! even if he's dead that will still happen, That's right isn't it?"

"Yes Joseph that is true BUT I would have preferred that Bass be alive.

24 Back Home

When I met Emily in Yarmouth a few days after we had docked in the Pool she told me what had happened after we had set sail on the Monday morning.

As Emily waved me on my way with a kiss she asked Mrs. Butterfield if she could have the day off to visit her parents in Creekmouth. As they walked back into the Kitchen past the washing room the following conversation took place.

"Of course Emily, in fact go and get a pony and trap to take you. It's only two miles so it won't be expensive and I'll pay"

"Oh no ma'am I cannot let you do that, I do have some money saved up and so I will pay for trap."

"Emily, be gracious, this is my gift to you. If you feel uncomfortable then let me pay one way and please, just accept this, you know you are more than just a maid to Charles and I."

"Thank you so much ma'am. It will make things so much easier and I can be back in time to help put the children to bed. I'll set off at nine o clock and be back by four"

"Emily, excuse me for asking but is this about Charles Jones"

"Yes ma'am, I know it's only a few days but I think I have fallen in love with him. Am I mad? Foolish, crazy or too young to know the difference"

"Well Emily, I met Charles in 1840 and it was love at first site. We began courting immediately but the family rule was that we could not be married until we both passed 21. That is Charles and I had both to be 21. Since I was two years younger than him we married in 1842. He was a rough but handsome character, always in fights with the help of his brother and others. He was a boarder in my mother's house on Heath Street. Both he and Joseph served as crew on the smacks. It was mad, foolish and crazy. He did not believe in God just like his Brother Joseph whereas I was a committed Christian. Joseph is a work in progress by the way. I will never give up on him for he loves my husband and they are great friends. How does Jonesy feel about you?"

"He says he feels the same way but he says that he has nothing to offer me since he is an orphan."

"My, oh my, you have discussed things deeply. Sensible talk too. Now Emily I cannot tell you the details but Jonesy, Chas and Billy together with the crew are going to learn something to their advantage on this cruise. In my opinion it is going to cause a lot of trouble with the other skippers and owners but Charles and Joseph have decided and I agree with what they are proposing. Did you know that a smacks value is divided into sixty four shares. Charles has sixteen as do I and Joseph has thirty two. This fact is involved but I will let Jonesy tell you when he gets back. I guess you are going to see your parents ~ yes"

"Yes~ but that is not going to be easy, my Mother will be fine or at least I think she will but my Father is very different. He was always very protective, kind of controlling in a way, particularly when I got into my teens. He had a way with me I did not like. Something happened. He did something claiming it was a game.

He groped my breasts. I did not like it. He threatened to beat me if I told my Mother. I told my Mother anyway but she is not a strong person and is controlled by my Father. I worry about Eliza, who is two years younger than me and just entering her teens. Things are not good in that house Mrs. Butterfield, not good at all. But they are my parents and so must be told. I think Jonesy and I will be engaged soon, though of course he has not asked me yet. There is something else Mrs. Butterfield. I am seventeen not sixteen and I will soon be eighteen. Charles thinks he is fourteen, perhaps nearly fifteen but he does not know because he does not have a birth certificate.

I think he is more like seventeen just like me. I told you that I was fifteen because I wanted the position, I liked you and your family and the job got me out of Creekmouth. I do not think my Father would let me take the position but then I found out he needed the money. I have to send half what I earn to him each month".

"What, well that I did not know. I knew that you were not fifteen Emily. Anyone who was observant could see that. Now; I have decided to come with you. I know what you are talking about. There is no need to go into detail. It is bad, very bad and you are right not to tolerate it. Perhaps you can see how things are with Eliza. Now you listen Emily, pay attention! You must never talk about this to Master Joseph, never, you understand. He will do your father harm Emily, great harm and so he must never know. Understand"

Yes Ma'am. Master Joseph is like my Uncle. I like him, I like him a lot but I know he can be difficult. The fight at the Fishing Smack proved that. His ways are just though, at least I think they are just, am I wrong?"

"No you are not wrong. Joseph has a very strong sense of justice and if justice is not done by the Courts it is always likely to be done by him. However he always listens to Charles, always. He often mocks him but as I have said before though they are different they are very close. Two years separates them. Charles is the oldest. He was born in 1815. Joseph looks the oldest due to all the fights. Charles is not always right. Joseph knows that my husband and I are on a different path to him but as I have said, Joseph is a work in progress. He has a truly big and generous heart. He is loyal to all his friends and they know this, but believe me there is history in the family over what you have told me and he would do for your father if he ever got to know. May I tell my husband what you have said?"

"Yes, oh yes, Master Charles is like my Father. I know he cares for me. I have never known security such as I feel in this house. Please tell Master Charles and thank you for coming with me today. It will make things so much easier."

"Good let's go and get the pony and trap, I can drive so that will save hiring a driver. What time shall we go?"

"I have to see to the children but say 10.00. That should get us there around 11:30; my Father is the foreman and often has a drink of tea at home around then."

"Right, what time is it, oh it's only half past seven. I'll go to Reuben Rogers and get the trap. I will also call on Mrs Shellito to see if she can sit the children"

Mrs Butterfield arrived at Rogers's ostlery at ten past nine but Mr. Rogers could not help her. All the traps were out and not due back till later. He then told her that Fred Barber had a trap that he sometimes let out. She was surprised to hear this. Frederick Barber was the father of Florence Scattergood, Fred Scattergood's wife.

Ann went to Smith Street as instructed but as she went down High Street and crossed over to Gascoigne Street she noticed that Tomlinson and Budd, the Barking Pawnbrokers that everyone used, had moved.

She glanced in their window. There was nothing of interest. She arrived at Mr .Barbers and sure enough there was a piebald pony harnessed to a trap in nice condition tethered at the gate. She knocked on the door. The door opened and there stood Mary Barber who Mrs. Butterfield knew since they both attended St Margaret's Church.

"Hello Ann, what a pleasant surprise, please come in and how can I help?"

"Reuben Rogers sent me here, I am in need of that trap because I have to go to Creekmouth today. Is it available?"

"I think it is but Fred deals with these things, he's out back. I will just get him. Sit yourself down. I'll make us a cup o tea and we can have a chat". A few minutes later Frederick Barber came in.

"Hello Ann. It was a great party last night. We all enjoyed it. My grandchildren loved all the games on the water meadow and my son in law was sober for once. In fact he's been sober since Charles and Joseph took him on. You probably know that my brothers and I made Fred Scattergood marry Florence. Well everybody knows. He got her pregnant with Arthur. I have eight grandchildren, four boys and four girls. I did a bad thing there Ann and I regret it. Fred's alright as long as he stays off the drink but he doesn't love Florence and he tells her this and anybody else who will listen. Her kids love her to bits for she has a gentle and kind nature. Did you here about the fight on Saturday night? It was a beaut. Charles, Joseph and Cut Bunton did for them all. It was a joy to see"

"Was it? Well all I can say is that Charles was in a right state when he came home. He is trying to put away his old violent ways and that fight did him no good at all"

"I know Ann, we all knew but Craddock did have it coming. Is Charles over it?"

"He sailed on this morning's ebb so that will keep him busy. I expect to hear from him later today"

"Oh, the angels ~ yes, good idea that, now how can I help?"

"Is the Pony and Trap free for hire "

"It is, how long do you want it for"

"For the day .I will bring it back around six."

They arranged the hire and Mr. Barber introduced Ann to Sugar, the pony.

"Sugar loves apples Ann, so take plenty with you. He is a good horse and will give you no trouble".

"Thanks, the Forges are no stranger to horses as I am sure you are aware. See you later"

She was about to depart when Mary Barber called out

"Ann, Ann please will you take time for tea. It's ready"

"Sorry Mary I was forgetting"

Mrs Butterfield entered the parlour and sat down.

"How are the grandchildren Mary, you have quite a big family now, four boys and four girls isn't it"

"Yes, Arthur, Alice, Frank, Audrey, Alfred, Evelyn, Frederick and Florence. Florence is the youngest"

"Arthur is in the Navy isn't he?"

"Yes, he is in Gibraltar at the moment. We got a letter the other day. Alice is courting Bernard Cross the Farmer and Audrey is courting Harold Hudson. The others are all at school except for Florence"

"So how are things Mary? I know that life is hard for Florence when Fred Scattergood is on the booze"

"Everyone knows. I just wish his Grandfather would close his tab at the Stanhope Arms and not give him any more credit. At the moment things are OK since he is not drinking. I thank Charles and Joseph for that. Did you know that Joseph has threatened him?"

"Err no I did not know that"

"One day when Fred was drunk Joseph saw him hitting my daughter with her children watching. He picked him up by the neck Ann, and took him round back. He told Fred that if he ever found out that he had hit her or the kids it would be Boys Oak for him. He has not touched her since."

"So you are not angry with Joseph?"

"Angry? No, no, he saved us, we are all really grateful. Now drink your tea and tell me about your news. Everyone really likes your new apprentices. Didn't Billy do well with his mouth organ at the dance?"

Ann stayed for another hour. "Must go Mary I have got to see if Mrs Shellito can sit the children so I will see you at Church on Sunday."

"Be careful with Mrs Shellito Ann, she is going through a hard time at the moment. She lost her job as a teacher because she was stealing. I am not saying she is doing that now but when push comes to shove and you have children to feed we can all be tempted".

"Thanks for that, I have used her for three years on and off with no trouble but for warned is for armed"

Ann knocked on Mrs. Shellito's door and she was free and so got on the trap and went with Ann to number twelve.

The journey to Creekmouth was completed without mishap. Emily told me that the stench from the Thames was bad, really bad and they used their scented handkerchiefs all the way. As they approached Creekmouth from the North they passed the allotment gardens on their left and the Navy and Army weapons magazines on their right.

Lawes Chemicals had built a village of 42 house and there was a school. Then there was the guano works. These were right alongside the Thames and each had a long pier going out to the landing wharf beyond the Ebb tide mud. They could see all of the ships in Barking Reach awaiting their turn at the Royal Docks. The pungent smell of coal gas was coming from Becton Gas works so there were smells of every sort. They arrived at number 22 at 11:30 as Emily had hoped. They saw her Dad walking from the Works for his morning coffee. Ann saw a tall and thin looking man with a very sombrous face. She and Emily waved and he waved back, though not with any great vigour.

"It will be four weeks since I have seen him, "said Emily.

As Mr. Byes approached Mrs Butterfield said she saw a change come over Emily. The confident outgoing Emily seemed to disappear and a sullen unsure and unhappy girl appeared. She automatically stepped behind Ann Butterfield seemingly seeking protection. Mrs Butterfield responded by stepping forward and holding out her hand.

"Good morning Mrs. Butterfield to what do we owe the pleasure. Neither of you is expected and so I hope my daughter has been behaving herself and doing her chores"

"Good morning Jethro and yes it's been a long time, about three years I believe. There is nothing for you to be concerned about. Emily performs her duties really well and has become part of the Butterfield family as we hoped she would. Now let us get down to the reason for of my visit. Charles and Joseph sailed this morning on the Lady Ann It is her maiden voyage out to the Holland Banks. Emily said she needed to see you and Ethel so since my time was free I hired the pony and trap and here we are"

> "Yes, we all saw the Lady Ann enter the Thames at Barking reach and head off east downriver. I must say she is a really lovely smack. We all liked the schooner bow. Please come in. Ethel gives me coffee this time of the morning and I need to get cleaned up anyway since I and some other blokes have been removing a steam boiler from the collier you can see tied up at the dock. It has had its best days but the boiler is ok. We will be wrecking it shortly, the ship I mean"

"I didn't know you were into ship engineering Mr Byers?"

"I can turn my hand to most things. The boiler is going to Hewitt's Engineering works on Fisher Street. They need a second boiler to cope with the work load they have. In fact I am taking up a post there as Chief Engineer in three months"

Turning to Emily he said. "Come give your Father a kiss Emily and welcome the news that we shall be seeing more of each other"

Mrs Butterfield saw Emily turn white. She shuffled to her Father and kissed him on the cheek. There was no love in the kiss. Her Father placed his hand on Emily's left buttock and puller her close, He then whispered something in her ear. As he was doing this Ethel Byers appeared and quickly went up to her daughter pulling her away from Jethro and giving Emily a bracing hug.

"What a lovely surprise dear and then turning to Mrs. Butterfield she said "Please come in Ann. It is lovely to see you. I don't get a lot of visitors so I hope you can stay a while and bring me up to speed on Barking gossip."

She pushed Emily in front of her and then gestured for Mrs. Butterfield to follow. Mrs Byers inserted herself between Mrs. Butterfield and Jethro deliberately. They entered a clean but modest house. It was one of the larger villas built by the Lawes Chemical Company for its workers. It was a semi detached house and had a front and back garden. Lawes had also built a School and village hall. Once inside all four sat down and the tea was poured out. All seemed relaxed. Emily's true character re ~ emerged and she seemed like her old self. At this point Jethro turned to Emily and asked

"So, daughter of mine what is the purpose of this visit; not that you need a purpose. Your Father and Mother are always pleased to see you"

"I have met someone and I know that he is the person for me and I intend to marry him. I am here to seek your permission."

"This is sudden. You were here four weeks ago and never mentioned anything then. Who is this person and how long have you known him?"

"His name is Charles Jones and I met him four days ago"

"Four days, four days, that is not long. What does he do for work?"

"He is an apprentice with the Butterfield's on the Lady Ann".

"An apprentice you say, that must mean he is from one of the workhouses. Does he have any family? Would your mother or I know them? Is he educated? "

"He is an orphan Father. All his family died of typhoid. He comes from Romford and he was in Romford Workhouse. He has worked on the collier barges unloading coal for Becton Gas works but he is now with the Butterfield's as an apprentice"

At this point Mrs Butterfield interrupted.

"We have taken on three apprentice's mister Byers. I interviewed many orphans for the positions but we were looking for boys with potential since, as you know we have to sign them for seven years. They join as children and leave us as men. It is our intention during this period to make them skilled sailors and fishermen. We also intend to teach them to read and write".

"So Charles Jones cannot read or write and he is from a poorhouse. What on earth do you see in him Emily? I am sure you can do better".

"It is not a case of doing better Father I am in love with Charles. He is a lovely person and a great artist and I want to be his wife."

"Do you, do you indeed, well let me remind you that you cannot marry anyone without my permission!"

Emily turned to her mother "Mother please help me. I do not want this. Please persuade Father to give us his blessing"

Mrs Byers remained very quiet. Looking directly at Ethel Mrs Butterfield said "Let me assure you both that Charles Jones has a good and financially rewarding future with us. I cannot tell you the details just now but when he comes to ask for Emily's hand in marriage you will see that he will be able to care for her, rent a home and so forth"

Turning to Mr. Byers Mrs Butterfield said "Emily is your daughter Jethro but she has become a member of the Butterfield household. Charles and Joseph are like her Uncles and that is how she thinks of them. They will not, I will not let anything threaten Emily's happiness or contentment. The community saw them together at the Picnic and later at the dance and everyone approves. I would have persuaded Emily to think twice about Charles Jones if I had any concerns about him or his intentions. You have nothing to fear and much to lose if you do not give your blessing. I know that this is a family matter for Ethel and you to decide but she has been with us for three years and it surely is not unnatural for us to care about her. Surely that is what you wanted when you said yes."

"You are right when you say it is our decision. I hope that Master Charles Jones is what you say he is. "

Turning to Emily he asked. "When did you say yes"?

"He has not asked me to marry him yet but he will, I know he will."

"What, what did you say, he hasn't asked you well perhaps he never will and so what is the point of this visit"

"I told him that I have fallen in love with him but I would only be really sure after his absence. He told me then that he loved me"

"But he did not ask you to marry him?"

"No. He said he had nothing to offer, nothing, just his heart, mind soul and strength and that was enough for me. It was later when Mrs Butterfield told me that he would have something to offer financially when he returned from the Lady Ann's maiden voyage but she cannot tell me what it is. I will learn from Charles when he returns from the shakedown cruise."

"When do you think he will visit me to ask for your hand in marriage?"

"I hope it will be a couple of days after the Ann ropes up at Barking Pool."

"Let's hope you are right. Ethel and I will look forward to meeting him. Let us hope he is what you say he is because if I he cannot support you I shall say No"

Mrs Butterfield looked at Emily and gestured for her to remain silent.

"Now I cannot stay any longer both of you since my time is up." He gulped down his coffee and left.

The door was slammed shut and Ethel looking dejected turned to Emily and said. "I am sure it will all work out my dear. I will say yes, since I trust Ann and your own good judgement. Now please sit down and let me take your travelling clothes and let's talk about something pleasant".

Emily grasped her mother hands and knelt down before her. "Mother Mrs Butterfield knows about my Dad's ways. I had to tell her. How is Eliza?"

Ethel started to cry and then began sobbing. "I do not understand him Ann. It is not right but what can I do. I have no money and this house goes with his job."

Looking at Emily she said "It is the same problem Emily. I can tell. She is so quiet when her Father is around".

Mrs Butterfield spoke up; Emily said that she had a very determined look on her face, a look she had never seen before. "Leave this with me Ethel. Jethro needs persuading to stop his bad ways. We will provide him with that persuasion. Now tell me some good news."

The rest of the day was spent in just talking and then at three o'clock Emily's brothers and sisters came home from school. Eliza was among them. On seeing Eliza, Mrs Butterfield spoke "Excuse me Ethel but just when does Eliza leave school?

"In about two months Ann, why do you ask?"

"Well I was thinking about getting Emily some help; the room she occupies will easily take two. I will take Eliza as a housemaid if you would be happy with this."

When Eliza heard this she immediately cheered up .Emily went off with Eliza into the back garden. They were gone for a while. At three thirty Emily and Ann departed Creekmouth heading back to Barking. As they were journeying away from the estate they heard a boat whistle. Emily turned to Mrs Butterfield and said

"That's the paddle steamer Alice on her way down to Gravesend with day trippers. If you look you can see the smoke from her funnel. There is a village party here three weeks on Saturday and if Charles has asked me to marry him that would be a good time to ask my Father, but whatever he says I am going to marry Charles Jones"

"Oh yes, I see it. First Colliers, then paddle steamers and finally the Railway from Barking to London. I wonder when steam will be used in smacks. Charles is always on about the massive docks project at Grimsby. He says that they are building fish pontoons right out into the Alexandra Dock and that ice wagons will be waiting to take the fish straight from the hold onto the wagons and then from there by steam engine to Billingsgate. The world is really changing, but I like Barking. All my family are here. I won't move unless we all move. Now, regarding your father's answer to your question. As the Law stands you cannot marry Jonesy without your Fathers consent. You could run away to Gretna Green in the Scottish Borders but that is a long, long way and not really practical. The Butterfield's will have to ensure that Jethro says yes. Now about Barking, there are some nice properties off Heath Street. Fisher Street is getting rough. I want us to move there but we shall just have to see how this venture with the Ann Goodman goes."

"Isn't Heath Street where your Father lives?"

"Yes, I have always liked Oak Cottage. It really is not a cottage at all since it has six bedrooms, two bathrooms, flush toilet and gas lighting. Ah, perchance to dream." They had a safe journey home talking all the way just like mother and daughter but the question about our marriage would have to wait because of what was about to happen in Great Yarmouth.

25 The Great Yarmouth Fiasco

It was my watch from four till eight am. Chas had gone to bed and I was sat next to the tiller just looking at the stars and watching all of the other smacks anchored and yielding to the gentle swell. Everything was at peace. We had fastened everything down just as we had been shown. There was nothing to do. I became thirsty. All of the deck drinking water had gone. The only thing Chas had missed. I heard movement downstairs below deck and footsteps heading toward the Mess Deck. I then heard a noise. Someone had been to the toilet. It became quiet again. About an hour later I just had to have a drink so after checking the sea and wind state as I had been shown I went below deck into the Crew Deck. I filled a tankard of water from the fresh water cask. To do this I had to pass the dead body of Zechariah Bass. He was laid on the mess deck table with his feet to the bulkhead and his head hanging over the end. The body was covered with a grey blanket. I lifted the blanket and looked at this horrible man. Then his head twitched. It scared me out of my skin and I ran for the Crew Deck door but stopped. His head was still uncovered. I retraced my steps intending to place the cover back over his head. As I was about to do this I noticed something white deep in his nose. Joseph always kept tweezers in the first aid draw for removing wood splinters. I gently inserted these in the Bass's nose and removed the white stuff. It was feather down. It had not been there when John had announced Zechariah's demise since we all carefully looked at the body. This was done so that if called to give evidence we would all bear the same witness. It must have been the twitching of the head. The only place on the Lady Ann where duck down feathers could be found was in the Norwegian Eider down quilt and pillows. As I stood looking I realised Zechariah had been suffocated. I was glad but I also knew it was murder. Zechariah was himself a murderer. I went back on deck and sat by the tiller bath. I decided to tell no one. I had to get my mind off what I had seen so I took the sketch pad Emily had bought me and continued filling in the garden scene I had begun just a few days ago. As I thought about Emily I filled in the shading and detailed Emily's features I thought deeply about her declaration that she loved me and would know how much when I returned. I decided that night to ask her to marry me though where we would live and how I would support her I did not know. But marry her I would. No one else would hold her and kiss her but me and that for the rest of my life.

Suddenly it was eight o clock and Billy came on deck.

"Joseph has made breakfast. You are to go down right now. We need to catch the eleven o clock high tide into Yarmouth and so will be underway in about thirty minutes. Is there anything to report for the ships log. ?"

"No Billy everything was fine. Mr Butterfield is expecting a sailing breeze this morning from the east so it should take us straight in."

When Master Charles was spelled at the tiller by Joseph he would go down into the Captains cabin and we would all be called in turn to give details of our watch. This was done three times a day.

True to the skippers forecast the easterly breeze took us straight into Yarmouth via the Corton and Gorleston road; deep channels in the sea bed. The approach was always difficult due to the shifting sandbanks. Fred Scattergood was in the bow sounding off the depth below the Ann Goodman's keel, but all went without any trouble. I had never been to Yarmouth before but it looked very busy. I saw the lighthouse on the port side.

There were several fishing smacks unloading their catch. Not all Skippers did fleeting. Skipper Kichin and Joshua Munn were on board as agreed. Brian Kichin had hailed the Ann Goodman just after I had gone down for breakfast. As we sailed down the River Yare towards Yarmouth docks a steam paddle tug passed us towing a deep sea smack to the river mouth. These vessels were unstable at sea according to the skipper but were very useful in towing working boats up narrow sea passages like the Yare.

We moored up without any trouble and I saw what I assumed was the harbour master approaching. The skipper climbed onto the hard to meet him. They stood and talked. I could see he was shocked. He turned round and ran back to the Dock Office.

"Right Brian, let's get this show on the road. You go to the Yarmouth Echo and the Daily News. Tell them about Bass throwing Nick Mountsel off the smack and him drowning in the site of the crew. Tell them about the crew's reaction but do not tell them about the beating. Were you doing any fleeting yesterday Brian?"

"Yes; but before you arrived. Did you pass the schooner on her way to Yarmouth?"

"No, but we would have been too far South."

"Good, so let's say Bass got injured during fleeting and that this put him in a bad temper so that when young Nick spilt the hot coffee he threw him overboard. This will explain the bruises."

At this point Joseph interrupted.

"YOU cannot tell lies not with your new found faith. You could never tell lies anyway; not even when were kids. You are no good at it. You will have a bad conscience and it will show. I on the other hand am an expert"

Master Charles then said "The Bible says I can be as cautious as a serpent and yet innocent as a dove"

"That may well be BUT you still have to be a good liar. I will go to the Police Station and I will tell them what happened. They will have Bass's corpse and they all know how dangerous fleeting is. He was alive when he came on board and died during the night, we all agreed? Brian?

"Yes, I will go to the Echo and Daily News as agreed"

"Josh, do this for your mate"

"You bet Mr Butterfield. I am glad he died."

"Good, you stay on board Charles" said Joseph "I will see you later"

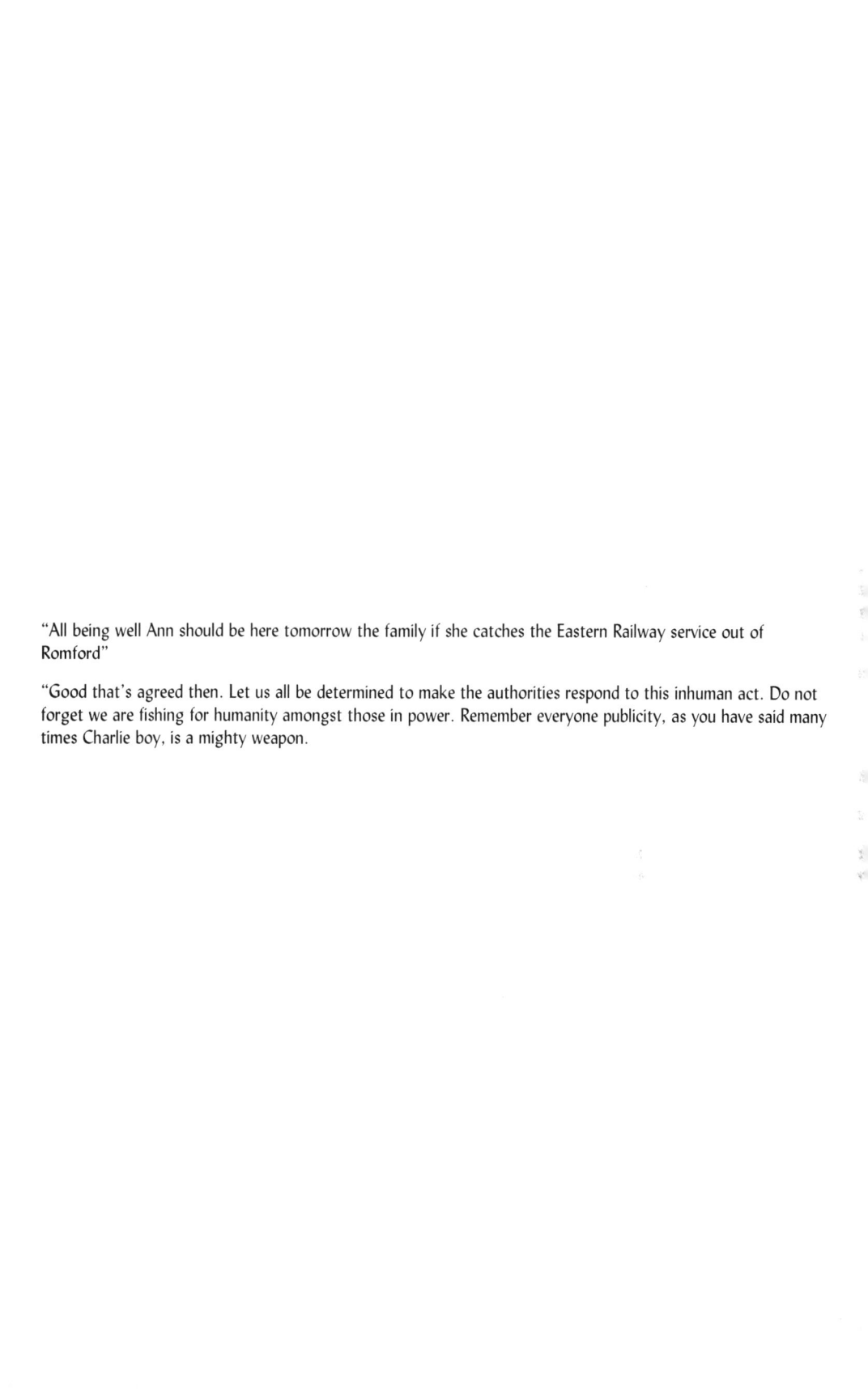

"All being well Ann should be here tomorrow the family if she catches the Eastern Railway service out of Romford"

"Good that's agreed then. Let us all be determined to make the authorities respond to this inhuman act. Do not forget we are fishing for humanity amongst those in power. Remember everyone publicity, as you have said many times Charlie boy, is a mighty weapon.

26 Back at Barking

Ann and Emily arrived back at Fisher Street at four o clock. Emily went inside and Ann took the Pony and Trap back to Mr. Barber. On her way she passed the pawnbrokers again and peered at the goods in the window. There was nothing of interest.

"Mrs Shellito are you there its Emily, Oh there you are"

She was in the washing shed.

"Are the children alright, I guess they will want their tea"

"Yes they are fine and I will be off, oh by the way one of the pigeons is back"

"You mean the angels don't you?"

"No I mean pigeon for goodness sake; why does Joseph call them angels"

"It's latin and means messenger. I will go and get the message.

Ann arrived back and Emily handed her the leather tube which she had detached from Naomi's leg. Inside there was a written message.

"Oh" said Ann "they are moored off the Holland Banks. Charles says it was a good cruise and the Ann Goodman handles really well". There was a pause and then she continued " Oh, they are becalmed but expect to sail back tomorrow. There is nothing for you Emily but then Jonesy has only had one lesson. Sorry, I am mistaken Charles has added a post script. It says Jonesy is completing a sketch of a young lady to whom he sends his warmest affection."

"Warmest affection indeed, that boy needs to learn to write for then I shall really know what he means"

"Patience my dear patience"

At that moment they heard the pigeon coop bell ring. Another Angel had returned.

"Oh dear, I hope that is not bad news. Please go and get the tube Emily."

Emily watched Ann Butterfield read the second message. She was distressed and then angry.

"We leave tomorrow on the Eastern Railways train for Yarmouth. We will have to take the children and you will have to come. Zechariah Bass has murdered Nicholas Mountsel and Charles is heading into Yarmouth with Bass's body. My goodness me will this cruelty never end?"

Early on Tuesday they took a cab to the Eastern Railways Station at Romford. They caught the nine thirty train to Yarmouth. They would have to change at Colchester taking the service to Yarmouth via Ipswich. It would take about 5 hours; so if everything went well they would the there around two o clock.

They had Charles junior, Alfred and Ann with them. The children were very excited about going on the train. The journey was uneventful but both Ann and Emily marvelled at how easy it was to travel. They had sent a telegram to Yarmouth and this had been delivered to Master Charles around ten in the morning.

Master Charles met them at the station with a cab and the family were taken to the Ann Goodman. Charles had decided that after the Coroners Court the family would cruise down the coast back to Barking calling in at West Mersea to see friends and join in the annual regatta. Ann and the children were to sleep in the Skippers cabin with him. Emily was to take the bottom hammock on the starboard side normally occupied by John Harrison and Joseph would take the top hammock normally occupied by Fred Scattergood. They in turn took Charles Adson and Billy Moreton's hammocks on the Port side. I was lucky in that I did not have to move and so would be able to see Emily tucked up in bed at night. Chas and Billy would have to sleep on the floor of the Mess Deck.

I was not there when they all arrived having gone into Yarmouth with Master Joseph. Joshua Munn and I were heading with him to the Police Stations.

We walked in through the front door of the Police Station and up to the public counter behind which stood a large fat man in a dark black uniform wearing a huge handlebar moustache.

"Good maarning sirs, how can I help ee" His Norfolk accent was very strong.

Joseph spoke

"My name is Joseph Butterfield owner of the deep sea smack Ann Goodman and I have come to report a murder"

"She will be thur boo wi'h thur schooner bow Ol guess. We all saw yow moor up. Fine boo do Ol do say.so"

"Yes she is, but did you note what I said. I have come to report a murder"

"Ol did hare waa yow said Mas'er Bu'terfield. Yow will be thur Bu'terfield's from Baarkin'? would Ol be roight and would Ol be roight in 'hinkin' tha an appren'ice fisher lad has died."

"Not died, murdered is what I said"

"roigh'y ho, roigh'y ho, le' me gi' some de'ails"

After some time he finished writing and then asked us to sit down. He disappeared inside the Police Station. Fifteen minutes later a thin bald headed man in a three piece pin striped suit opened the side door and asked us to follow him.

This was Inspector Jeddah Trouble.

Once inside the Police Station we were taken to a small interview room and the three of us were asked to sit down. A second police constable joined us with a police note pad. This was Constable Bell.

"So Mr Butterfield you claim that a murder has taken place"

"Yes, though I did not see it, Young Joshua Nunn here did, he being an apprentice on the fishing smack Dragon who's Master was Zechariah Bass"

"You say was, as if he were dead"

"He is dead. He died last night on the Ann Goodman from his injuries during fleeting"

"This is very serious Master Butterfield. Where is Bass's body?"

"It's in the Mess Deck on the on my smack "

Turning to Constable Bell he said

"Go and get Sergeant Madden and then go with him; take two other constables and remove the corpse to the Mortuary on Castle Street.

Turning to me Inspector Trouble said "Who are you and what are you doing here?"

"My name is Charles Jones, they call me Jonesy and am an apprentice to the Butterfield's. I was present when Joshua Munn explained what happened"

"Right, I see, not a material witness" Turning to Joshua he said "You had better tell me what occurred Master Munn. I want the truth now and nothing but the truth, do you understand"

Joshua went white. He told Inspector Trouble exactly what happened just as he had told Master Charles.

"Are there any other witnesses"

"Er yes, the whole crew saw what happened but they are off the Holland Banks waiting for the wind. I have been sent by the Master's mate."

"Where is the body of young Nicholas Mountsel"

"He drowned sir before anyone could get to him. The wind was not strong and though we were anchored there is a strong current; he could not swim. He was thrown over the side near the stern and we saw it all" At this point Joshua began to cry and shake with emotion. "It's not right sir, it's not. Skipper Bass just threw him over the side like some piece of trash. It could have been me. I am really glad Bass is dead "

"Ok, ok, I have got the picture. I will have to send a steam packet out to the Dragon to get the other statements. My problem is there is no body. You know what is going to happen Joseph. It will be death through drowning because Mountsel could not swim. If he could swim, it will be argued, he would not have drowned. That is what the Coroner will place on record. There is one chance to fix this. If you get George McGregor as Coroner you might get what I guess you want, which is condemnation of Mountsel's treatment.

McGregor had lost a nephew at sea just a few months ago. He was dragging for Mussels on the Pioneer out of West Mersea. He was swept overboard by a breaching wave. Did Bass know Nicholas Mountsel could not swim?"

"Yes sir, none of us could swim. None of the crew, not even the mate"

Turning to me he said

"Take this as a warning Jonesy and learn to swim"

"I can swim sir, Master Joseph has taught all three of us to swim and use the Kisby rings on the Ann Goodman"

"Has he now, well that is good news"

"Now Joshua tell me about what the crew did."

"We had all been mistreated sir, all of us. Since the strike crews are not willing to be mistreated though some do put up with it because they are afraid. We apprentices got the worst of Skipper Bass's temper but he would not listen. The schooner came out to the fleet around three o-clock and Mr Bass got onto the Dragon's fleeting boat. He said he had business with the Captain of the schooner. When trying to board the schooner he slipped and got trapped between the fleeting boat and the schooner's hull. That's when he broke his arm. When he got back on board the Dragon he was in a foul mood and then Nicholas's knee gave way and he spilt the coffee. After he had thrown Nick overboard we all wanted to give him a good pasting. He is a big man sir and though angry and hurt he made it below deck to his cabin. Later the Mate reported that he was having trouble breathing and so when the Ann Goodman arrived Skipper Kichin took Bass to the smack since we all knew she was on her first sail and would be heading back".

"Where is Skipper Kichin?" asked Inspector Trouble

"I have sent him to the Echo and the Daily News. I have also sent a message to Barking to see if John Dill of the London Mail will attend the hearing."

The Inspector replied

"Now that Mr. Joseph Butterfield is good news. I'll get McGregor assigned as Coroner"

"How are you going to do that?" asked Joseph.

"I have my ways Mr .Butterfield, just as you have yours BUT there are to be no fights in this Town, understand"

"Yes, I understand, but what makes you think I am going to get into a fight?"

"Joseph, Joseph, this is a fishing community. Everyone here know what you did to the Gnats crew and in any case Nathanial Bunton was just here two days ago"

"You mean Cuts in Yarmouth? "

"No, he moved on, but not before knocking two skippers senseless over the treatment of their apprentices. They were in hospital but have now gone back to sea. They wouldn't press charges and so I had to let Mr Bunton go. He spent a night in the cells. We had a good chat".

"Where is he now?"

"He was after Craddock who had beat up a young apprentice in Romford after he left Barking. Craddock still smells rank Joseph. Bunton heard about it and then caught the train to Colchester. When he couldn't find him there he went on to Ipswich and then ended up here. "

"Where has he gone to?"

"Sergeant Bell escorted him to the train station. He told Bell that Craddock had gone to Lincoln so he went back to London to catch the Eastern Railways service to Lincoln"

"Um, we will be in Grimsby in about three weeks time so perhaps we can find him and see what the crack is"

"Now I will have to do a full investigation into Bass's death. I will also have to notify the relatives. This is going to take more than a few days. I'll get back to you on the date of the inquest on Mountsel. Bass is another matter. He died on the Lady Ann so you cannot sail just yet. I will be as fast as I can. A statement from your Brother and the other members of the crew will probably be enough to let you sail on Thursday. Joshua Munn is the only witness concerning Nicholas's death but once he has testified and the crew testimonies are read he can go back to sea. One of the packet boats will take him."

We headed back to the smack and Skipper Kichin joined us on the way.

"How was it Brian?"

"Great, both papers will have reporters at the inquest. The Editors seemed to want to get on board with our campaign"

We arrived back at the Ann to find a hearse taking Bass's body away to the morgue. Sergeant Madden stepped in front of Joseph and stared him face to face.

"I know all about you Joseph Butterfield. You cannot come to Yarmouth and carry on like you do in Barking. I'll do for you and that's a promise. Stump Slater is a relation of mine and I know what you did to him though I cannot prove anything"

"He shouldn't try to sink ships Sergeant Madden and you want to be careful. You are an Officer of the Law and your duty is to protect me, a law abiding citizen. It is all hearsay and gossip unless you have proof. We all have to sleep you know and the nights are dark in Yarmouth who knows what can happen"

"Don't threaten me Butterfield"

"See you at the inquest" said Joseph "and bring your notebook"

With that exchange Madden left. Suddenly we heard children's voices.

"Uncle Joseph, Uncle Joseph, we have been on a train and tonight we are sleeping on the Ann Goodman. We've got your hammock". Then they stuck there tongues out and shouted "So there".

Joseph jumped onto the deck. " We'll see about that come here the three of you"

They screamed; "We've got your hammock so there" they said again. Then once more they all stuck their tongues out .

Once Joseph was on the deck he chased after them." We'll see about that come here the three of your"

With that they all disappeared below deck with screams of delight and Joseph quickly followed.

Then I heard a voice from the bow. "Good afternoon Mister Charles Jones. Thank you for sending me your affection"

"Oh! Emily, Emily, how lovely to see you. I am so pleased. I thought you would still be in Barking. Joseph and the rest of us have just been into Town. Let's take a slow walk, I saw a little cafe, oh, I have no money" I felt so sad.

"I have money and you soon will have. Let's go"

She stepped off the deck onto the hard and we set off hand in hand just like a regular couple. My heart was pounding

Emily spoke "My, your hands are warm, very warm, missed me then?"

"Oh yes, but I kept looking at the portrait of you that I had started and focussed on that. It really helped. It got me near to you, if you understand"

"Yes, I understand, did you finish it?"

"Oh no, I am taking lot's of time, perchance to dream"

"I heard Mrs Butterfield say that, where did you learn it"

"It's from a poem. It was read to us in the Workhouse. When did Mrs Butterfield say that and where?"

We arrived at the Coffee Shop and went in. Emily chose a table for two by the window. It was cosy.

"We were on the way back from Creekmouth. After you sailed I decided to go and visit my parents. I had to tell my Father about us. He is a very jealous and possessive man. He had to learn about you from me. I was not looking forward to it but Mrs. Butterfield seemed to detect my fear and she got the truth out of me"

At that moment the waitress arrived and we ordered

"Eh what truth?"

"My father is a very wicked man Charles. He did something to me when I was fourteen which I did not like. He threatened me with violence if I told anyone. I told my mother"

"I don't understand; what did he do?"

"He touched me where Fathers shouldn't and that is why I had to get away. He would have stopped me but he needed the money. That is why he accepted Mrs Butterfield's offer. Please don't ask me anymore. Nothing happened really. It was just not right. I believe Eliza is having the same trouble. There is an end in site to that because she leaves school in two weeks and is coming to Fisher Street as second maid"

The coffee and cake came. I held Emily's hand really tight and put my arm around her. She dropped her head onto my shoulder and began to cry.

"Are we alright Charles? I didn't cause it, I didn't, I really didn't"

"I am in love with you Emily Byes, heart soul mind and strength and yes of course we are alright though what your father will say when he finds out its me. I have no prospects and am an orphan. He is bound to ask about that"

"Mrs Butterfield told me that something is going to happen that would change things for you, for us, but that it was something you would have to hear from Master Charles and Master Joseph"

I was really intrigued. What was I going to be told?

"Now tell me about this murder."

27 Shares

We arrived back at the smack around two o clock. We climbed on board to be greeted by Fred Scattergood who was roping up.

"High Jonesy and hello Miss Emily. We have been waiting for you the Butterfield's want all of the crew in their cabin"

We followed Fred and went down the steps into the Crew Deck. Once in the Crew deck we turned round and headed for the Butterfield's cabin at the stern. They were sat at the table. The children were on the floor playing. Chas, Billy and John Harrison sat in the other chairs Fred Scattergood and I stood.

"Charles, call Emily for me" said Ann Butterfield.

I went through the crew deck into the mess deck which was now bright since the deck boat had been moved forrard and roped down again so light was pouring in through the skylight. Emily was sat down reading. She looked up.

"Mistress Anne wants you"

"Ah Emily please take the children and do their ABC's. We will be about an hour"

"Yes Maam"

After the children had left Master Charles began.

"Now let's have some good news. We all need it after what has just happened. After the strike a seaman's wages were set at 16 shillings a week for men and 18 shillings a week for Mates. Now John and Fred you know there is no mate on board the Lady Ann, My brother, my wife and I have decided to set the rate for you two at 18 shillings per week" .

A big smile swept over their faces. Turning to us he said

"Normally apprentices are just given room and board with no wages whilst at sea. We think this is wrong and so in addition we are going to pay the apprentices five shillings a week each. This will be increased gradually to ten shillings a week as their skills improve."

Chas, Billy and I could not believe our ears and we began to say thank you together.

"Wait, I have not finished. We are heading to the Faroes in a few days and will be gone about two weeks. As you know the Ann Goodman is the longest keel double mast fishing smack ever built. She is twelve feet longer than most smacks because Joseph and I wanted a good cabin. She has been fitted out to a very high crew standard. Where we are going is big cod country with the seas to go with it. This means that we shall all have to work hard, really hard and be exposed to great danger IF we do not take advantage of all the safety features fitted to the Ann. Whenever we are at sea everyone and I mean everyone will be fastened to the safety rope that goes down the centre of the deck. Even though the Ann has a schooner bow she still has little freeboard.

We were intending to fix that but did not have the time. So when she breaches in bad weather the sea will sweep over her deck. Cod is fetching very, very high prices and king cod is fetching the best prices of all.

The best prices are paid in Grimsby and so once the hold is full we shall head there as fast as possible in one continuous sail. I reckon it will take twenty hours. During this time we will only get about four hours sleep per watch; less if the weather is bad. It is for this reason that Mrs. Butterfield has equipped all of the hammocks with warm bedding from the Faroes and all of the necessary warm undergarments. Joe and I do not like bunks so that is why all of us have hammocks. Bunks do not swing with the ship. Hammocks will provide more comfort and hence better sleep.

SO; to continue .We have decided to give you a share of the catch after costs are deducted. A smack is divided into sixty four shares. This allows the owner to get cash during low season by mortgaging these shares. This does not apply to us. We are well funded. Joseph owns thirty two shares, Ann and I own sixteen each. As I have said this refers to the ownership of the smack but we have decided to adopt a similar structure for the catch. It will be divided as follows;-

Joseph will have twenty shares.
Ann and I ten shares each. So the Butterfields will have forty shares.
Then there will be nine shares each to John and Fred so that makes fifty eight shares.
The apprentices will have two shares each thus totalling sixty four shares. Is everyone on board with this?"

"Excuse me Master Charles but none of us can add up" I said.

At this Billy spoke up

"I can do my ten times table sir but am not much good at subtraction or division"

"Right!" said the skipper.

Turning to Ann he said

"Put that down on your things to teach these lads Ann"

"Charles, I have already begun working on that with Emily"

"Good, now let me give you some figures taken from the smack Endeavour. Let me see. Last year the Endeavour yielded the following profits per voyage. I could give you all the months but the winter months are best

January	four cruises	One hundred and ten pounds eight shillings
February	four cruises	One hundred and thirteen shillings.
March	four cruises	One hundred and thirty seven shillings.

So for these three months the catch value was three hundred and sixty two pounds two shillings

For the year it was one thousand and sixty pounds. Let's say that the Lady Ann catch value was the same. Set against this is the cost of running the Ann Goodman. We estimate that it will cost around six hundred pounds a year. So the pot to be divided will be four hundred and sixty pounds."

He sighed as he looked at our blank faces.

"I can see that this is too much information. I will try and make it simpler. Each quarter or every three months Mrs. Butterfield will add up the earnings from fish sales. She will take away the costs of repairs and provisions and what's left is the profit to be divided as stated. So, if we were to sell three hundred and sixty pounds and two shillings worth of fish at Grimsby and if the costs were as I have estimated then the profit would be roughly two hundred and twelve pounds. That would mean that each share was worth three pound twelve shillings. I arrive at this by dividing two hundred and twelve pounds by sixty four. Joseph would get sixty two pounds and four shillings. Ann and I would get the same. John and Fred would get twenty eight pounds and eight shillings and each apprentice would get six pounds and twelve shillings. This is on top of your wages. This would take place four times through the year "

All were silent.

Joseph spoke,

"For God's sake does anyone have anything to say"

Billy spoke up

"if I get five shillings a week and I multiple this by fifty two weeks then I shall earn fifty two times five which equals two hundred and sixty shillings. There are twenty shillings to a pound so that would be?"

He looked at Ann Butterfield

"Well done Billy, that would come to two hundred and sixty shillings divided by twenty shillings to a pound or thirteen pounds in a year"

Carrying on she said

"On top of that you might get four times six pounds and twelve shillings provided the costs of running the Lady Ann are as forecast at around six hundred pounds a year"

Billy spoke:"that comes to" he paused and seemed to be thinking "wow! more than twenty four pounds. In total I would earn thirty seven pounds a year. That cannot be true!"

Joseph was getting angry

"Well it IS true Billy, but mark my words all of you, this will be damned hard work. We do not know how long this price will last. Fish is popular because at one time England did not eat meat on Friday. We all eat fish, or at least the believers did" I saw him nudge Ann "on Fridays".

Though theses old customs are on their way out people still love fish and they love cod most of all. Once the fish hold is full we have to get to Grimsby by Wednesday. We enter Fish Dock number one and moor up alongside the pontoons. The fish is boxed right in the hold and then taken onto the pontoon fish market and then from there to Billingsgate in London. It must be fresh hence the fast sail when we are full"

The silence continued. We were all amazed. I was amazed most of all because I could after all ask Emily Byes to marry me.

"Right" said Joseph "I have had enough of this, back to work all of you, ungrateful bastards that you are"

"Joseph! There is no need for that" said Ann Butterfield giving her Brother in Law a withering stare

"Sorry Ann, but silence?"

Turning to all of us she said "I know that you are all stunned into silence. When you have recovered perhaps there are questions you might like to ask, I can give you advice on opening a Bank Account. We have thought about this for a long time.

"Excuse me Mrs Butterfield but what is a Bank Account?"Billy asked.

"It is a place where you deposit money earned and where you can borrow money from. It is not easy to open a Bank Account especially if you are under eighteen or are an orphan but there are ways round it. Basically we would have to become your guarantors. This does not apply to John and Fred but only to fishing apprentices".

We all nodded our heads. It was as clear as mud.

28 The Coroners Court

Inspector trouble had succeeded in getting the Coroners Court set for Wednesday and he had also succeeded in getting Mr. McGregor as the Coroner. Wednesday morning came and the Butterfield's, Joshua Munn, Brian Kichin and I headed to the Lees Head Hotel where it was to be held. John Dill from the London Times was in the Room when we arrived as were other reporters. Mrs. Bass was there with her husband Wilfred who everyone in Barking called Wimpy.

The Court was called into session by Mr. McGregor and he stated its purpose.

"This Coroners Court has been summoned to pronounce the cause of death on a young apprentice named Nicholas Mountsel. He was indentured to Mr and Mrs Wilfred Bass and the Court has secured the apprentice documents. Nicholas was delivered to the Bass household, according to this document in December of last year. He has cruised with the Dragon three times. Is that correct Mrs Bass"

"It is sir, but he was a lazy boy"

"We will come to that in a moment"

The clerk spoke out "Will Joshua Munn please take the stand". Joshua stepped forward.

"Now Mr. Munn please tell us what you saw"

Joshua repeated what he had said to us.

"Did Skipper Bass know that Nicholas could not swim" The Coroner asked

"Yes Sir"

"Thank you; this is corroborated by the attached statement of facts document signed by the crew of the Dragon"

Turning to the Clerk he said: "Please enter this into the Record" pausing he now said "Joshua please tell the Court what life was like for Nicholas"

"Mrs. Bass sold all of the sea gear given to him by the Marine Society sir. He had neither waterproofs to wear nor any sea boots". She, Joshua pointed at Mrs Bass "sold them all".

The Court was suddenly interrupted by Mrs. Bass standing up and shouting "He lies, he lies, they all lie, scum of the earth they are not worth a jot"

"If you interrupt me again Mrs Bass I shall find you in contempt and you will spend a night in the cells"

Looking at Mr. Bass he said "Come on Wimpy, keep your wife in order there's a good fellow"

I wondered how Mr McGregor knew Mr. Bass's nickname. Everybody laughed.

"Continue on Joshua" said the Coroner.

"There was nowhere to sleep sir but on wet matting and then the skipper seemed to get a fix on Nick. He kept hitting him and punching him but it was the kick in the knee that caused his death sir. He could not walk properly after that, that is why he spilt the hot coffee and now he's dead"

Mrs Bass stood up in Court and shouted at Joshua "You lie, there was bedding, there was and you and the crew of the Dragon murdered my boy so you did"

At this McGregor turned to Constable Bell and said: "Take her down to the cells right now. Bring her in front of me after I have pronounced the cause of death. With the power laid upon me by the state I pronounce that Nicholas Mountsell died through drowning. Though there is no corpse we have heard how he could not swim"

There was a great outcry in the Court. Joseph, Charles and Ann looked at one another; stunned.

"In my role as Coroner I am allowed to comment on the circumstances of Nicholas Mountsell's death. Further investigation by Inspector Trouble has yielded additional information for which the Court is grateful. Charles Pigrome was the replacement Skipper of the Dragon. Inspector trouble informs me that skipper George Stiggles who took the Dragon out of Barking hurt his leg on the outward voyage and so Mrs Bass contracted with Lester Pigrome to replace him. He was sent out by steamer from Lowestoft and took Stiggles place. When Pigrome joined the Dragon all of the apprentices were in a bad state. Pigrome wrote a letter to Mrs.Bass informing her of the situation and asking for the two apprentices to be relieved. The Court has a copy of this letter. Instead she relieved Pigrome by sending her son Zechariah Bass. I have a copy of the letter that Mrs. Bass wrote to Pigrome in reply. It reads in part as follows "I don't know what you mean, you must work yourself. As for the boys you expect them all to be like men. You must not let them eat so much."

At this McGregor addressed the Court: "Did you ever hear of anything as abominable as that". He continued reading "If I can send some I will but I am not sending a man. There is as much help as anyone else. If you come home I must do what was done by the Madcap crew"

The coroner looked up and said "she sent them to prison." He continued to read "Tom's frock and Bob's frock and the boots were sent out. The frocks came by Alert and noon board the Foam."There is no doubt in my mind that Zechariah Bass was a very wicked and cruel man. And you Mr. Bass are not fit to employ any seamen in this dangerous trade. If Parliament had granted me the powers I would have you committed for murder. But as it is Nicholas Mountsel died at sea through drowning because he was thrown overboard by Bass who has, in turn, died aboard the Ann Goodman"

"They killed him, the Butterfield's, they killed my son" shouted Mr. Bass.

"Bring Mrs Bass up constable Bell"

Mrs Bass entered the room. "Please stand here Mrs Bass. I fine you fifty pounds for contempt of Court. You must pay now or be held over".

The caspell was banged and the Court was closed. The verdict had been given. The Hotel room began to clear. I saw that the Butterfield's had got some of what they wanted and I was glad.

Joseph and the rest of us walked together back to the smack.

When we arrived Joseph said: "Thank you Brian and thank you Joshua please stay here while I get Charles"

Turning to me he said. "Jonesy please go and get my Brother".

I went down the rear hatch onto the crew deck and then knocked on the Butterfield's cabin.

"Hello" was Master Charles voice.

"Master Joseph wants you topside skipper"

"Right, are you coming my dear "he said to Ann "Most certainly Charles; I must know what occurred just like you"

Once on the dockside all was explained. I could here them talking but could not make out what was said. I heard Emily's voice in the Crew Cabin and went in.

"What took place Jonesy?" I responded "I thought it was to be Charles when we were on our own" "Sorry, what happened Charles?" I explained the verdict and how the reporters dashed off after the Coroners caspell crashed. "It should result in bad publicity for the Smack owners and help in making everyone aware of the cruelty but all are agreed that somehow the Law has to be changed. We are sailing on tomorrows tide"

"Yes I know. Mr Charles has booked that paddle steamer to tow us out and we are then heading on a cruise to West Mersea. Master Charles wants to show the children the regatta. It should be nice and we will have more time together"

"Yes, I have the late watch from eight to midnight and the barometer is showing high pressure"

"You know how to read a Barometer?"

"Yes we all do, Master Joseph showed us"

"I am trying to learn the alphabet using Joseph's sea shanty. It does help."

"Good, that will mean you can send me messages of affection!!!!

"I will be busy tomorrow because we are long lining on our way down to West Mersea and though I have been shown how to do it I have not done it before and in any case no one is allowed on deck that is not roped up. But if you come on deck during my watch after dinner we can talk. There is much to tell you. I am to get a share of the catch. Master Charles says it will be a moonlit night tonight with a rolling calm sea."

I winked at her "Just right for romance."

"There is going to be romance is there, not just affection"

"Will you meet me at the bow where you stood before?"

"Yes of course"

"If we stand in the lee of the staysail we shall be unseen so that will suit me"

"You don't want us to be seen then?" said Emily

"No, but please don't ask any more questions since it will spoil my surprise"

"Oh, I see, there is to be a surprise, is the picture finished?" Emily's heart was bursting for she suspected, hoped and dreamed that Charles Jones was going to ask her to marry him.

"Not yet but it is coming on well, now please stop asking questions, ok"

29   The Steam Paddle Tug.

Early in the morning on the ebb tide the bow of the Ann Goodman was hooked up to the paddle steamer tug. She bore the name Formidable. We set the Ann free from the dock and the tug moved off gently turning the Ann so that she faced downstream of the Yare. It was simple and fast.

We repeated the sail procedure shown us at Barking and as soon as we left the Yare Mouth we cast off the tug and turned south. The Wind was blowing from the North East so the boom went out to starboard on the main and mizzen masts and off Lady Ann went at a good pace. It was a following sea and so there was not much breaching.

I was sent below but only after I had got some boxes ready in the fish hold to take the cod we hope to catch. There was no ice but it was still cold down there. I said goodbye to Emily, who was with the children and Joseph teaching them their ABC's and then climbed in my hammock around ten in the morning and went to sleep.

I was awakened at two in the afternoon since all of the crew were required on deck for the long line cast. We were about twelve miles west of the Dogger Bank. I stood by Fred Scattergood who had the line ready. There were one hundred snoods and hooks ready to attach to the line and each had a tallow lure on the end of it. The hooks were hung over a wicker basket and in the basket was a line with twenty five snoods attached. The long line was tethered to a deck cleat on the starboard side of the smack. The booms of the main and mizzen mast were out over the starboard full and by.

The long line was coiled; one thousand feet of rope ready to be cast.

Master Charles was at the tiller when the command "shoot" was given. The line tip with its weight buoy was cast over the side. Immediately the line began to run out. The first hook left the nest and then a few seconds later the second. This continued for about 15 minutes until all 40 hooks were overboard. We ran like this for twenty minutes and then the command came to "Haul"

The long line was looped around the long line capstan and then fixed to a deck cleat. Billy Chas and I now inserted the capstan leavers into the slots and began to turn the capstan. The stay brace clicked in the notches and very slowly the line began to wind round the capstan. It was very, very heavy work but the line was gradually coming in. Billy was sent to get the fish boxes. There would be twenty fish to a box. There was a cheer from John Harrison and Fred. The first fish was a cod and a good size it was. They gaff hooked it on board it was disconnected by Fred and hurled down into the fish hold .The snood was picked up by Billy to be re bated and then placed in the nest. John Harrison was making sure the line was coming in free and true and it became clear that it had been a good run for once the line was in we had caught thirty eight fish.

The line was recast and once again hauled in but this time there were 40 cod.

It was cast again and this time we hauled in 36 cod.

Chas and I were starting to feel the strain but we had been made to do press ups on the way out. In the end after many weeks at sea, with all this exercise, good food and sleep we were very, very strong in what Master Joseph called the upper torso. Big chests and big arms with strong hands just like him.

30 The Proposal

Before we left Yarmouth, after we had eaten dinner, which Ann and Emily had prepared from the smack stores. It was my watch. I excused myself and went to my hammock. In the cupboard on the hull side I extracted the curtain ring. I had looped the silver string around the ring in one place and then made a kind of rose out of it. On the day I took the ring there was some red velvet on the floor and I had taken that. I now placed the ring inside the red velvet and then went on deck to relieve Billy. Fred Scattergood was on the tiller but Master Joseph would be up relieving him soon. We were not skilled enough to take the tiller without John, Master Charles or Master Joseph present.

"Anything to report Billy?" I asked. "No, Fred wants another 100 snoods loaded into the baskets for tomorrows shoot before we go into Brightlingsea and then Mersea Island. Check with Master Joseph, oh there he is now"

I turned and saw Joseph Butterfield step down into the tiller bath. Billy left me and went below deck but they had to wait at the hatch whilst Emily came on deck. She stopped and talked to Master Joseph for a moment and then headed toward me at the bow.

"Hello my sweetheart, glad you could come" I said. She was wearing a hat and cape in dark blue with a light blue dress underneath. She looked beautiful. Lets step into the lee of the staysail and then we are on our own".

The moon was shining white and its light reflecting upon the sea was amazing. On occasion it went behind the clouds and that caused beautiful delicate moonbeams. They looked like search lights being sent out from lighthouses. It was not cold but just breezy, perfect sailing weather.

Joseph Butterfield

When Emily came on deck she had stopped to talk to Joseph.

"You look nervous Emily are you well, not seasick I hope."

"Oh no Master Joseph I love ships and the sea, always have"

"Call me Uncle Joseph Emily when we are alone indeed please call me that when the family is gathered. I am very, very fond of you dear as are Charles and Ann. I am sure you know this"

"Yes Uncle Joe I am really happy at Fisher Street and love being included in the family"

"So what is happening tonight my dear? I notice Jonesy is waiting in the lee of the staysail. Look! What is he doing with his pocket?"

"I am hoping, dreaming, aching for Charles Jones to ask me to marry him. He asked me to meet him at the start of his watch. He said he is going to explain something to do with shares in the Ann Goodman"

"Not shares in the Goodman Emily but in the catch move along now. I too share your hope. You two are a good match"

The Proposal.

It was eight o clock on Wednesday night and so I went topside to relieve Master Joseph.

"Good evening skipper anything to do other than keep watch."

"Eh well yes but I want to check the long line snoods so just go forrard and check the halyards as you have been trained and then just keep watch. There is some wake from the paddle tugs but other than that all seems well"

I went forrard and was checking the lines when I heard light footsteps on the deck. I turned and there was Miss Emily Byes as arranged and on time. "Hello sweetheart, you look lovely.

She was wearing a cape with a hood tied at the neck with a bow. The hood framed her face and I knew that her long hair was down because curls were showing on her forehead. Her hair was normally brushed back. Underneath the cape was her normal blue maids dress with the tight waist again fastened in a bow. It was a beautiful moonlit night with moonbeams shooting through and lighting up the river yare. The town lamp lighter was making his way back along the quay.

"So here I am and you have a surprise, or so you said"

"Yes, but it's too busy, I'll see if we can walk to the lighthouse, just wait a moment"

I approached Master Joseph with my request. "Sure but don't be longer than half an hour, I will be done here then and I want to check on the angels"

We walked along the wharf to the mouth of the river yare and then stood at the foot of the lighthouse on the North Sea side leaning against the railings looking out to sea. As we walked I told Emily about the shares I would get on the catch and what Billy had said we would earn. I now knew that with her wages and mine we could definitely start a home together. I would have something good to tell her father. She was pleased.

"Look Emily look to the east on the horizon"

She looked and saw what I saw, it was a fishing smack long lining with its sails full and bye caught in the full light of a moonbeam. She smiled.

"You have a lovely profile Emily Byes and you are truly beautiful in every way. Since I now have prospects I need to ask you something" With that I dropped down on both knees and holding both of Emily's hands I looked up into those amazing eyes and spoke these words "Miss Emily Byes, will you marry me, will you be my wife ?"

"Yes, oh yes, you gallant and humble man I will be your wife. Now please stand up, you're only supposed to go down on one knee. You look as if you are praying, I am not a goddess"

I stood up and reached into my pocket and took out the red velvet parcel and gave it to her. She looked pleased but puzzled. As the ring became visible she smiled.

"Oh Charles it's wonderful. Did you make it?"

"It's a curtain ring and yes I made the silver rose"

"Charles, please put it on my finger"

She removed her glove and I took the ring and placed it on the third finger of her left hand. Just as I was dong this a moonbeam lit up where we were standing. Emily looked staggeringly beautiful but unaware of this as she always was.

"When I have made some money we can get a proper gold ring with a jewel"

"Maybe, but that will be a dress ring. This will be my engagement ring for the whole of my life. Nothing will be able to replace this. Now get up and kiss me."

I got up and kissed her on the lips and she kissed back. It was the loveliest sensation. We held each other for a moment and then I stepped back. I saw the stuff on the floor when Chas, Billy and I we were taken by Mrs Butterfield into her sewing room. I hoped that one day I might get to use them and now I have".

"So you were thinking like this day's ago on the night of the dance"

"I have been thinking of you all the time, really, ever since you did the curtsy So when I have got some money, as I have said, we will get us a proper engagement ring Emily"

"Yes, yes but once again that will be a dress ring for others to see. This for me will always be our true engagement ring. Given in the moonlight on a lovely breezy evening by the boy or should I say man I love. Hold me tight"

I held her close, heads together, arms locked. As I stood holding Emily I began thinking of the conversation I had with Master Charles before Skipper Kichin came on board. I had talked with him about Emily and the reaction of everyone on the night of the dance when we had kissed. He had told me that there are four Greek words for love and not just one. He said that *Eros* was sexual love, intimacy though I do not fully understand what he means. Apparently it is not just having sex but the moment two persons become one flesh. He said if it is done right with each seeking the others pleasure it is a kind of spiritual experience. When I asked him how I would know he simply said that it was to do with possession, at least for the man. Jealousy is mostly bad but not when it concerns the affections of the one you love and who loves you. They are for you and you alone. I think he means sexual affections. I have much to learn.

He then said that the next word was *philia* which in English means friendship. He said that husband and wife should be good friends. They should do things together. This should and would be natural not forced. Both should seek to share each others interest they should not pursue interests that separate. He said that *eros* dies, it is eroded by age but *philia* lasts forever .

He then said that *storge* means family love. You can choose your wife, your friends but you just get your relatives. He said it was a bond of blood even though relatives often do not get along. Not all brother and sisters get along. I always thought that they would. Mine have all died so perhaps I will never know.

He then said that the greatest Greek word for love was *agape* . He said that this was doing right because it was right. He said it is motivated by a love of principle. These principles could be learned by studying the Bible. He was trying to get self control under provocation, long suffering over bad things. He was now always seeking to find joy in even small things, moonbeams, a good catch, flowers and pigeons. Take nothing for granted. He was trying to show kindness even to those who did not deserve it. He was trying to seek peace of mind and heart which was sometimes difficult. As far as it depended upon him he sought peace with all. Ann had told him that he and Joseph had good hearts in that they tried their best to help others. The apprentice cruelties were an example of this. He was striving to secure Faith in God the Father of Jesus Christ and that is why he had to find his name. It was something to do with what he had read. The verse was something like "I am the way, the truth and the light, no one gets to the Father except through me" He said it had something to do with Hallelujah which we sang in church. He said that faith was a belief in things hoped for a conviction that things would happen that had been promised but you could not see. He said that another quality to get was mildness. He said that having a quiet and mild spirit was like a steel sword in a velvet sheath. He finally said that all of these must be present in a marriage since it is the merging of two souls. He told me that the man was the head of his household NOT because he was better or wiser than his wife but because God wished it to be that way.

A man was to love his wife as his own body. He who loved his wife loved himself and no man ever mistreated his own flesh but feeds and cares for it. He said that affection really mattered and that it should be practiced often. Apparently the Bible says that whatsoever a man or woman sow this they shall reap both good and bad. Sow affection and you are likely to reap affection. It was hard to take in. Not wrong but you had to listen carefully. Now I was to be a husband and I wanted to be a good husband and father.

"Charles, where are you" she asked looking intently into my eyes.

"I am here my love beside you as I will always be. I was thinking about a conversation I had with Master Charles about you"

"About me?"

"Yes, but about marriage. I hoped you would say yes, I was sure you would but"

She placed her fingers on my lips and said "Shhhh, I understand. You must tell me what he said later but now let's get back to the Ann"

As we got to the Ann Joseph was looking for us, "Hello you love birds, glad your back, can I can go and see to my birds now"

I thought as I looked at Joseph, who would ever think that this enormous muscular seaman who I had seen dispensing hard justice had such a soft side for those he cared about.

Emily has a huge grin on here face as she said "excuse me Uncle Joseph, Charles has asked me to marry him and I have said yes"

"I suspected as much. Everyone is waiting on the mess deck. I told them where you had gone. Let's all go down below. Topside will be OK for ten minutes but I regret no longer, you know what my brother is like."

Emily entered the mess deck cabin first and they were all there. Mrs. Butterfield and her husband seemed very keen and curious.

Emily looked at them all with pride "Charles has asked me to marry him and I have said yes, she took off her glove and showed them our ring"

"Well I am so pleased and so happy for the two of you" said Ann.

Charles shook my hand and kissed Emily, "Joe lets toast the young couple, get out Goodman's Goblin".

We all went into the Mess Deck and Joseph unlocked the stores cupboard and brought out a barrel and placed it on the metal cooking table.

"Get your cups lads" We got our cups of their hooks and Joe brought two glass goblets out of the stores locker and gave these to Emily and Ann. He took a bottle of lemonade left over from the picnic and filled Fred Scattergood's cup. He then opened the tap of the barrel and filled the glasses and cups. Once this was done Master Charles stepped back and said in an emotion filled voice

"To the happy couple, remember one another and always be friends and lovers"

I saw Ann Goodman Butterfield look at her husband with the most gentle and kind face. I knew then that they were friends and lovers and would be our example."

Everyone said "Cheers" and then we all began to talk.

Joe turned to Ann and said. "1850 was a good year for the Goblin Ann this is really rich and tasty with a kick like the staysail in a force four"

Ann Goodman Forge had been making wine for many years. Her mother had taught her. It was made from blackberries and rose hips with great care and attention paid to the recipe. It fermented for at least six years and was known by all of Barking as Goodman's Goblin for it had brought down many a man who did not listen on the matter of quantity. Charles was a shy man when it came to romance. I learned that Ann Forge loved him from the day he had knocked a seaman out who was bothering her. At first she was angry but as she rebutted his violence with a throw away remark about Jesus saying to turn the other cheek she had noticed a great change come over him, almost bitter regret. He had said that he knew she was right and would try to do better. She told me later that was when Charles humility and desire to be better won her heart. He had lived as a boarder for years but was so slow in making advances that Ann decided to introduce him to the Goblin. It did the trick. He told her that he had wanted her from the day they met. He had bared his soul to Ann and it was then that she had learned of his determination to make life better for the apprentices.

As a seaman he had witnessed first hand the cruelty. It was then that she learned about the death of his younger brother John. He had been fleeting between smack and schooner and had fallen into the sea and had drowned. He and all the other seamen were away at sea for four months at a time.It was then that she also learned of his disgust at the sermon preached by the Vicar of St.Margarets Church saying God had taken his brother to heaven to be with Jesus. Ann had said she shared his disgust and that such a sermon wouldn't comfort any family particularly since she knew, being a regular attendee that Joseph and Charles were three wheelers, that is only attending Church for birth's deaths and funerals. Joseph had never been seen at Church though she had seen him round the town and also when he came to see Charles. A deep bond had been formed the night that Ann Goodman Forge told Charles that his brother John was in the death sleep, like Lazarus. Like Lazarus he would be resurrected. No heaven, no hell, no purgatory just death. Lazarus was raised just a few days after he died but his body already stank. John would see life again once the Devil's power had been broken.

"Now about tomorrow, Ann has changed her mind and is going back to Barking on the train with Emily and the children"

At this was came a deep sigh from Charles junior who loved to be at sea.

"I know Charles but it will be better for all. We don't really have time to call in at Brightlingsea. Uncle Joseph, the whole crew and I have the long lining tests to do on our way down the coast. During that time you would all have to be below decks anyway. You will be home on Thursday and we should be at the Pool Friday. We can send the fish to Billingsgate, re-provision and then set sail for the Faroes Monday"

Ann spoke "This is much better, we will have the weekend together and then they will be gone for a month maybe three weeks hopefully if the catch is good"

Emily smiled and whispered "We could go and tell my Father and Mother about our engagement and then that job will be over"

"Yes that is what we'll do now that I do have prospects, very good prospects as it turns out"

Ann turned to Charles and said "let's go to your cabin dear I need to talk with you about something"

After they entered his cabin Ann asked Charles to sit down and listen. She then told him about Emily's conversation with her about her Father. "I have just heard them arranging to go to Creekmouth on the Sunday before you leave for Torshavn"

"Umm, they should not go on their own, we shall go with them and you can say that you wanted to finalise the arrangements concerning Eliza", said Charles. "Ann, Joseph must never here about this from anyone, I am sure that Joseph would do for Mr. Byes even if it meant his own death."

"Yes Dear, I have made this clear to Emily but you are going to have to talk to Jonesey about keeping his temper if her father get's up to his tricks with Emily in front of him"

"Good point; I'll do that on the sail home".

Charles and Ann emerged from their cabin. "We are all going out for a meal" said Ann. Charles is just going to arrange for the Port Master to fix a watch on the Ann then we can go.

Emily spoke;"I need to go back to the lighthouse just for a while. It is such a lovely night and I just want to take a moment by myself and enjoy what has just happened."

I took hold of her hand: "Is everything good Emily?"

"Yes everything is more than good it is wonderful"

Ann spoke "Make sure you are dressed for the meal. I have brought the dance dress. It is in the cabin I will just go and get it. Be there for seven o clock"

All was arranged and the family had a lovely meal at the Crewe and Harpur. The next morning Ann, Emily and the children caught the train south and we sailed down the East Coast in a following wind. The Ann Goodman just flew and we caught a lot of fish.

31 The Temeraire
    Joseph William Mallord Turner

By Friday we were sailing down the Thames Estuary in a faltering wind when I noticed a paddle steamer tug enter the Thames on our stern from the Medway. She was towing an old wooden ninety eight gun three decker. Many of the ships that fought at Trafalgar in 1805 were being broken up. I knew that she was headed for Beatson's yard at Rotherhithe. The ship turned out to be the Temeraire. She was in fact a Second Rate and yet bigger than the Victory who, with 100 guns was a First Rate. I learnt that she was built in 1793 costing £73,241 pounds and taking five thousand trees. Her sail area was vast six thousand five hundred and ten square yards of canvas. Eliab Harvey who was the Senior Captain of the fleet had been in command. He was known for his daring and had joined the Navy at thirteen becoming Captain of his own ship by twenty five. There were seven hundred and twenty men on the Temeraire that day. One of them was Alexander Brennan a Midshipman. Though now in his fifties he worked at Lawes when I was there. It was from him that I learned all this history and what happened on that glorious day. Nelson in the Victory had crossed the French battle line with the French First Rate Redoubtable on his starboard and Bucentaure the French flagship with Rear Admiral Villeneuve on his port. Victory passed at a perilously slow rate due to the wind and was taking fire from the rear guns of the Bucentuare, and from the forward guns of the Redoubtable.

The French were in fact preparing to board the Victory as she passed until Harvey took the Temeraire to the starboard of the Redoubtable, coming up on her stern. Harvey was intending to draw fire away from the Victory which he did. The Temeraire raked the ship with grapeshot killing most of her crew. As the Victory passed between both French ships she opened up with a withering repeated one hundred gun broadside until the bow and forward decks of the Redoubtable were ripped apart and the stern of the Bucentaure was decimated.

Then Captain Harvey pulled alongside the Redoubtable battering her with broadside after broadside. A Spanish seventy four came alongside the Temeraire's starboard. She was the Fouguex. Shot after shot was sent into the Temeraire's hull. The French and Spanish crews on either ship could not put up with the withering broadside from the port and starboard guns of the Temeraire at pistol shot range. Temeraire carried on pounding both ships until they were wrecks eventually shattering the Redoubtable's main mast. Harvey signalled the Redoubtable to strike her colours so that there could be an end to the appalling death rate but her Captain sent riflemen aloft to carry on the fight. It was one of these men that shot Lord Nelson on the Victory not so far away. The withering fire was devastating to both ships which eventually struck their colours and surrendered. Both vessels, though in British hands, sank in the storm that followed Trafalgar.

Rear Admiral Cunningham on the Royal Sovereign, lead ship of the lee column saw this through his glass and bewailed the end of the Temeraire. Imagine his astonishment and pride when two hours later the white ensign flew from the mainmast of all three ships. Forty seven of the Temeraire's crew died that day and seventy six were injured. She survived the terrific storm that followed the battle of Trafalgar and eventually limped home to the Nore in the Thames Estuary. The damage was enormous. Every sail and yard had been destroyed, only the lower masts were standing and they had been shot through in many places. The rudder had been shot off together with the starboard cat head from which the starboard anchor should have been suspended. Eight feet of her hull on the starboard side was stove in and the quarter galleries on both sides of the ship had been destroyed as she was crushed between the French and Spanish seventy fours. Upon its return to the Nore the public flocked to see the battle scarred ship, many from Barking since there were many old salts in the Town.

32 Fish, Shares and Bank Accounts

The Paddle Steamer Alice passed us and the paddle steamer tug towing the Temeraire. It was going west down the Thames and then the wind dropped. We eventually lay mid-stream becalmed. The tug and the Temeraire passed us and we bobbed in their wake. I looked at the shore and noticed a man with an easel, he waved. I waved back. I could see the Lawes Chemical works jetty in the distance and the ships moored in Barking Reach. Just beyond that was the entrance to Barking Creek.

The light was beautiful and the clouds magical. One day I hoped I would be able to paint them such scenes, one day. We all made it home without incident and once the Ann Goodman was moored up in Barking Pool Charles went to see his father in law John forge and ordered another set of jib sails. He also asked him to check all of the rigging with Chas. He then came back to the mooring.

"Right Jonesy, go and get the fish boxes from the back garden at Fisher Street so that we can place the fish in them for delivery to Billingsgate"

As I stepped up the companionway onto the hard I saw Emily pushing the wheel barrow with six boxes on it.

She stopped in front of me. I said in fun. "No wonder you have got such a good bosom Mrs. Jones but six boxes will not do. I shall need another six at least"

"You need to be very, very, careful Master Charles Jones, we are not married yet and do not forget you have to treat me like your own body"

"I know but I drive my body really hard look" At this I showed her my new arm muscles.

She winked at me and said "Shall we go to see my Father after Church tomorrow and then you can show him your new found strength. I am sure it will impress him"

"Sorry love, I was just fooling about"

"I know, I know you stupid boy and anyway fooling about comes after we are married"

"Will there be any training for that, I have had to be trained to go to sea"

"Will there be training, will there be training, no, it will be a snagging cruise just like the one you have been on and that, only after you have got our certificate." She said.

"Right, well the crew of the Lady Ann have just had a great cruise free from any real problems"

"Yes, and that's what you get with a good crew and we are a good crew."

"Are we talking about the same thing, you know Eros"

"Oh it's Greek now is it, well I know what Eros is Master Charles Jones and yes we are talking about the same thing. Here take these boxes while I go and get the others"

The boxes arrived and Emily did no more than send me into the fish hold to hand her the fish which she then placed into the boxes. When done she took the barrow to the nearest ice house and came back fully loaded. We iced the fish and then the skipper returned.

"Well done the two of you, I knew the shares idea would work"

"How much will these be worth at Billingsgate skipper?"

"Well there not king cod but they are good fish. I would be disappointed if we did not make fifteen guineas after cruising costs. You will have to ask Ann".

"What's a guinea skipper?

"Twenty one shillings"

Emily quickly worked out our share and was very pleased. "You need to open a Bank Account Charles because I need; I mean we need to save for our bottom draw"

"I already have a bottom draw in my bedroom and on the Ann"

Grabbing me by my shirt top Emily came close and then said, "It is an expression, an illustration a figure of speech. The bottom draw I am talking about are the things we need to start a home, pots pans, clothes blankets, soap scent and a nightdress for Eros, got it"

"Sorry, I am just so stupid but yes please open a Bank Account in our name"

"What do you mean in our name?".

"Mrs Butterfield has explained it should have my, our complete names"

"Your name is Charles Jones isn't it?"

"My full name is Charles Daydreamer Jones"

"Daydreamer Jones? You never told me that was your middle name"

"Would you tell anyone unless you trusted them?"

"Eh no, but I like it. Charles Dreamer Jones shall be the name on the account, we'll drop the Day bit but why my name as well. It's normally the man's name, just the man's. My middle name by the way is Millicent"

"Master Charles told me that Mrs Butterfield has shares in the ownership of the Lady Ann. She has sixteen shares. Her maiden name was Ann Goodman Forge and so I thought you might like to include your maiden name, is that ok."

"Well yes it is OK, so it shall be Charles Dreamer Jones and Emily Millicent Byes but why?"

"The two shall be one flesh is what the Bible says doesn't it. After marriage we shall be one and that is what I want for us to always be, one. I will be no good without you Emily. You inspire me"

"What a wonderful thing to say. But there is a part of me that will always be Emily Millicent Byes even after I am married to you."

"Good, that is what I want. I never wanted to be shacked up with a yes woman, though I suppose now and again would be a nice thing"

"There now, you have just spoilt it, shacked up, shacked up with me is that how you think of our engagement

Oh dear the fire was lit, how was I going to put it out? At this point the Skipper stepped in "You are arguing about words. Stop it. You both love one another don't you? Ann and I have seen it BUT the tongue can be a soothing balm or death dealing poison. The latter is the case when emotions get aroused. With a dagger I can hurt you at three feet, with a sword at ten with a longbow at two hundred with cannon at five hundred but with my tongue I can injure you on the other side of earth, in Australia. Bible Bashing Butterfield has read "a word at the right time is like apples of gold in silver settings, but at the wrong time it is like a gold nose ring in the snout of a pig. Anyway I have to check on something see you at Fisher Street".

"Sorry sir, you are right so Emily where will our bottom draw be located."

"Oh, well there is a spare sea chest and I had thought of my room at Fisher Street"

"What a good idea, we shall need a list. Let's make such a list when we get back home. We can do it in the kitchen. I can't write yet but I am sure I can add to the list"

"Good, that's better" said Master Charles turning back. "You don't get paid in real terms until I get paid but since we are at sea for months at a time most traders will allow you to set up a tab. There is, however, great danger in this. Once you are in a trader's debt he can feel like he owns you. Especially rich people like Bankers. They are not all bad BUT most are greedy. The love of money is the cause of much evil. The treatment of the apprentices proves this. They can also think that all people are motivated by the same love. Did you know John Hennekee's step Father was offered ten guineas if he would call off John Dill of the London Times over reporting the inquest. So please be careful. If you take my advice Emily ask your mistress to train you to be a milliner and dressmaker. You always dress well and that talent can make you money. Now there is just one other thing. From now on you are not to be on your own in my house. There must always be a chaperone present."

I looked at Emily "What's a chaperone" She blushed deep red.

"Ah yes I am forgetting Charles that you are still building on your library of words. You have proposed marriage and Emily has said yes, that is commitment. Commitment leads to privileges. Privileges like kissing and holding hands and holding one another closely. Such actions cause other things to happen. Such things can lead to the pair of you doing things you shouldn't do until you're married. The risk of such unwise but delightful action is pregnancy. This affects Emily more than you and will lead to loss of standing in the community. You do not want that and certainly even if you are married you do not want a child straight away. Becoming one flesh takes time.

Chaperoning is a mechanism which prevents these unwanted results. You must never be on your own, the chaperone need not be so close as to spoil things but those are the rules in my house. It is not bad or evil to experience passion. In fact your marriage would be bland and unrewarding without it.

Enjoy your courtship don't spoil it by loss of self control. Discover one another but stick by the rules. Fornication leads to a bad conscience and you do not want that"

"Yes Uncle Charles we will do just what you say. I will open the Bank Account when I am eighteen in three months time and we will do what you say, we promise" said Emily and she meant it.

"Right take the fish boxes and put them on Balfour's hatch boat since it looks ready to sail on the evening ebb.

We did just so.

Balfour's three sons were on board.

"Hello mates, off to London are we?"

"Yes Jonesy. We were going today but father has secured another cargo so we won't be going until Monday, on the same ebb as the Ann. I believe we shall follow you down. Will the fish keep?"

"Yes, tell your father to bill Mrs Butterfield will you"

"Yes, indeed, how are the brogues?"

"Good your father did a really fine job. I am wearing them to Church tomorrow and then Emily and I are going to Creekmouth with the Butterfield's. Oh by the way Emily and I are engaged did you know"

At this Emily blushed so I grabbed her hand and put my arms round her.

"You smell of fish" she said quietly.

"So do you, have I upset you again and anyway we all smell of fish until we get clean"

"No, not at all, I am glad you want to tell everyone, that's the way I feel"

"How could we" said Balfour's boys, you've been away, but we are not surprised"

"Why is that?" asked Emily

"We saw you spooning at the dance. It was great to see. Congratulations "

"Why thank you, thank you mates nicely done; now we must head to Fisher Street. If we don't see you again have a nice time in London".

When we entered Fisher Street there was great activity. The kitchen was the place to be as usual. Billy went upstairs and went to bed having been on the morning sailing watch. Emily and I were talking to Mrs Butterfield about opening a Bank Account when Charles walked in.

"Where is Joseph?" he asked of no one in particular.

"He said he was going to the telegraph office, something about Nathaniel and Lincoln" said Ann Butterfield turning to me.

Master Charles said "I think we should go to Creekmouth tomorrow after church"

"Yes skipper that is what Emily and I have agreed, so are you coming to?

"Yes, Ann wants to finalise the taking on of Eliza as a maid when she leaves school. I have got us a trap. We shall go straight after Church."

"Emily" she turned to look at me "after Church tomorrow I need to go home and get the art materials you bought me before we head to Creekmouth"

"Why do you want them, I am sure that I will not be in the mood to be sketched"

"I wasn't thinking of sketching you and I will not be sketching at all if things do not go well with your Father. The light is good there and I saw a rotting hulk in the mud near Lawes Jetty so I thought I might sketch it"

"Well if Father is awkward we will have Master Charles and Mistress Ann on our side and they do know what the problem is. My mother has already said yes to our marriage. I think it will be ok and in any case I am going to marry you no matter what my Father says. It will give me time with Eliza so hopefully we can both do what we want"

33　I meet Mr. Byes

After Church we set off for Creekmouth. The wind was from the East and so the smell from the stinking Thames was not bad. The meeting with Emily's parents went well especially when Mr. Butterfield explained the shares arrangement. The tension decreased even further when her Father learnt that the marriage would not take place until we were both 21 some three years hence.

We stayed for lunch and whilst Mr. Byes explained about his new position at the engineering yard in Barking and the fitting of the slave boiler Emily took Eliza for a walk. I set myself up on Lawes Jetty and I began to sketch the hulk. I had been there about twenty minutes when a man walked onto the wharf with an easel and various bits of kit and promptly came and sat within six feet of me. He set himself up and then came and stood behind me. It was really off putting.

"You've got the perspective right and the foreground looks good. The mud's the real problem since it is so boring but not bad, not bad at all, which school are you with?"

"Thank you, but what do you mean which school am I with. My name is Charles Jones and I am apprenticed to Charles and Joseph Butterfield who own the fishing smack Ann Goodman."

"Are you indeed, I saw the her yesterday father down the estuary. You were passed by that paddle steamer tug towing the Temeraire to her graveyard. My name is Joseph Mallard William Turner and I am a painter with the Royal Society of Arts. Did you notice the sky yesterday?"

"Eh, yes and I also noticed you. We lost the wind just as that tug caught up with us"

"Yes, so you did and that was good for me since it helps the composition. I am doing a new painting and it just so happens that the Temeraire gives depth to my real passion, the sky. Would you like to see the basic sketch"

"Please"

"He placed the sketch on the easel and stood back, what do you think being a sailor"

"Oh yes, I see what you mean, but the Ann can only just be seen and then not very well. You've put the Alice in as well but just as a black outline."

"I know but it will be the sky that everyone will love. I am famous for my skies."

"I am sorry Mr Turner; it's all lost on me. I am self taught and at the moment cannot read or write though I am being taught"

"Good that is an essential skill and everyone should have it, self taught ay well then it's very, very good. Stick at it."

"What do you think of this" I showed him the sketch of Emily leaning on the lighthouse at Great Yarmouth with a fishing smack bathed in the moonbeam at the +mouth of the Yare.

"That young sir is exceptional; I would say your true talent lays in the depiction of the human form"

At that moment Emily walked onto the jetty. We both turned. Mr. Turner said "Ah the lady in question, pleased to meet you my name is Jethro Mallard William Turner. I am doing a preparatory sketch for a new painting which I am going to call the Fighting Temeraire".

"Pleased to meet you Mr Turner, I am Emily Millicent Byes, Charles Jones fiancée"

"This sketch of you shows real talent, I would suggest that is where the future of your fiancé lies and not in fishing"

"My apprenticeship is for seven years so that is what I shall be doing." I said.

"I understand. Here is my card. Please send the finished sketch of Emily and the hulk. I will see what I can do"

Emily spoke up, "Excuse me Mr Turner did you paint Rain, Steam and Speed?"

"Yes, have you seen it?"

"Yes my Mistress, Ann Butterfield took me to see it. It's one of her favourites. We went to see it after the opening of Barking station."

"I am pleased, do either of you know why I am calling this work the Fighting Temeraire. Her crew you see called her the Saucy Temeraire"

Emily said "No" but I said "yes sir, I worked with one of the Midshipman who was on board at Trafalgar, he is still working at Lawes"

"Well, good, perhaps you will tell Miss Emily later, in my opinion it is the Temeraire that should be saved for the nation and not the Victory but the problem is that Lord Nelson died on the flagship. So here we are forty one years later and the Temeraire is being scrapped. You may or may not be aware Miss Emily that it was Lord Nelsons belief that once his fleet engaged the enemy his Captains and Admirals were to be left to themselves as to how they fought. In the melee Captain Harvey who was on the Temeraire was boarded on the starboard by a Spanish crew and on the port by a French crew. 74's. He later named building's on his Estate after the Redoubtable and the Fugaux. Rear Admiral Cunningham saw what was happening though he too was engaged in massive conflict with the Santa Ana. Imagine his surprise when two hours later the white ensign flew above all three ships. Hearts of Oak had achieved an amazing victory. Now in here we are in 1856 and she is being taken away to be destroyed. In my opinion she should be saved for the nation but it would seem I am too late. So my new painting is to place in England's memory what happened on that ship".

Emily spoke "I am sure it will Mr Turner, I should love to see it once it's finished wouldn't you Charles"

"I surely would"

"And so you shall, in fact you two shall be the first to see it. I shall send a courier and you shall come to my London studio and see the Fighting Temeraire before it goes on exhibition.

"You are so kind Mr Turner. I am sure Mrs Butterfield would like to see it to"

"And so she shall but when it's on show, not as you will see it. By then Charles you should have finished both sketches".

Emily spoke "Well, we have to go, that's why I am here. Charles and Ann are ready to go home but what a lovely surprise, I, we both have had to meet one of England's greatest artists. Some say you are as good as Constable"

"You are both so kind and we shall meet again in a few months. I hope to be finished by October"

We said goodbye and Jethro Mallard William Turner settled on his chair by his easel and took out his oil scallop and became absorbed in the light. That astonishing light spreading across the Thames estuary to be forever fixed in his painting of the Temeraire. We were back home by five o clock. After dinner Emily and I went into the front room. She got out a paper pad and we began to make a list of the things need for our bottom draw. The front door closed. It was Master Joseph. He had been gone all day.

34 North to the Faroes

It was Monday morning and we were storming up the east coast of England in a south westerly and the Goodman was showing her heels. There were white caps on the wave tops and every sail was drawing full and bye.

A long white wake trailed behind the Ann. Off to the east I could see the smacks fishing off the Dogger Bank. The Dogger was one hundred and forty miles long and was to be respected. The sea was breaching over the schooner bow of the Ann but the deflection panels prevented most of the swell from sweeping across the deck. All of us were roped up for safety. The Ann was leaning severely over to her starboard side but the rush was on. We were all wearing our wet weather gear so we were all fine. We had passed Yarmouth twenty minutes ago and now were rushing on towards Boston. The Wash, that great Norfolk bay was on our port side but soon we left that and Boston behind. At three o clock Charles was relieved at the tiller by Joseph.

"Close in now Brother let them see the Dock Tower"

Joseph winked and laughed "Aye, aye Captain Dock Tower it is"

"Jonesy, Chas and Billy downstairs now"

We all went below deck.

"Get your chalks and boards it lesson time"

For the next two hours we were taught how to read and then how to write. Billy asked to learn his numbers so we all had to go through numbers. The only thing that made it interesting was I finally could work out how to calculate my share of the catch. We suddenly heard Joseph's voice.

"Deck there Grimsby Dock tower on the port side about 8 miles"

Once on deck, the day being clear and bright we all saw the tower on the horizon. This was two hundred feet high and was the tallest structure on the east cost. The tower stored the thirty thousand gallons of water required to operate the hydraulic cranes of the Royal and Alexandra Docks. This, then, was to be our frequent destination once loaded with King Cod. By early Tuesday morning we had left Scotland behind. I had seen the Shetlands and Scapa Flow off the Port side on the horizon. It was not dark. Charles and Joseph had been on the tiller for thirty hours when finally the Faroes came above the forward horizon. We headed straight into Torshavn and moored up alongside the quay. The dock manager Lars Morst Ericsson welcomed us. He was Swedish and knew Joseph from the days when he was an apprentice. The Goliath often called in at the Swedish ports on her way back home. Joseph told me he was always playing around with electricity and switches. There was a guy called Almon Strowger who had invented a method of connecting Alexandra Graham Bells telephone without human assistance. Lars reckoned he could do it better. He called it Crossbar.

"Welcome Joseph, yah, we have been expecting you for months, ju are here now, this is good yah I have set a watch for the Ann so please all come with me."

The crew followed Lars into the small town and it became clear we were headed for a particular place. Everything about Torshvaal was clean. It smelt clean and fresh. It had those same odours as Barking but they were pleasant and comforting.

We entered a Hotel and headed to what appeared to be a drinking room. There was a crowd and they all cheered. Most were Norwegians and a few spoke English. They were all fishermen. Joseph was made more of than Charles, if that were possible. I could not understand what was being said even though Lars Ericsson was translating. It appeared though that Joseph did understand Norwegian because of the animated way he was talking and using his hands. What I pieced together was that several Norwegian smacks had seen the Ann Goodman whilst at sea on their stern horizon. They new it was the Ann because of her schooner bow. I got to understand what an incredible community spirit those who caught fish enjoyed. Norway did not have the problem with apprentices because its Government had passed laws to protect its orphans. The Faroes fishermen knew of the Butterfield's stand on the subject. Lars spoke in his stilted English

"Now my friend's ju sail west for twelve miles and then turn east and set all long lines with weights to run at forty feet yes"

Joseph spoke "Forty feet that's deep.

"Jah but they are running deep and are truly big. I have caught one weighing one hundred and thirty pounde. Set for sixty fish a line and no more. I do not know how ju English weigh the cod but they are as heavy as a six year old child. With three lines stern running I tink that twelve runs will fill your hold".

Charles spoke next. "So Lars you thing we can get tow thousand one hundred and sixty king cod in twelve runs"

"Ja, but you will only manage four runs a day. The fish are big and heavy but ju can do this I know."

Lars was right, exactly right and after three days the hold was full but all of us were very tired. We eat like horses and Joseph was put to it keeping us well fed. We were in Torshavn loading with ice when I asked Joseph to hold one of the cod we had caught. The cold white snow of the Faroes set against the calm blue sea of the harbour was truly a visual feast. After this all of us went to sleep. The run to Grimsby would take place the next day which was Monday. We would arrive into the fish dock early Wednesday morning so that our King Cod were part of that day's auction. When that was finished they would then be loaded onto the Ice wagons for the fish train journey to Billingsgate. During the long lining and on the run to Grimsby Chas proved to be the fastest rope and line splicer anyone had ever seen. Twice he had spotted a frayed section of the lines and had cut and spliced them without anyone really noticing, On the run to Grimsby the staysail halyard parted and Chas secured, spliced it and had it deck cleated within minutes.

It was Wednesday morning and Grimsby Dock Tower had been visible since dawn. We entered the Fish Dock sea lock along with five other smacks. The sea gate closed and we were raised fourteen feet to the fish dock level. The dock gate opened and we and nudged in on the forestay and staysail up to the fish dock pontoon and moored off. There were several young apprentices stood on the pontoon waiting for the fish hold hatch cover to be removed. This was the case with the five other smacks, all of them with single masts. Chas and I lifted the fish hold hatch cover and immediately six apprentices came aboard and three jumped down among the fish but it soon became clear that they could not lift the fish. Recognising this foreman jumped into the hold shouting "Its King Cod boy's the Butterfield's have brought home Fisherman's gold. The word spread and within fifteen minutes the boxed fish had all been labelled and were in the auction shed. Charles and Joseph were on the quay and watched what was taking place, making sure that the boxes were clearly marked LA Butt. They were gone in ten minutes for three hundred and twenty guineas.

We were pleased, very pleased though all of us were exhausted.

"Right Charles I'll go and get re-provisioned" said Joseph and set off for the other side of the dock.

"OK, I will go and secure the cash, John and Fred get the Goodman clean and tidy. Chas, check all the rigging. Billy clean up downstairs and Jonesy go up top and check all the pulleys and ropes. We are all to be in hammocks by two o clock. We need ten hours sleep ready for the run north tomorrow."

At six o clock the next day we left the sea lock gates and having cleared the sand banks we turned north for Toshavn. I watched the dock tower fall away as we sped north. We did this three times and the word got out helped by Joseph telegraphing ahead from Torshavn on our expected arrival into Grimsby. The fish merchants came from all over the East coast, from Lowestoft in the South to Kirkaldy in Scotland. The prices secured were astounding. King Cod was fish gold. I cannot do justice to the frantic activity in Grimsby. There were hundreds of smacks at the fish dock. So great was the demand that the Manchester, Sheffield and Lincoln Railway Company had begun the construction of Fish Dock number two.

There were many, many, businessmen who became boat owners. These would then secure Skippers and empower them to recruit seamen and of course to apprentice orphans to the seven year contract of slavery. The treatment of these apprentices was worse, far worse than Barking. The Butterfield's were fishtocracy and like others who owned their boats were seen as above the employed skippers because the catch was theirs. It was on the third visit to Grimsby within as many weeks that Charles and Joseph became more determined in their goal to change the Law. Though we had docked late in the day the fish were boxed and re-iced ready for the morning's auction. We were to head south for a week's rest in our home port which everyone was looking forward to. I burned to be with Emily, hold her close and feel the passion. Charles paid an apprentice to watch the Ann and he, along with the rest of the crew walked along fish dock number one and then along Alexandra Dock, across the railway line to Cleethorpes and down towards Riby Square. Joseph had said he was going to Riverhead and would see us on board later. Many of the suppliers had stores and warehouses at Riverhead.

Master Charles shouted after him "Don't be later than nine o clock Joe we leave by eight"

Joe waved but did not turn round; he seemed most determined and was walking at some speed.

35 Riby Square

The scene was shocking. There was fisher lad's everywhere. Many were sleeping in doorways or on the streets which of course the traders did not like. The Square was full of drinking houses, brothels and gambling dens all designed to relieve the fishermen and apprentice boys of their pay off money. Skippers contracted crew for a cruise. Apprentices had no choice about sailing again with the same skipper. It was that or before the Courts and then to Lincoln jail. It was different for the registered seamen, they could choose but the same people that fleeced the apprentices set the same traps for the seamen. Charles took everything in but we were not calling in at any of the places in Riby Square. We headed for Garibaldi Street and the Mariners Compass. We had been there before but during the day, never at night time. It was run by Thomas and Mary Howlett though the real powerhouse was Mary. Thomas was the son of Charles Howlett the shoemaker who had made all of our wet weather footgear and had left Barking for Grimsby some years before. We were not there long. Mary ran a coffee house attached to the pub. It was not big but that was where Fred Scattergood was placed while we got lemonade and Charles got his pint of ale. The ale was made on the premises from good Lincolnshire barley.

Mary was serving coffee when Master Charles joined us at the table "Good pint Mary, really good"

"Where's Joseph?" she asked.

"He's gone over to Riverhead to get provisions"

"Still looking for Nathaniel Bunton then" she said.

"Are there no secrets Mary, yes I suppose he is, though I think Cut will be in Lincoln and not Grimsby if he is in Lincolnshire at all."

"Henry Ready saw him on Freeman Street two weeks ago"

"Did he now, I had heard Henry had moved but the crack in Barking was he had settled in Gorleston"

"Aye, well that was the plan until he brought the Foam into Grimsby and made the best money ever on his catch. He lives on Cleethorpes Road. Doing quite well, so I hear, but still gone for months, bloody fleeting, it's the curse of all fishing families. Home for a few days and then nine months later another child, not for me thanks. You don't do fleeting or so the crack goes"

"No, but then Joseph and I are fishtocrats aren't we .We own the Lady Ann and the catch and things are going well "

"So I hear"

"I am shocked at the treatment of the fisherlads, it is far worse than Barking; at least the lads had a home with the fishing families, somewhere to be, even if they were not well treated. But this place is like the Klondike in Alaska"

"It is, it is, and everyone in authority is in on it Charles, everyone. It is not right, but what can anyone do when even our Member of Parliament is turning an eye to the corruption. Lots of decent skippers come here at the end of a cruise. None of them can stomach Riby Square. This Town is owned by the Railway Company,even our streets are named after them"

"So I see, what's being built as you cross the railway line into the road leading to Riby Square.?"

"Colonel George Tomline is said to be planning to build some three storey villa's to get fishtocrats like you to move to Grimsby, its just talk. I know the ground has been prepared. I have seen it. I shop at Kime's for groceries. His shop is just before Riby Square. It will, in my opinion, be some years before they get building there but then who am I. There are houses going up everywhere, England is moving to Grimsby Charles as you have no doubt seen"

"Yes, I can see but we go home tomorrow. My life would be easier if we lived here but Ann will not move or at least she will not move unless all of her family move. It's the same for me, my Mother, Father and Aunt Sarah live on Axe Street, My Brother John is buried in St Margaret's and his wife Ann is still in grief. She still runs the Upton, nice little smack that. The Spashett family have a good business there in Barking"

I was glad Master and Mistress Butterfield were not thinking of moving. I needed time to complete my engagement to Emily and plan for marriage. I was sure the years would go quickly. There was so much to do. I wondered if she had set the Bank Account up. It was on the way back to the Goodman that it happened. Charles saw a skipper kicking a fisher lad trying to bed down for the night in a doorway. We all heard the threats the skipper made "you will sail tomorrow you scum, you cheeky little bastard, your apprenticed to me and sail you will or it's Lincoln Jail for you. First though a little discipline is called for"

"Hay you! Leave the child alone. He has enough to cope with. Go home" said Master Charles.

"Mind your own business Butterfield, who do you think you are, this boy's apprenticed to me and he has got to learn whose boss, so mind your own business"

"How do you know my name? As far as I am aware we have never met before. See these three lads, they are my apprentices. I treat them as human beings and not as trash. You should do the same." Turning to the boy he said "You should sail with your skipper if you are his apprentice, Please tell me why you are refusing"

At this the skipper grabbed Charles arm and turned him round. Master Charles remained calm.

"What you about! I told you to mind your own business"

"When you mistreat children it is my business for Jesus said "Let the children come unto" me so that is what I am doing".

"Piss off Butterfield before you get into something you will regret, I have many friends in this town"

At this Charles stepped forward and grabbed the man's privates. He gasped in pain. He then used his other hand to grab the man' shirt at his neck and then lifted him completely off the ground.

"Listen to me" he said in a cold, calm and yet determined voice. "I am not your enemy, but what you are doing right now will make me your enemy. I smell drink, Go home sober up and then see the lad tomorrow. He is a child, treat him with kindness and train him to be a seaman. That is what I am doing and it is what you and all of the other skippers should be doing. Now I am going to release you do not try violence. I used to be a street fighter and was good at it. I have put skippers in hospital before and I can certainly put you in hospital but I am trying to change so please help me with this"

The man calmed down. Charles released him "Please go home, do you need help to get there?"

"No, I will be alright. I do not live far away, just over there on Garibaldi Street number twenty six."

"Good, have a peaceful night, perhaps I will see you again. I go to the Mariners Compass when in port so look me up"

The man walked off. There was a big sigh from Master Charles. Turning to the apprentice he said "now why won't you sail?

"He treat weh horrid fre three months ah divvent knaa what aa've dyun to be tret leik tha an tha bloody fleeting, Ah saw three apprentices droon so ahm not followin them. It's Lincoln jail fre me. Ah will then hev somewhere to sleep"

"What's your name?"

"Jeremy Pickersgill, they calls me Jem. Ahem frem North Shields"

"How old are you"

"It says fourteen on me ticket but aa've have been at sea fre two years so ah reckon ahm sixteen"

"Have you any family Jem"

"Ne Master Butterfield them is aal dead. Ah caught a collier from Shields thinking ah might get work heor but once ah arrived and they seedah ain't got ne folks they put me in the poorhouse an then they apprenticed me fre fishin the bastards"

"Well that is really difficult since if you made your mark on the form the skipper has got you for seven years"

"Ah knaa. Ah can read an write much canny good it dyun me. William Brace taught me, tried to larn me the Bible te but ah wasn't hev any of that. Two years aa've I been gunna sea but ah I ain't gannin ne more ne matter what oos says"

"I will try and buy your apprenticeship off your skipper before we sail tomorrow. In the meantime please come with me. John, Fred take the lads back to the Ann and don't go via Riby Square. Go to the end of this road and then up Tomline Street and then take the docks road. See you in a bit"

"Aye aye skipper"

"Come on Jem bring your stuff and follow me"

"Weor are wi gannin"

"We are going to the Mariners Compass where I just came from. Mary Howlett's mother Jane Porter used to take lodgers I want to see if you can board up for three months.

"Aa've not got no dosh Master Butterfield. Ah spent it aal on them tarts. Twenty minutes id al ah got an it wez gone. Mind yee sheh wez canny good shag, smelt nice to"

They arrived at the Mariners Compass and Mary Howlett confirmed that her Mother Jane Porter still took lodgers and she had a room free since a boy had just gone on a three month cruise. Charles knocked on the door of sixteen Kent Street and Jane Porter answered. Charles explained the situation and paid board for three months for Jem.

"Now once you're free of your apprenticeship Jem you'll still need a job. How do you feel about working on the Fish Pontoons, I know a bloke there who might take you on"

"I divvent mind hard work Master Butterfield"

"You said you could read and write is that true?".

" Aye, but could be betta but it gest weh through."

"Writing is a good thing and you could be taught to improve"

"I can teach him" said Jane Porter. "I could add it to the board"

"Do that then. I will call in when were in Grimsby. That should be every three weeks or thereabouts. Now Jem how are you with numbers."

"Ahm greet wi numbers. Me da wez a gambler so Ah lorn'd real fast. Ah can add, subtract, multiply an divide in me heed. Me da played darts an taught me"

"That's settled then," said Mrs Porter "and now young man you need a bath for you really do smell"

"Aa've na had no bath a six month. Will it be cold?"

Mrs Porter bent down and looked Jem in the eye." No Jem Pickersgill it shall be hot and there will be soap and a towel. There will also be some new clothes or at least new to you. I have had many lads staying here between cruises so I should be able to fix you up good. They are clean, I washed them myself, now say goodbye to Skipper Butterfield and lets get you clean".

"Thank yee for yer kindness Mr. Butterfierld. Let me knaa about the Fish Pontoons job aye and ah will dee me best"

"Jem look out for the Ann's telegraph. Make sure we get a good berth. Middle of the pontoon is best"

"Ah will dee me best sir"

"Listen to me Jem, Charles knelt down and faced Jem eye to eye. "There are to be no more tarts, no drink and no more swearing. Do you understand me, do you?"

"Agh that's hard tha is. Thinks you've bowt me dyer well yee ain't. Ahm Jem Pickersgill an if yee think yee Aan me think agyen"

"I do not want to own you Jem but you are on the wrong road. The good book says that whatever a man sows he reaps both good and bad. Nobody not even Queen Victoria escapes that rule of life. You need to start sowing good. Hating the past is like trying to push water uphill. The only thing any of us can do anything about is the now. Time travels one way Jem it comes from the future, is present and then becomes history, our history. Even the future is affected by bad habits. Change!.

"are yee a prophet leik Mr.Brace. Ah divvnae know. What yee syah makes sense. I will change. See yee in three weeks"

Master Charles paid fourteen guineas to the skipper he had threatened. This sum bought Jem Pickersgill out of his apprenticeship. He got Jem the job on the fish dock pontoon. Joseph would telegraph from Torshavn telling Jem when the Ann would arrive. He gave him a letter stating that he was the Ann Goodman's mooring agent and he was to get a mooring mid way down the Fish Dock pontoon. That simple deal made Jem Pickersgill a rich man. He never forgot the good done to him by Master Charles as you will learn from Ann Kimes diary.

The drunken skipper had done alright to. Fourteen guineas to take the boy on from the poorhouse and now another fourteen to set him free.

We left Grimsby for Barking on the morning's ebb. There was no fishing on the way home and the angels were set free as we past each point. By Friday we were sailing up the Creek and everyone was looking forward to the rest. I could tell you about the cruises for the rest of 1856, through to 1860 but they were all basically the same. The Ann became famous and King Cod ruled Grimsby. The Butterfield's and I and indeed all of the crew became comfortably off. In the spring of 1859 we all moved to Oak Cottage on Heath Street. The Forges lived just four doors down. It had coal gas lighting, flush toilets, though the sink hole was still in the back garden but right at the bottom away from the house. Master Charles had a brick covered walk way built with a wash house building off of it. There was an apartment at the back of the Cottage with a sink, kitchen, bedroom and cuddy. This was where Emily and I lived after we were married in 1860 when we were both twenty one. Mrs Butterfield had all of Oak Cottage decorated but she really went to town on the kitchen. She had the decorator place scheen green flock wallpaper on all four walls. This set off the black cooking stove and fire place. She and Eliza were always black leading the kitchen equipment and it showed. There was one thing which continually annoyed her. It was a patch of damp high up on the outside wall of the kitchen. It was darker than the rest. It dried out in summer.

Oak Cottage backed onto St Margaret's Church cemetery but that didn't bother any of us since we all now believed in the death sleep. No ghost's or wild spirits. John Forge died in March of 1858 and then William Tudsbury Haggis died the following year. Mary Forge ne Haggis was the chief benefactor in his will for she was William's only relative. As William held the mortgages on several smacks these past to Mary Forge and so Mary kept the Sail making business going. Her eldest son George Hall Forge really ran the business but things were changing. Several fishing families had already left Barking for the East Coast ports and in 1859 George Hall Forge moved the business to Grimsby. Elizabeth Forge stayed in Barking and came to live with us at Oakfield Cottage. Elizabeth Ann Forge ne Spashett moved with her Brother to Lowestoft where the Spashett's began a new business. In that year she was able to pay off the mortgage which she and her husband John Butterfield had taken out on the smack Upton. It sank in the great storm of 1863.

Once I had completed my apprenticeship in 1860 I told the Butterfield's that I had bought a small farm just outside Ilford. My art business was doing reasonably well and we had enough money for Emily to move her dress making business from Oak Cottage to a little shop in Barking. We had four children by 1871 but the Butterfield's were long gone by then. Emily and I kept in touch with them by letter and we once took the children to see them by train in 1869. They had been there four years. They were living at number 7 Worsley Buildings on Pollitt Street. Charles daughter Ann was running the house though she was engaged to be married to George Kime who had the Grocers shop on Cleethorpes Road. She eventually married him in 1870 and lived in Horncastle. Neither I nor Emily liked Grimsby. We never went again.

The Butterfield's fight against the fisher lad's slavery carried on but not even they could have imagined what was going to happen. The slavery ended in 1888 though neither of them lived to see it. They did live to end it and end it they did. That is Ann Butterfield's storey.

This is the end of my story.

Charles Daydreamer Jones

36 Incidents

During the years there were several things that took place which I thought were good, unusual and then bad and then very bad. Here is the list.

June 1856
*Mistress Ann tells Master Charles that she is pregnant. Everyone is delighted. Walter is born the following year. Mother and child are both well.

August 1856:
Charles discovers the name of God. He is reading the forward of the King James Bible and reads the note that the name was removed to conform with tradition. It remains in two places. In the King James the name is Jehovah but he later reads that it really is Yahweh. He discovers both retain the four Hebrew consonants YHWH. Charles prefers Yaweh because he has sung Hallelujah all his life. He told me that the real name for Jesus is Jehoshuah but every one knows Jesus but very few know the Fathers name and so Yahweh is better.

September 1856.
I receive an invitation from William Turner to view "The Fighting Temeraire". It is a big painting. The composition and technique are inspiring. The sky is probably the best he has ever done. No one knows that the fishing smack in the picture is the Ann Goodman. The black smudge which is the Lady Alice paddle steamer is the only painted record of that boat which was sunk in the Thames when it was rammed by a coal barge going down river. Hundreds died.

William Turner takes my drawing of Emily and the Hulk and places them on exhibition with other artists. The Hulk is sold in ten weeks for a nice sum.

February 1857.
Alfred, Charles and Ann's third child dies aged 7. He is buried in St Margaret'. The Vicar's sermon emphasis the resurrection, Albert is no flower in God's garden. Both parents grieve but the death of children was a common family experience in those days when the Thames was an open sewer

March 1857
Charles and Ann's fourth child is born. A boy, he is named Walter.

July 1858.
The Great Stink.

The summer is so hot that the Thames ferment's. Michael Faraday declares that it is just an open sewer. Cholera strikes the City. The Government passes a Bill in weeks funding the London sewer network. Ann Butterfield develops a really bad cough which lasts all summer and only goes away in the late autumn. It never really went away.

Spring 1859
Charles and Ann move into Oak Cottage. We visit Mr and Mrs Byes and I ask for Emily's hand in marriage. Mr Byes says yes. Do not like that man. Mr. Byes still lives in Creekmouth.

Summer 1859

Emily and I marry. Master Charles gives Emily away because Mr Byes is dead. He dies under very strange circumstances. He was found hanging from Boys Oak at Creekmouth. His private parts had been removed. The police knew he had been murdered but there were no witnesses and anyone who might have had a grievance could prove where they were. The Butterfield's were at sea when it happened.

January 1860

Ann Butterfield dies. Her cough suddenly gets worse. Charles is away at sea. She is buried alongside her son Albert. Charles has a brick barrel made and placed on the grave slab. Charles is grief stricken as is Joseph and indeed all of us. She is missed by all in Barking. There were hundreds at the Service.

March 1862.

Charles Butterfield junior joins crew. Head strong boy. He is 14.

June 1862

William Butterfield; Joseph and Charles father dies aged 82. The death was expected, He was old and satisfied with life but his aching bones made him miserable. He told his sons he was ready for the death sleep.

February 1863.

The greatest winter storm ever recorded struck the Barking fishing fleet on the Holland Banks. 100 boats sank. Many, many families were plunged into poverty. Barking finished as a fishing centre.

December 1864.

The Butterfield's move to Grimsby. Aunt Sarah won't go. She chooses Romford workhouse where she dies in 1872 at the age of seventy six. Emily and I say a sad farewell to the family as they leave Barking Pool on the Lady Ann headed for Grimsby. Her fish hold had been cleaned out and lined with hessian and that is where all of the furniture and stuff from Oak Cottage was placed. Barking had become a place of bad memories Before I close this my account of our lives with the Butterfield's I will expand on three of the incidents and hope they will help you the reader of these my notes.

1865

Mary Ann Butterfield, Charles and Joseph's mother dies in Grimsby. She is buried with at Ainslie Street public Cemetary. The fight for justice for the apprentices was not finished. In fact it became intense, much more intense. Grimsby was where it got resolved but that story belongs to Ann Butterfield later Ann Kime. She was as beautiful as her mother and very, very strong. She had twelve children.

May 1867.

Charles Butterfield junior dies at sea off the Faroes. Swept overboard whilst long lining. Not wearing safety rope. Joseph dives into the sea with Kisby Ring but the rope is too short. He sees Charles drown less than fifty feet away. The sea is bitterly cold. Joseph gets pneumonia and nearly dies. He is rushed in a mad non stop sail of over thirty hours to Grimsby and is saved by the Doctors at the new hospital.. Joseph never returns to Barking. When he recovers he joins Jem Pickersgill and they form a business together buying and selling fish. Joseph never goes fishing again. This is covered in more detail In Ann Kime's diary.

The death of Mr Byes.

Mr Byes started work in July of 1856 at the Hoskins Shipyard. He supervised the installation of the second boiler in the newly built works extension but he still lived at Creekmouth. He would leave on Monday morning and go home Friday night. Emily and Eliza would often see him around Barking though he never came to the house on Fisher Street. He would walk home it being only two miles. The Road followed the way of Barking Creek it went through a copse of trees and then entered Fisher Street. The Creekmouth end of Fisher Street was where the Engineering Works were located. There were many factory buildings both sides of the road. There were no street lamps. That end of Fisher Street, past the Fishing Smack Pub was a bad place for fights and stuff. Mt Byes was not liked. He was a bully. If he did not get his way both men and women were fired. He made a lot of enemies,

One Friday after he had left work he called at Fisher Street and of course Emily opened the door. Master Charles was away. Emily told me what happened.

"Hello my dear, glad to see your father?. Your special friend. Is Eliza at home? for I would love to see you both? You never seem to have time to visit when I see you in Barking"

"Yes Father Eliza is at home but we do not want to visit with you and you know why, so please leave"

At that moment Ann Butterfield called out "Who is it Emily"

"It's my Father Ma'am, he wants to visit"

Mrs Butterfield immediately came to the door. "Go inside Emily and finish off the dinner pots"

Emily did as she was told. When she got inside Eliza was shaking. Emily put her arms round her and both went and sat near the open fire. Emily took Eliza's face in her hands and told her that she was safe. That nothing would be allowed to happen and that their father would not be allowed inside the house.

"What are you doing here Jed, Charles told you NOT to call?"

"He did, he did but he is away and I haven't visited with my daughters Mrs. Butterfield for some time. I have said yes to Emily's marriage and have kept away as asked but a father needs to see his daughters. I am sure you understand this having children yourself"

"True, but Mr Byes there is no way that you are entering my house to see your daughters. No way. I know what you have been doing to them and so does Master Charles and you are not coming in here.

"Whatever they have been saying is not true. It is all in their mind. Children make up such stories don't they"

"You mean stories about touching their breasts and so on. They are not stories Mr. Byes. I believe you are a wicked man and I am warning you not to try and see the girls at any time."

"I see. Do you have any witnesses to these alleged acts of mine. If you do you should have me arrested. Did my wife ever see me do anything to my daughters? No she did not. I will go but I shall get to see my daughters Mrs Butterfield. I see them in Barking regularly and shall find the time to visit"

"Listen and listen very, very carefully Mr. Byes. You are not to visit with your daughters in Barking or anywhere else. Not at any time. If you do not do as I say there will be severe consequences for you and I am not talking about the Law. Charles will be home on Friday. You were told by him to leave the girls alone. I shall tell him of your visit and I can assure you that YOU will get a visit from my husband. I repeat once again that you are to have nothing, absolutely nothing to do with Emily or Eliza. Is that clear? Do you understand?

"Yes, I understand. Good day to you"

Ann heard him say something under his breath something about "skin" and "rat". When she came into the kitchen she was angry. Not upset, but angry.

"Now it's dealt with so please calm down especially you Eliza. I shall talk to Master Charles about this. Emily please come into the parlour. It's at times like this that I understand Joseph's thinking. He's the forge hammer of God you know. He likes Joshua in the Old Testament. He is a funny bloke my Brother in Law, I love him dearly. Now please listen to me young lady for now you are both to avoid going into Barking at least until Master Charles has seen your Father and gone over the rules again."

They did just so. Charles went down to Creekmouth on the Sunday after Church to see Mr. Byes. No one knows what was said. All that Mrs. Byes could say was that her husband became bitter and even harder to live with. He was determined to see his daughters and that is what he did.

He did not see them for over three months but he was seen by many people in Barking watching them. The restrictions laid upon the girls were eased and they once more enjoyed the company of the townsfolk.

It was late one Thursday night on the way back from the pawn shop on Gascoigne Street that Mr. Byes visited. Whatever happened the sisters would not say and never did. Emily refused to talk about it. All I could get was that there was no physical contact. Four days later on the Friday Mr. Byes never made it home. After a brief search he was found hanging from Boys Oak. He had been severely beaten and his privates cut off. They were seen lying on the fat pools of the Creek. No one was ever charged. It certainly was not the Butterfield's for Charles and Joseph were at sea. Here is my theory, though I have no proof. Everyone thought Joseph did not know. I did not believe this. He became very protective of both Emily and Eliza after Mistress Ann and Emily had been to Creekmouth. Yet, how could he know for I never told him and I know that Charles and Ann would never tell him. He had taken to reading a bedtime story to Eliza.

When he was sat on her bedroom floor he always kept the door open, never shut. We could all here the stories that he read. Moby Dick was the current one. When Joseph and Eliza went out she would often just walk up and take Joseph's hand. He would squeeze it and they talked as they walked. Eliza really liked the angels and took great care of them and the other pigeons. Like her sister she was truly beautiful. Emily told me that neither Eliza nor she ever spoke to Joseph about the visit of their father but I still felt that somehow Joseph knew.

The autopsy of Mr Byers showed he had several broken ribs. It was the kind of wound that a street fighter might inflict. His liver was damaged but it was the broken neck that had killed him. Then there was the desecration of his body. Someone knew what he had been up to. None of us went to the funeral. Mrs Byes went but her children stayed at Fisher Street. I recalled the night I saw Joseph leave the fish pontoon and head toward the Riverhead in Grimsby. About five minutes later when Joseph had crossed the dock bridge I witnessed Charles leave the Ann and walk in the same direction. Since I was off duty I followed.

The Riverhead was being developed and many new houses were being built. There was also a shipyard which built fishing smacks. The yard was open and on the starboard side of a newly built double mast smack called the Esther, which was almost ready for launching I saw Joseph talking to Jem Pickersgill. Suddenly a thick set man stepped forward. I could not see him clearly because he was in the lee of the smack. It was set on its keel propped up ready for the launch.

It looked like Nathaniel Bunton but I could not be sure. The discussion was short, no more than ten minutes and then they parted. Jem walked over the road bridge and set off to Kent Street along Cleethorpes Road. Joseph shook hands with the thick set bloke, pulled him close and seemed to be whispering in his ear. They parted and Joseph headed back in the direction of the Ann. Charles in the mean time was stood with his telescope looking at the Esther or that is what anyone would have concluded since he kept moving the glass around not fixing on one spot. He was some way off. The thick set bloke headed for Grimsby Station. Charles walked quickly and approached him as he went up the station steps. They disappeared into the Waiting Room. About thirty minutes later Charles came out and I saw the bloke enter the ticket office. He came out walked round to platform two and got on a waiting train. At seven thirty the train left. It was an Eastern Railways service.

I ran onto the platform once Master Charles had left and pretended to miss the train on Platform two. The station master approached me "Damn I said I have missed that train to Lincoln"

"No you have not young sir, that's the train to Peterborough with change to London"

"To London you say"

"Yes, it terminates at Peterborough ; nearly all the passengers have forward tickets to London even the last one to board"

Oh yes, the thick set man"

"Yes, wouldn't like to meet him on a dark night. The service to Lincoln runs every hour. The last one is nine o clock"

"Thank you."

As I walked back to Fish Dock number one and the Ann I came to this conclusion. I believe that Joseph and Cut met because they had discovered where Craddock was living. Somehow Jem Pickersgill was involved. That story belongs to Ann Kime.

Charles had intercepted Cut who was intending to catch the Lincoln train but had asked him to go to Barking and frighten Mr. Byes. I believe that Mr Byes was caught by Bunton leaving work, taken into the copse and then it all went wrong for Mr Byes. Bunton did for him. I do not believe that Cut intended to murder him. I cannot explain how Cut got him to Creekmouth which was at least two miles distant. Cut was known in Barking and so any attempt at a horse and trap would have been known about. All that can be said is that a hay wagon crossed the West Road bridge from East Ham loaded with hay and that there were fresh cart tracks down Fisher Street as far as East Marsh Pond. It was a wet night and the driver was hunched over against the rain. I do not believe that Cut would have desecrated Mr. Bye's body, but somebody did and whilst it was hanging from Boys Oak. I never saw Cut Bunton again and as I have said after 1870 I stopped going to Grimsby. All of this happened not long after Mr Byes visited with his girls.

Engagement party 1856

The Butterfield's held an engagement party for us when we returned from the cruise. All the family were there. The Forges, the Spashett's, John Harrison, his wife Kate and their three girls Dorothy, Gladys and their only boy Alfred George. Fred Scattergood was also there with his with his wife Florence and their seven children. Arthur his first born had gone deep sea. Alfred, Frederick, Frank, Alice Audrey Evelyn and the youngest who was still a babe in arms and named after her mother. A good time was had by all. At this party Emily showed them the new engagement ring which we had chosen on our visit to London together. It was a green emerald with a diamond cluster. She didn't wear it that night, no; she wore the curtain ring I had made. She always wore the real ring amongst family but wore the dress ring when we went out.

The next day Emily received a note from her mother explaining that the community at Creekmouth had also arranged a party at the village hall and would we attend. It was planned for a Saturday. I did not think we could go since I was due on another cruise but the Butterfield's delayed the departure until the Monday so we did go and it was a lovely day. Emily's father was there but he was well behaved and so we both enjoyed the party.

Predestination

This is the last of my notes. There are many, many more but it would be too much. One evening in Torshavn when I was on watch Master Charles came on deck. It was late afternoon and the weather was pleasant with a warm breeze. The conversation which follows is to the best of my recollection what was said.

I came to believe in the death sleep after this conversation but I was never to become an active believer a regular Church goer.

"Ahoy Jonesy, beautiful afternoon. I see you are writing, what are you writing about?"

"I have been writing about your fight to end the apprentice slavery and how hard it is because the Law has to be changed and you and Joseph don't know how to get this done. I have just finished writing about Alfred's death. How can you be so sure you will see him again?"

"That is a big question and in some ways I cannot answer it unless you have faith in the Supreme Being, Yahweh"

"You mean God"

"Yes but Yahweh is his name, Do you know what it means"

"No"

"It means 'I Am'. But I have read that a fuller description is" I shall prove to be what I shall prove to be". It is really a statement of action. In the nation of Israel's case they needed a Saviour to deliver them from slavery in Egypt and that is what Yahweh proved to be to them. It also applies to us, if we have faith. Yahweh will prove to be what we need to get through life. It does not mean that Yahweh is a crutch for weak willed people. Weak willed people cannot be Christians because they have to do God's will, walk the narrow path."

"Oh yes, Mrs Charnock used to tell me about that. Only those on the narrow path who have been called and chosen will be saved, the rest of us are doomed like my Father and Mother and the rest of my family"

"Well that belief stems from a man called John Calvin. You see Jonesy there is a big challenge for the believer. Millions of people have lived and died without ever having read the Bible and so did not know about Yahweh or his Son Jesus Christ. They were ignorant. It was not that they did not believe in a god but that they did not believe in the True God'

I said "They were not all bad then, they did believe, they just were not Christians."

"Yes, that's true but what you believe shapes your attitude. Many Religions teach bad things and so the actions of the believers reflect this. Wars, many wars have been fought over Religion. It is not a source for peace but conflict. There is another thing, if religions are like the spokes of ships steering gear all leading to God then there can be no such thing as Truth because they all teach different things. Jesus said that only the Truth could set us free".

"Set us free, free from what?"

"Free from the greatest lie ever told. This single simple lie has shaped mankind's history but it's complicated because not many people know that something nearly all religions teach is a lie".

"What Lie?"

"Umm, I am not sure Jonesy that you are ready for this"

"Why do you say that, I have asked the question and I am writing about Alfred's death and how you and Mistress Ann dealt with it"

"In the book of Psalms it says the fear of God is the beginning of wisdom. What it really says is the *phobos* of Yahweh is the beginning of wisdom. You remember when we talked about how Florence Scattergood hated going outside and I told you the word was agoraphobia"

"Yes"

"The phobia bit comes straight from the Greek word '*phobos*' and in the case of agoraphobia means morbid dread of open spaces. There is another meaning and that is what occurs in the Psalms. In this case it does not mean morbid dread but means wholesome fear. A better word would be reverence or respect. All sailors have to respect or revere the sea. We are not in morbid dread of it for it can be both beautiful and fearsome. It does though have the potential to kill us if we as sailors do not respect it. That is why we all wear the safety ropes. Understand"

"Eh yes, I think so. Are you saying we should treat Yahweh like the sea?"

"In a way, yes, reverence is the creature standing in awe of something. It can be the sea and it can be God himself. This reverence is based on reasoning. It is an emotion and can and has made both of us feel very small and insignificant when we are facing enormous seas. This emotion has the effect of making us teachable. We listen and obey. I am always thinking in mountainous seas if everything is in its right place. Have I done all I can to make the Ann safe. Have I applied the rules of the sea? Yahweh can teach us when we are in this reverential frame of mind. He can teach us to benefit ourselves by teaching us HOW to live, what to place first, what is valuable and what is worthless. What stands or can stand against this is our free will"

I asked him "Why do you think I might not be ready?"

"Have you ever experienced *phobos* reverence of Yahweh, God as you say?"

"Eh, don't know"

"Lars tells me that there should be a great display of the Northern Lights tonight. Take your time and look at them. They were here before you were born and will be here after you are dead. I'll talk to you later"

That night I watched the Northern Lights and in the middle a shooting star shot across the sky. Then I heard the sound of a whale and thought of the Albatross following us for days without beating its wings. It dawned on me that I was surrounded by things that I took for granted. I was affected but I don't know if it is this *phobos* or reverence, I think it is because Emily has changed me. Emily' eyes and hair. Her great beauty and yet sweet nature. I have been surrounded by miracles but not appreciated them. There is so much bad in the world though, surely if there is a loving God he would do something about it. Not to do so would be a crime against humanity, why, even I am trying to end the fisher lad's slavery. I shall have to talk with Master Charles some more. Several days later after we were back at Torshavn and were topping off the king cod with ice for the dash south I went up on deck. It was Master Charles watch. It was the same time of day. He was writing up the ships log.

"Hello skipper, can we continue our conversation"

"Certainly, did you watch the Northern Lights?"

"Yes"

"Did you experience reverence; I was going to join you and then decided it should be private"

"I think so; I will certainly not take the wonderful things that I see for granted any more. But my experience won't change anything. Bad things are happening everyday"

"That is another question. Jonesy I want you to understand that I don't know all the answers. I like you have many, many questions and so I keep on looking for the answers. Now about the lie and the narrow path. I think you might be ready. Let us see. There is an incident in the Gospels where the Pharisees are basically saying that Jesus is a bastard. In his reply he says something which when reading the account you can miss. He says to them "Ye" that is the Pharisees "are of your father the devil and the lust of your father ye will do. He was a murderer from the beginning and abode not in the truth because there is no truth in him. When he speaketh a lie he speaketh of his own: for he is a liar and the father of it'. So Jonesy according to Jesus Christ Satan the Devil has the dubious distinction of being the Father of all lies. All the lies ever told spring from him and in some way there is a lie that is the father of all lies"

"So what is this lie, as you say is the father of all lies"

"You will not die"

"I don't understand"

"In Genesis Adam is told not to eat the fruit of the Tree of the Knowledge of Good and Bad. He is told that if he does he will die. Death is only mentioned as a consequence of ignoring this law"

"Oh yes, the story of the stolen apple"

"If you think of it as a story and only a story I don't think I can help you. It wasn't an apple tree it was just a tree set apart by a command. There was no harm in it. There were thousands of trees in the Garden of Eden. When tempting Eve the Devil said "you will surely NOT die for you will become like God knowing GOOD and BAD. That is the lie that has fathered all of the lies because it has led to mankind believing he has an immortal soul that survives him after he dies."

SO

Now comes the really big problem. What happens to this immortal soul after death?"

I answered "Well if you have been chosen you go to heaven and if you haven't you go to hell"

"What determines your destination?"

"What you do in this life, you go to heaven if you do good and hell if you do bad"

"How do you discover what good is since it seems to determine your everlasting destiny since the soul, according to some, cannot die"

"Mrs Charnock said it was all in the Bible and that's when I told her I couldn't read"

"So if you had not learnt to read and write you would have lived in ignorance of what the Bible has to say"

"Yes, that's true. Does it matter?"

Well there are millions of people who have lived and died without knowing anything about the Bible. They were ignorant. Now since salvation, according to the Bible, and indeed according to Jesus statement that he was the way the truth and the life and that no one got to the Father Yahweh except through him, it becomes very important.

"John Calvin reasoned that since God was all knowing these millions were never meant to know. They were locked into false religion, which they had chosen with their free will. They would never change and God new this so he abandoned them to everlasting hellfire on the basis of their ignorance. It was he and another preacher called John Knox that coined the phrase the 'elect'. Now there certainly are many passages in the Bible that talk about the elect. The teaching has certain benefits. It extols God's knowledge and his control of things and yet seems very unjust. Here is a very good question but if you are not a believer it will make no sense, but here it is.

Jesus blood according to the Bible saves us from SIN .Not murder theft or cruelty. They are acts of sin. The English word sin translates the Greek Harmatia which means "You have missed". We were made in God's image, in his likeness but have missed being in his likeness or image. Are you with me?"

"Yes, a bit deep but I see what you mean. I was born a sinner, Not that I was evil but that I would miss being like God. Why would I miss?"

"That's another question and I don't know all the answers to that one. The question is could the blood of Jesus have saved all mankind that has ever lived. The millions who were ignorant, OR, did it have a limited capacity. Now the answer must be that it could save all. SO why didn't it"

I answered "because all didn't know"

"That is right! So if you had paid a price that could save all but saves but a few. Would you be happy with the results?"

"No"

Tell me Jonesy, did they read any poems to you in the workhouse.

"Eh well they did read stuff at Christmas"

"Do you mean Christmas Carols"?

"Yes"

"Did they read to you any of England's great poets?"

"No"

"Not long ago I read a poem written by Ann Bronte on the subject of the Elect. I memorised it. Would you like to hear it?"

"Is it deep?"

"Yes but you will understand what she is saying" He began "Its entitled 'A word to the Elect'

"You may rejoice to think yourselves secure;
you may be grateful for the gift divine-
That grace unsought, which made your black heart pure,
And fits your earth born souls in Heaven to shine.

But is it sweet to look around, and view
Thousands excluded from that happiness
Which deserve at least as much as you-
Their faults not greater, nor their virtues less ?

And wherefore should you love your God the more,
Because to you alone His smiles are given;
Because He chose to pass the many o'er,
And only bring the favoured *few* to Heaven?.

Master Charles raised his voice when he spoke the word *few*.

And wherefore should your hearts more grateful prove,
because for ALL the Saviour did not did die?
Is yours the God of justice and of love?
And are your bosoms warm with charity?

Say, does your heart expand to all mankind?
And, would you to your neighbour ever do-
The weak, the strong, the enlightened and the Blind
As you would have your neighbours do to you.

And when you looking on your fellow men
behold them doomed to endless misery.
How can you talk of joy and rapture then?
May God withhold such cruel joy from me.

That none deserve eternal bliss I know;
Unmerited the grace is in mercy given;
But none shall sink to everlasting woe,
That have not well deserved the wrath of Heaven.

And, oh! There lives within my heart
A hope long nursed by me
(And should its cheering ray depart,
How dark my soul would be!)

Master Charles then paused and crouching down so he could look me in the eyes said

"That as in Adam All have died,
In Christ shall ALL men live;"

He raised his voice when he said ALL and then continued

        "And ever round his throne abide
        Eternal praise to give

That even the wicked shall at last
be set free from Satan's lies;
And when their dreadful doom is past
to life and light arise

I ask not how remote the day,
nor what the sinners woe,
before their dross is cast away
enough for me to know

That when the cup of wrath is drained
the metal purified,
they'll cling to him they once disdained,
and live by him that died"

"Wow! I said. "She wrote that"

"Yes she did though I have changed just one stanza"

"Eh what on earth is a stanza?"

It's a verse. I have changed a verse

"That even the wicked shall at last be fitted for the skies to :-

That even the wicked shall at last be set free from Satan's lies"

I have done this because no one gets everlasting life without exercising faith in Jesus and that faith is derived from accurate knowledge. The teaching of the immortal soul is the problem since it teaches that it is what you do in this life that determines your future. THAT is the Father of All lies and makes God cruel and partial. It is NOT true.

It is true that what you do in this life has an effect but Jesus spoke of a resurrection from the sleep of death and he spoke about the righteous and the unrighteous coming back to life again. Real life here on earth as sentient thinking human beings. It would be in this new life free from the Devils influence that ALL will be taught Yahweh's truth's through Jesus Christ in his Kingdom"

"Oh the Lords Prayer" I said "thy will be done on Earth as it is in heaven. There is going to have to be an enormous change.

"There certainly is. It's called the Great Tribulation and leads to Armageddon. Yahweh's demonstration of power and might."

"So millions die at Armageddon at God's hands"

"Uhm, that is another question. Those who are the direct tools of the Devil will probably die at God's hands but not ordinary folk that is those who are ignorant.

 I do not believe Yahweh would kill them. Any way not everyone accepted Predestination because they thought it was so unjust. So the teaching of Armeniasm arose. This is the teaching that if a person though ignorant does what is right according to his conscience then this will save him and he will get to heaven and if he doesn't listen to his conscience then he will go to hell.

This has certain benefits, it emphasises Yahweh's love but the same reward is given to those with faith in Yahweh and those without. Now since faith in Yahweh has rules and some have died keeping these rules it all seems very unjust. Take the British and Foreign Bible Societies Missionary activity. Before their missionaries go to China, most, being ignorant are saved. The missionaries go to China and no one or very few believe. All lost to hellfire so the Good News becomes the Bad News. Get it"

"Yes, yes I see it now. The problem is ignorance and the belief that our destiny is determined by the life we live on earth now. Whereas, if we do not have an immortal soul we simply enter the death sleep. From this sleep all of us that have ever lived will rise back to life through what did you say it was?"

"The resurrection, and then that is where the knowledge of the Lord will cover the Earth like the waters cover the sea"

"Oh Mrs Charnock used to quote it proving that she was known about. So is everybody coming back like Isaac Newton and Emperor Nero, I mean he persecuted the Christians didn't he?"

"Everyone is coming back as long as they have not sinned against Yahweh's spirit. Such people will not be coming back Yahweh has forgotten that they existed. They are gone forever. All that was lost in Adam is saved in Jesus Christ who is recorded as saying 'I have come that they might have life in abundance"

"Wow what a fantastic purpose but will it be them"

"Most certainly with all their memories, loves and hates otherwise they will have been interfered with. Got it!"

"Sure, I mean yes and what a great comfort"

"Now there is just one last thing and then we must finish getting ready for tomorrow"

"Did Mrs Charnock read the temptation of Jesus to you?"

"Yes he had gone into the wilderness after his baptism"

"That's it; the important bit is when he is on the battlement of Herods Temple about two hundred feet above the Kidron valley. In Luke it says that the Devil showed Jesus all the Kingdom's of the World in a moment of time and then says 'All this power I will give thee, and the glory of them: for that is delivered unto me; and to whomsoever I will I give it.' What is really interesting is the phrase "moment of time". In Greek it does not mean now at this moment but means that it is like a snapshot of history. The Devil has always been in control. He has woven a web of deceit becoming an angel of light to mankind nurturing our selfishness which is the ruin of us all. Jesus DID NOT say they were not Satan the Devil's to give; which he certainly would have if the claim was not true. He answered by simply quoting the first commandment "get thee behind me Satan for it is written thou shalt worship the Lord thy God and him only shalt thou serve.

Mark my words Jonesy there will not be any fish left in the North Sea if we carry on like we are. There is no way. Steam is going to change everything. There is going to come a time when this planet will be on the edge of destruction as we sail our destructive course. Then when all seems lost we will come to see that Yahweh's way is best and that the use of our free will has limits.

It is then that Yahweh will demonstrate is awesome power and become or prove to be to humanity's saviour. The Devil will be destroyed and peace and happiness will break out like a lovely morning sunrise."

"How did you get all of this knowledge Skipper, It is a bit deep for me though I can say that I do now understand"

"It began when I met Mrs Butterfield, Ann Goodman Forge. I was a bad man Jonesy. Joseph and I were very good at street fighting. Cut's counsel on knocking your opponent out was one I enjoyed. All fishermen are strong Jonesy; all of us have big chests and mighty arms but few like fighting. I however did like fighting and oh dear oh dear, so did Joseph. We worked together. We would get people to fight so we could knock them out. The two of us put a man in hospital over something only to find out it was the wrong man. We had picked the fight. It was after that when I started to want to be different. Ann is a good student of the Bible and she really helped me to change. Joseph is changing to but for a different reason. It all came to a head when my Brother John died. He loved Elizabeth Ann Spashett with all his heart Jonesy, with all his heart. She was pregnant when he went to sea in 1851 and he died at sea never seeing his newborn child. At the funeral the Vicar at St Margaret's said God had taken him. I did not believe it then and I do not believe it now. That's what started it all. Now we had better get finished for we sail home tomorrow"

"Aye, Aye Skipper "

Well that is it. I spoke with him many more times, not always about the death sleep but though I believed in that I just don't know about the rest.

So ends my notes.

PS
You should read Ann Kime's book about how the Butterfield's finished the Fishing Apprentice slavery. It is a ripping good yarn. It tells the story of how the Butterfield's with the help of Colonel George Tomline ended the fisher lad's slavery. Ann Kime (Butterfield) died in 1934 at the age of 84. She had twelve children.

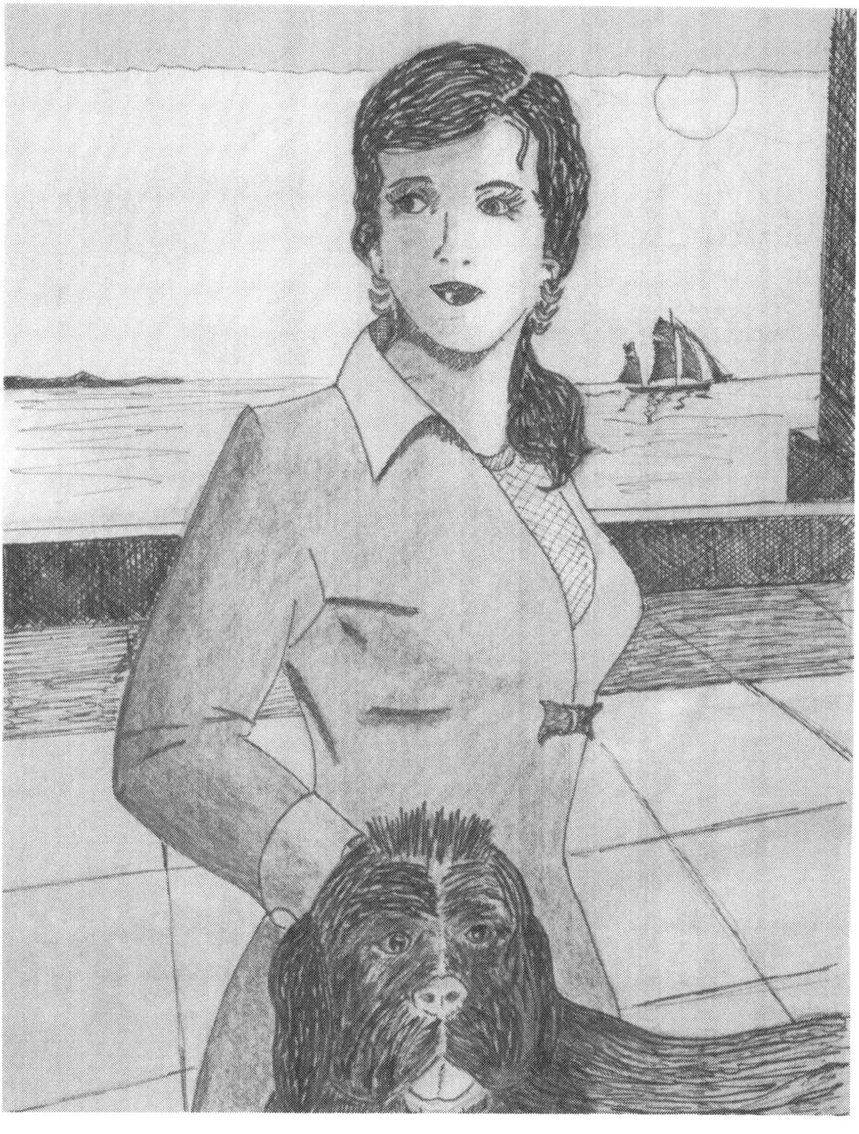

APPENDIX

Fleeting

The practice of keeping the fishing smacks at sea for up to three months. Each smack had a "tub" boat. The fish was loaded into boxes as illustrated and then two men would row the catch to the Schooner which would then take the fish back into Grimsby. It was very dangerous work.

This is how the Ann Goodman would have looked with the exception of the schooner bow

The mayhem of the Dogger Bank. Hundreds of smacks trying to catch fish

Emily Byers dressed for the Dance

She was part of the Butterfield's family though she was a maid.

Emily Byers at Yarmouth Light.

Contemplating Charles Jones proposal of marriage.

She had already said YES

Charles Thomas and Ann Goodman Butterfield going to the dance.

They were known and loved. Ann is buried in St. Margaret's Church with her son Alfred.

Cut Bunton, Elizabeth Chalk (Ann's Sister) and Lizzie Butterfield (Spashett) Ann's Sister in Law) heading for the dance.

Joseph Butterfield with has niece Ann heading for the dance

This is probably how the brothers looked

Charles Thomas   Joseph William

I loved inventing the personalities of both men

Printed in Great Britain
by Amazon